THE BODY IN

MW00834343

"You brought me here to see this hovel?" The claustrophobic room reeked of alcohol and sweat. I turned to leave.

"Not so fast." Esther moved to a small door and pushed it open. "I brought you here to see this."

I was presented with a partial view of a white porcelain bathroom sink. "A bathroom? Really, Esther. This is a complete waste of both our time."

Esther beckoned me closer with her finger.

I decided to take a look, if only to humor her before having her committed to an institution. This was Philadelphia. There had to be at least one mental hospital in the area with a vacancy.

JJ Fuller sat on the ground, his back against the wall, his knee against the toilet bowl.

"Please tell me he's passed out drunk."

Esther waited a beat before replying. "He's passed out dead is what he is…"

Books by J.R. Ripley

DIE, DIE BIRDIE

TOWHEE GET YOUR GUN

THE WOODPECKER ALWAYS PECKS TWICE

TO KILL A HUMMINGBIRD

CHICKADEE CHICKADEE BANG BANG

HOW THE FINCH STOLE CHRISTMAS

FOWL OF THE HOUSE OF USHER

A BIRDER'S GUIDE TO MURDER

Published by Kensington Publishing Corporation

A Birder's Guide to Murder

J.R. Ripley

LYRICAL UNDERGROUND
Kensington Publishing Corp.
www.kensingtonbooks.com

To the extent that the image or images on the cover of this book depict a person or persons, such person or persons are merely models, and are not intended to portray any character or characters featured in the book.

LYRICAL UNDERGROUND BOOKS are published by

Kensington Publishing Corp.
119 West 40th Street
New York, NY 10018

Copyright © 2018 by J.R. Ripley

All rights reserved. No part of this book may be reproduced in any form or by any means without the prior written consent of the Publisher, excepting brief quotes used in reviews.

All Kensington titles, imprints, and distributed lines are available at special quantity discounts for bulk purchases for sales promotion, premiums, fundraising, educational, or institutional use.

Special book excerpts or customized printings can also be created to fit specific needs. For details, write or phone the office of the Kensington Sales Manager: Kensington Publishing Corp., 119 West 40th Street, New York, NY 10018. Attn. Sales Department. Phone: 1-800-221-2647.

Lyrical Underground and Lyrical Underground logo Reg. US Pat. & TM Off.

First Electronic Edition: November 2018
ISBN-13: 978-1-5161-0620-2 (ebook)
ISBN-10: 1-5161-0620-2 (ebook)

First Print Edition: November 2018
ISBN-13: 978-1-5161-0621-9
ISBN-10: 1-5161-0621-0

Printed in the United States of America

Acknowledgments

First and foremost, thanks to Bill Thompson, III. *A Birder's Guide to Murder* happened and Amy, Esther and the gang went to Philly because Bill sent me an email with the subject line: Crazy Idea.

That idea was to have a book in A Bird Lover's Mystery series take place at the American Birding Expo. The ABE is a very real event that is now held annually in Philadelphia. Murders rarely occur at the Expo unless Amy is attending so please don't fret about going. And if you love birds and birdwatching, you should go.

The ABE is presented by *Bird Watcher's Digest* Magazine, of which Bill Thompson, III, is Editor-in-Chief, and the American Birding Association. My thanks to Jeffrey A. Gordon, president of the ABA, and the ABA staff for their kind assistance.

Thanks also to Emily Jones, Ben Lizdas and the entire staff of BWD, and the volunteers who help make the Expo possible and patiently answered all my questions; to the John James Audubon Center at Mill Grove and Carrie Barron, Assistant Director/Education Manager, in particular; and Richard Crossley for his unique birding guides and friendship.

1

Derek flipped rapidly through the pages of *A Field Guide to the Birds of the Carolinas.* "What did you say was the name of that bird we saw earlier, Amy?"

I sipped and set my beer mug on the side table. "Which bird?" The scent of pepperoni and hops hung in the air.

We had gone on a late afternoon bird stroll near Ruby Lake and along Lake Shore Drive, the town's main thoroughfare. Near sunset, we ended our walk at Brewer's Biergarten, which was next door to my own shop, Birds & Bees. Both businesses are located on Lake Shore Drive.

Our group at the table, included Esther Pilaster, Floyd Withers, Karl Vogel and me. There had been more of us on the birding walk. The rest had retired for the evening. The small expedition had been part of our monthly Birds & Brews meeting.

The meetups had been the brainchild of Paul Anderson, one of the biergarten's owners—the tolerable one. The intolerable one was his partner, Craig Bigelow, my ex-boyfriend.

I had been reluctant initially to take part in the whole birds and brews thing but Paul had been right—birds and beer went together rather nicely.

Paul skipped the walk that evening, claiming he had too much work to do at the biergarten—his usual excuse.

We had seen dozens of birds and close to a dozen different species. I had been particularly delighted to see a variety of warblers, bay-breasted warblers, magnolia warblers and Tennessee warblers.

At Brewer's Biergarten afterward, we talked birds, ate wood-fired pizza and drank one of the house brews selected by Paul. Tonight's beer was a small batch IPA. The focus of the night's conversation was supposed to be the red-eyed vireo. We had seen a number of the olive green and white songbirds hopping limb to limb in the lush canopies of the majestic oaks near the edge of the lake.

However, the topic that I had so carefully chosen drifted further than a rufous hummingbird in a hurricane.

Esther sat stiffly, knitting something out of gray yarn that looked suspiciously like a cat-sized sweater. Floyd and Karl had their eyes fixed on a replay of an Alabama stock car race on the big screen TV hanging in the corner of the bar.

Esther Pilaster, or Esther the Pester, as I called her on occasion, although never to her face and sometimes affectionately, was a tenant of mine. I had inherited her when I'd bought the house. The previous owner had made her remaining in the building a condition of the sale.

My nickname for her had stemmed from her annoying ways when we'd first met. We hadn't exactly hit it off. To be fair, I think she had found me just as annoying when she'd inherited me as her landlord.

"The one that was rummaging around on the ground next to the shops. The gray and white one," Derek replied in answer to my question. He riffled some more through the guidebook.

I had to give Derek credit for trying. He had been coming on more and more birding outings with me. He'd have been just as happy if we had been carrying golf bags over our shoulders and walking the back nine at the local country club chasing a little white ball rather than LBJs. That's little brown jobs, not former U.S. presidents.

Little brown jobs is an affectionate term birders give to small, nondescript birds whose identity cannot be readily determined, either because they had flown past too quickly, there was insufficient light or maybe—as was often my case—you just plain didn't know what the heck it was.

I squeezed Derek's arm. "The same one whose name I told you not five minutes ago."

Derek scratched behind his ear. He looked like a big, ole adorable puppy dog. "Tell me again."

"Besides, we don't call that rummaging, Derek. We call that foraging." Floyd never took his eyes off the race cars on the screen as they banked a steep turn. Floyd is a retired banker and a widower with thinning gray hair and a bushy moustache. "Right, Amy?"

We slapped our palms together. "Right, Floyd." He had been one of my first customers. I own a shop catering to bird lovers and bird watching enthusiasts in the small town of Ruby Lake in western North Carolina.

Floyd's wife had been a bird watcher. He had taken up the hobby in her memory.

"Right, foraging." Derek persisted in turning the pages of the glossy guide. "The one making that high-pitched twinkling noise."

I arched my brow. "In the first place, what you call noise, is trilling. It's music to my ears. Bird song can mean many things from a male trying to get the attention of a female, to defending their territory."

"Maybe you should try whistling to get Derek's attention, Amy." Karl hooted.

"She's already got my attention," Derek said with laughter and more in his eyes. He cupped his hand over mine.

"I'll give you a hint," I said. "A dark-eyed..."

"Right, right. A dark-eyed..." Derek snapped his fingers thrice. "Shoot." He ducked his chin. "I forget."

"Again?" Esther snorted. "What do you see in this guy?" She pointed a lavender knitting needle in Derek's direction.

"Free legal advice," I joked. Derek, like his father with whom he shared a practice in town, is an attorney.

Derek is also TDH: tall, dark and handsome, six-foot-two and eyes of blue. There was nothing nondescript about him, at least not in my guidebook.

A thick row of holly bordered the fudge shop at the corner shopping center across the street. Dark-eyed juncos had been busily scratching through the leaf-littered ground beneath the bushes.

"Remember the pneumonic I told you." My boyfriend looked at me blankly. "Gray skies above, snow below? Must be a..."

Nothing.

His beautiful blue eyes stared into my tired blue ones with a complete and utter lack of comprehension.

"Rhymes with below?" I hinted.

Still nothing.

Derek squeezed his brows together. "It wasn't a crow, was it?"

I smacked my hand against my forehead.

"I'm glad I don't need any legal advice." Esther's knitting needles clickety-clacked as she spoke, eyes on her work. She's a small, narrow-shouldered, elflike septuagenarian with a hawkish nose, sagging eyelids covering her gray-blue eyes and silvery hair normally pulled tightly to the back of her head in a four-inch ponytail.

She was garbed in loose-fitting tan slacks and a black Birds & Bees branded sweatshirt. Definitely not runway worthy but definitely not going to frighten our feathered friends either.

Whether Floyd was frightened by her or not, I couldn't say.

Karl pointed to the TV screen. A racecar had bounced off the racetrack's outside wall and two more cars like a careening steel ball in a pinball machine. Car one was now limping back to the pits. "That car's done. They'll probably have to *junk* her."

We all glanced at the screen.

"Yeah, she's *junk*, all right."

I finally understood what Karl was up to. "No helping, Karl. What is it with men?" I aimed my question at Esther. "They can remember who won the 1962 World Series—"

"Yankees, four games to three." That was Karl chiming in. Thick, black-rimmed glasses framed his gray eyes, which color-coordinated nicely with his own silver locks. "Over the San Francisco Giants."

Karl lives in a two-bedroom bungalow at Rolling Acres, a senior living facility near the outskirts of town. Floyd and Karl are good friends. Floyd has a condo in the same community. He'd moved out of his house and relocated there not long after his wife passed.

"And how many cubic inches in a '56 Corvette—"

My point was interrupted again. This time by Floyd, who held up his hand for silence as he squeezed his eyes shut. "Two hundred and fifty-six," he said proudly.

"They didn't go up to two eighty-three until '57," Karl added.

"I believe that was one of the first mass-produced automobiles to reach the golden one horsepower per cubic inch ratio," Derek contributed.

I folded my arms across my chest. "It was a junco. A dark-eyed junco. And no, I do not know how many cubic inches it is or how much horsepower it can produce or even what its zero to sixty speed is."

"Right, a junco." Derek flipped to the page in the bird guide. "Yep, that's him." His index finger landed on the picture of a gray and white bird resting on a bare tree limb. "Thanks, Amy."

"Don't mention it."

"I tried to tell you." Karl wrapped his hands around his mug.

Paul ambled over carrying a half pitcher of the night's brew. "Anybody need a refill?" Paul is about my age with brown eyes and wavy brown hair. He was Mr. Cool in his usual work outfit, a pair of designer jeans, polished black boots and a black Brewer's Biergarten shirt.

"No, thanks." I was tired. The meeting had devolved into talk of baseball and cars. If I didn't get some sleep, my eyes would be as red as that of the red-eyed vireo we were supposed to have been discussing. "I'm ready to call it a night."

"I'll take some." Karl raised his glass.

"You got it." Paul topped off the ex-chief's glass and shuffled away.

Derek scooted back his chair. "Come on, Amy. I'll walk you home."

Esther picked up her pink knitting bag. "Wait for me."

"How about staying for one more round, Esther?" Floyd suggested. "Karl and I will escort you home afterward."

"No, thanks," Esther replied.

Floyd was crestfallen as Esther stood.

Karl and Floyd used two modes of transportation. One of those modes was the Rolling Acres shuttle bus. The other was the humongous 1956 Chrysler 300B that the boys had purchased together as a project car. It was bright red with a capacious tan leather interior that must have required the sacrifice of a small herd of cows.

The two men loved tooling around in the antique automobile. How they managed to steer the chrome-embellished behemoth around town without bumping into everything in sight was beyond me.

The darn thing took up two parking spaces when they parallel parked. The Chrysler practically occupied parallel universes.

As for Floyd and Esther, I thought they would make a cute couple; him a widower, her never married—so as far as I knew. Esther was keeping a wall between them.

"Good news!"

I turned at the sound of a familiar voice. My mother stood on the sidewalk. My best friend, Kim, was at her side. The outdoor seating area of the biergarten was separated from the sidewalk by a brick pony wall.

Asia had its Great Wall of China. The Town of Ruby Lake had what was becoming known as the Little Wall of Beer. The occasional customer leaving an empty mug on the low wall had turned into a growing custom. Some nights, the wall was lined side to side with empty beer mugs. Paul thought it was cute and now actively encouraged the behavior.

"Mom? Come on in." I waved for them to join us.

A waitress asked if they'd like anything to eat or drink. Both declined although Kim grabbed a triangle of cold mushroom pizza from the aluminum platter resting in the middle of the table.

Esther was annoyed that our departure had been delayed.

"What's up, Mom?" I scooted over and Derek brought a chair from an empty table and set it beside me.

"Thank you, Derek." Mom sat. "Amy, do you remember that nice woman we met at the Outer Banks last year?"

"You mean at the Wings Over Carolina Bird Festival?" Mom, Esther and I had attended the fall bird watching event for several days the previous season.

"That's right."

"We met a lot of nice people there, Mom." Though Esther had done as much to drive away people as she had birds. Her people skills were even poorer than her nonexistent bird watching skills.

Esther made Derek look good by comparison. Our first morning out on the marsh, she had chosen to wear a snow white jacket and a bright red hat. From a distance, her skull looked like the Angry Red Planet. And both colors were scaring the birds away.

I'd had to buy her a pea green jacket and hat in Nags Head just so she would blend in better with our surroundings and not freak out the birds—or the tourists.

"I'm talking about Phoebe Gates."

I inclined my head and thought a moment. I pictured a tall, athletic blonde in her early forties. She had led several of the shorebird field trips. "Sure, I remember Phoebe."

"I remember her, too," Esther said none too kindly. "She kept suggesting that I invest in a new pair of binoculars. She got to be so annoying, I thought she might be a saleswoman working on commission."

To be fair to Phoebe, Esther's binoculars looked like something Captain Nemo might have used to spot land when the *Nautilus* surfaced to look for the Mysterious Island. I'd seen steampunked pairs with more modern touches.

Kim plunked herself down between Floyd and Karl who were only too happy to have her join them. She stretched her long legs. "How are my two favorite men tonight?" She planted a friendly kiss on each man's cheek, leaving a smear of pink lipstick on each.

Floyd blushed. Karl cackled.

Was that a tinge of jealousy I had seen in Esther's eyes when Kim kissed Floyd?

"She telephoned a few minutes ago. She wants you to call her back right away."

"What for?" I barely knew the woman. We'd shared a couple of conversations about birds and a cup of coffee or two over the course of the trip, nothing more.

Kim tossed down the crusty bit remaining of her pizza and licked her fingers all the way out to the tips of her lavender fingernails. She was always watching her weight. Why, I didn't know. Kim is gorgeous. I, on the other hand, look like I lost my gym membership.

Best friends can be so annoying.

Kim's blue eyes flashed as if reading my mind and gloating over that fact. "Remember when you told me about the American Birding Expo?"

"Of course." The American Birding Expo was going to be held in Philadelphia this year. I had attended the first expo prior to opening Birds & Bees. Seeing the level of interest in bird watching evidenced by the attendees had been one of the deciding factors that had led me to finally take the plunge and open my store. At the time, the ABE was being held in Ohio.

Looking back on that time, planning my move back home and taking the plunge going into business for myself, I must have been crazy. While I had a passion for birds, I knew nothing about running a business.

The Expo billed itself as North America's premier, all-encompassing gathering of birding-related products, services, companies, destinations, and organizations.

Mom and I had talked about attending the ABE again sometime, maybe even getting a booth in the expo hall to represent Birds & Bees.

What could it hurt to attend, except the wallet?

"We'll have to check it out someday." The store needed to expand, find new sources of revenue, if we were going to survive—especially since the payroll had grown with the addition of Esther and Kim as regular staffers.

Attending the American Birding Expo might give us some ideas. Not to mention, get the word out about our little store in the heart of North Carolina. Our state, with its diverse systems ranging from the ocean to the mountains with the piedmont in between, offered a wide variety of bird watching opportunities. There ought to be some way we could sustain our modest business. We needed some opportunities of our own.

"Phoebe said there's been a last-minute cancellation," Mom announced.

My brow quirked up. "Really?"

Mom drank from an untouched glass of ice water. "She said to let her know right away if you want it."

Not only did the American Birding Expo sound like fun—I hadn't had a real vacation since long prior to buying my house and starting my business—but a trip to Philadelphia sounded like just the ticket. "It could be a vacation and a marketing opportunity all in one."

"Like they say," Karl began, "kill two birds with one stone, Amy."

"You know I don't love that expression, Karl."

"Who came up with that saying anyway?" Derek turned to me for the answer.

I didn't have it. "Definitely not a bird lover."

"What are you going to tell Phoebe, dear?" Mom asked.

"It's a big decision." I mentally weighed the pluses and minuses and came up with a big fat zero, which was no help at all.

"Judging by that look in your eye, I take it you're in?" Kim said from across the table.

"Well..." I suddenly thought of all the work involved and my heart popped like a red latex balloon against the tip of one of Esther's knitting needles.

"I hear the sound of waffles," Karl said.

"That's *waffling*, dummy." Floyd jabbed Karl with his elbow.

"I'm not waffling," I replied. "It's just..."

"Just what?" Mom set down her glass.

"Who is going to watch the store? And what about marketing materials? We need, I don't know, new business cards, a poster or a banner or something. Maybe some packaged birdseed."

We sold seed in bulk, plus packaged our own Birds & Bees mixes. "We have nothing prepared."

"I'll bet the quick print place in town can make up most of that stuff," offered Floyd. "The bank used to use them all the time. I can give them a call."

"Good idea, Floyd," Mom replied. "Thank you."

I rubbed my neck viciously. "And the expense. Just think of it."

"The expenses will be minimal," assured Mom. "Phoebe says the hotel rooms are paid for."

"And she's giving us the booth for half price," Kim added to the pot.

"It sounds too good to pass up, Amy." Derek squeezed my shoulder.

"I guess." I turned to my mother. "Rooms? Plural?"

Mom nodded. "Phoebe says the exhibitor that had to pull out has booked several rooms at the Eagle Inn. Nonrefundable. She specifically said that we should all come. You too, Esther."

"Me?" Esther pinched her eyes toward her hawkish nose.

Mother nodded. "Phoebe remembers you quite fondly."

I didn't know what to say to that. Apparently, neither did Esther. She looked dumbfounded and annoyed all in one gray-haired bundle.

"*Eagle* Inn," Derek said smoothly. "That sounds like an omen to me."

"Omens can be both good and bad." I knew. I looked deep into his eyes. "Do you really think I should do this?"

"Absolutely."

"Can I come?" Floyd looked at me expectantly.

I jerked my head. "You want to come, Floyd?"

"Sure." He rubbed his hands together. "I could use some action. A little road trip sounds like just the thing." His eyes fell on Esther who wasn't returning the look.

"Well…" The whole thing seemed so overwhelming, so daunting.

"I think it's a great idea," pressed Derek.

"Why?" I narrowed my eyes at him. "You're not trying to get rid of me, are you?" Derek's ex-wife, also an Amy, lived in town and was desperate to get him back.

"Are you kidding? Never. In fact…"

"Yes?"

"I thought I'd come."

I gasped.

Derek blinked at me. "If you'll have me."

"Of course!" Suddenly this trip was looking more like a vacation than a chore.

"Okay." I slapped my palms on the table. "Let's do it." I smiled broadly. "We are all going to Philadelphia and the American Birding Expo!"

"Does that mean we get to share a room?" Derek wriggled his brows.

I blushed brighter than the brightest robin red breast. I mean, Mom was sitting right next to me. "I'll be rooming with Mom," I managed to squeak once I found my voice.

"No, you won't," Mom said. "I can't go. I have a checkup with Dr. Ajax later this week."

My mother had developed adult-onset myotonic multiple sclerosis with type 2 myotonic dystrophy. Dr. Ajax was her neurologist over in the neighboring town of Swan Ridge.

"Besides," Mom continued, "I don't think I'd fare well on such a long road trip. Not to mention, somebody has to stay home and keep an eye on the store. You said so yourself."

I studied my mother. We look a lot alike, especially since she'd stopped dyeing her hair blond and gone back to chestnut brown, the same as me. Mom has brown eyes. I have blue eyes, as had my deceased father. I have a few inches on her height-wise. I'm thirty-four so Mom has a few decades on me time-wise. She says she is older but wiser.

She's right, but I'm not telling her.

Because of her illness, Mom did tend to tire easily but I hated to leave her alone and said so.

"I'll keep you company, Barbara." Kim reached across the table and helped herself to the dregs of my beer.

I looked at her in surprise. "You don't want to come?"

Kim was always up for a vacation, whether it involved travel or not.

"Nah. I'd rather stay home. I've got a lot on my plate right now. Plus, you don't expect your mother to handle Birds and Bees by herself, do you?"

I had a feeling that what was on Kim's plate was her blossoming relationship with Dan Sutton, a local police officer. "I would feel better knowing you're here too. If you're sure you don't mind?"

"Not at all," Kim assured me.

"Okay, then it's settled. Me, Derek, Esther and Floyd. We'll take the Kia." The Kia was my somewhat trusty old minivan. I vowed to myself to have it serviced before the trip.

"Great!" Floyd thumped the table with his palm. "Me and Derek can share a room. You and Esther can share the other."

Esther and I shared a look.

That look was DISMAY.

"Not so fast." Karl waved his hand in the air. An unlit cigar rested between his index and middle fingers. He had carefully avoided lighting up. Not because it was against the law, which it was. Karl, as the former chief of police, felt himself above such things.

No, the last time he'd lit a cigar in the biergarten, Paul had dumped a full mug of beer in his lap, extinguishing the cigar in the process.

Paul maintained it had been an accident. I wasn't so sure about the accident part. Neither was Karl, apparently, because he hadn't lit up inside the joint since.

"What is it, Karl?" I asked.

"If Floyd gets to go, I do too." He stuck his chin out defiantly.

"Fine." Suddenly everybody wanted to go to a birding expo? "I don't suppose that's a problem. You and Floyd can share a room. Right, Floyd?"

"What about me?" Derek wriggled his eyebrows at me again.

"It sounds like there are more than enough rooms to go around. You, me and Esther will have our own rooms."

It didn't mean we had to stay in them.

Floyd turned to his best mate. "If you snore, you're sleeping in the bathtub."

Karl smirked. "And I suggest you not snore."

"Why is that?" Floyd made the mistake of asking.

"Because," Karl answered with a twinkle in his eye, "I'll be packing heat." He jammed the wet cigar between his lips.

"No, no, no!" I waved my hands at Karl. "Nobody is packing heat on this trip. That's all I need, a trigger-fingered half-blind septuagenarian waving a loaded weapon at passing motorists."

"Aw." Karl waved his hand dismissively. "I haven't done anything like that in ages."

I stared the former cop down. "You were packing the last time we all went to the Tuesday movie matinee. No guns, Karl. Let's all survive this trip in one piece." Karl opened his lips to retort but I cut him off. "And by *one piece*, I mean hole free."

"Fine. No guns." Karl folded his arms over his chest and pouted. "Take away a man's only source of happiness."

I turned to Derek and rolled my eyes. "See what you've gotten me into?"

"You're not changing your mind, are you?"

"Not a chance." I pictured romantic evenings with Derek, along the Delaware River, intimate dinners and late-night rendezvous.

I turned to Floyd and Karl. "You'll have to pitch in and help, both with the trip preparations and at the Expo."

"Absolutely." Floyd nodded his assurance. "We'll be glad to help out, won't we, Karl?"

"You got it, Amy. We'll be like deputies," he promised. "You tell us what to do and we'll do it...Chief." He held his hand over his heart. "Scout's honor."

Chief?

I liked the sound of that.

Derek planted his hand on my knee. "When exactly is this American Birding Expo?"

"Let's see, today is Monday and the Expo is—" I turned to Mom for the answer though I feared I knew it only too well.

"Friday, dear," Mom filled in. "The Expo runs Friday through Sunday. Ms. Gates, Phoebe, said for you to plan on being there on Wednesday, or Thursday at the latest, to set up your booth."

I groaned. "It's probably, what, an eight-hour drive from here to Philly?"

"More like ten," Kim corrected.

"I'm glad you find this funny," I said when Derek laughed.

"Hey, I'm not the one who has to set up an entire booth."

"No?" I said sternly.

Derek lifted his chin ceilingward. "I wonder if there are any good golf courses near this Expo thing. I might bring my clubs."

I grabbed his jaw and forced him to look me in the eyes. "I expect you to pull your weight, mister."

I grabbed my jacket from the back of my chair.

Derek's shoulders sagged. "Oh. Right, Chief." He grinned sheepishly at Floyd and Karl who were sniggering.

"It looks like we've all got a lot to do and very little time to do it in." Derek came to his feet. "I'll let my dad know I'll be out of town for a few days."

I gripped his hand and held him back. "Are you sure you can come? I mean, absolutely sure?" Half the reason for going was to spend a little quality time with Derek. If he backed out now...

"Don't worry. Things are light in the office. Dad can handle the casework." He looked past me to my mother. "And don't you and Dad have dinner plans tomorrow?"

"That we do." Derek's dad, Ben, and my mother were casually dating. I don't think either of them were sure how far they wanted to take things.

As for me and Derek, I knew exactly how far I wanted things to go. And there was nothing *casual* about it.

"You had better telephone Phoebe Gates right away to let her know you'll be taking the booth." Mom handed me a slip of paper with a phone number scribbled on it.

"You don't want her to give the spot to somebody else," Kim chimed in.

"I'll call from the apartment." I closed my hand around the slip of paper. "Tomorrow morning we'll make a list of everything we need and see if we can remotely get things together in time. I hope we know what we're getting ourselves into."

"Next stop, Philadelphia!" Floyd climbed to his feet and grabbed his jacket from the table behind him.

"Not me," snapped Esther.

"What?" I looked at her, nonplussed.

"I don't do Philadelphia."

"What do you mean you don't do Philadelphia?" Karl blinked at her. "That makes no sense."

"Make sense of this." Esther balled her right hand into a fist and waved it in front of Karl's nose.

The retired chief of police threw back his head and brayed.

Floyd joined him. A pair of old goats enjoying a good joke.

"Come on, Esther," Floyd said. "Stop joking around. Of course you're going. This is Birds and Bees business, isn't it?"

"That doesn't make it my business." She returned his stare eyeball for eyeball.

"But you *are* the assistant manager," Floyd persisted. "It seems only fitting that you represent the store."

Esther has no respect for the concept of a pecking order, let alone the one at Birds & Bees. In a short period of time, she had gone from renter to employee, to self-proclaimed assistant manager to partner.

If I wasn't careful, she'd end up owning the business, lock, stock and birdseed and I'd be sweeping the floors for her.

I didn't know what was going on in Esther's head at the moment—then again, I never did—but I couldn't imagine why she would not want a free trip to Philadelphia.

I leaned toward her. "Are you worried about your apartment?" Esther may or may not have a cat. I claimed she did. She claimed I was nuts.

Technically, cats are a no-no, unallowed according to the lease. Then again, that was when I thought I was allergic to cats. I had recently learned, much to my chagrin, that I was allergic to goldenrod.

The few times I'd been in Esther's apartment—something both she and I avoided as much as possible—the sneezing I had experienced had been due to her goldenrod night cream.

Not a cat.

"I'm sure Mom and Kim will be more than happy to keep an eye on... *things* for you," I said. Why Esther would not just come out and fess up to owning a cat at this point, I couldn't imagine.

Esther tossed her knitted bag over her shoulder and folded her arms. "There is nothing in Philadelphia, Pennsylvania that I wish to see."

"How about the Liberty Bell?" Karl suggested.

"Cracked," Esther was quick to reply. "Who cares?"

"Independence Hall?" Derek put in. "You can see the very room where the Declaration of Independence and the U.S. Constitution were signed."

"Boring," Esther snapped. "Leave it to a lawyer to think *that* would be interesting."

Derek shrugged at me as if to say *I tried*.

"They have a lovely Museum of the American Revolution," Mom said. "Your father and I took you when you were five. Remember, Amy?"

"Vaguely," I confessed. At that age, I remember thinking that one museum looked pretty much like any other.

"Esther doesn't need a museum on the American Revolution," Karl bellowed. "She lived through it."

"Very funny, *old* man." Esther shook her fist at Karl while Floyd shot him a withering look. "I said I'm not going and I'm not going. Take no for an answer already, people."

I didn't bother to scold Karl. He and Esther were always taking potshots at each other. It was all meant in good, clean fun.

At least it would be until Esther decided to run Karl through with one of her knitting needles.

"Aw, Esther." Floyd had only shown an interest in going because he expected Esther to be going.

"Who knows what we might learn at the Expo, Esther," I found myself saying. "The contacts we might make. Maybe get some new ideas for the store. I could really use you there." I didn't know why, but the more she resisted the idea, the more I was determined to drag her along.

"Philadelphia is for the birds," Esther said.

There was a joke in there someplace—I mean, we were talking about the American Birding Expo—but nobody laughed.

I was about to give up and suggest we head for home when Kim spoke up.

"You know, if it was me and I was going..." Kim's voice trailed off as she waited for everyone to give her their undivided attention.

"Yes?"

Kim glanced quickly at Esther then winked at me. "I'd hit the casinos after hours."

"Casinos?" Karl leaned forward, planting his elbows on the table. Esther stilled.

Did Kim know something about Esther that I didn't?

"There are casinos in Philly?" Derek said. "I didn't realize."

"Gambling casinos?" I asked, as if there could be any other kind.

"Several big ones have opened there in the last ten years or so. Mom and I have been a couple of times." I knew that Kim's mother had a fondness for games of chance. That explained her many marriages.

"I'd never gamble." Mother folded her hands in her lap. "I like to keep my money safe, not chance it to a pair of dice, a spinning wheel or a deck of playing cards."

"I'm with you, Mom. Nobody here cares about gambling away their hard-earned money, Kim."

"It was just a thought," Kim replied.

"I've got a few bucks lying around burning a hole in my pocket," Karl retorted. "I might visit one of those casinos and take a chance." He turned to me. "If the chief gives us any time off."

"We'll see, Karl. We'll see. Like they say," I teased, "time off is for *good* behavior."

Floyd held his breath and glanced furtively towards Esther.

Esther jumped to her feet, pocketbook in one hand and knitting bag in the other. She started purposefully to the exit.

We looked at one another.

At the door, Esther paused and snapped her neck around. "What are you all sitting there like lumps for? We've got a load of work to do and very little time to get it done in."

Esther pointed a knobby finger at Karl and Floyd and we hushed. "I expect to see you two buzzards at Birds and Bees bright and early."

She shifted her bag. "And by bright and early, I mean 8 a.m., not 10 a.m., not 9 a.m., not 8:30."

Karl nudged Floyd in the ribs. "Tough old bird, ain't she?"

Floyd barely noticed. He was wearing the biggest smile I had seen in ages.

2

Improbable as it seemed, Wednesday morning we were ready to roll. We hit the road at daybreak. After a grueling twelve hour plus drive, we reached the outskirts of Philadelphia.

"Man." Floyd pressed his nose against the glass. "That's what I call the big city."

"She's big all right." Karl squeezed his face next to Floyd's.

"Took us long enough to get here." Esther's knitting needles gnashed almost as loudly as her teeth.

"We could have shaved down our trip time if only some of us would have thought to go to the bathroom at the same time we were stopping for gas," I noted.

We were going to have to work out a better system for the return voyage of the damned.

"Don't worry, guys." Derek studied his cell phone screen. "According to the GPS, we've only got a few miles to go. We'll be there soon enough."

"I hope so." I put my foot on the brake pedal as traffic on I-95 morphed into bumper to bumper gridlock. "I hope so."

A few miles and an hour later, we pulled up on a quaint, very narrow street in Philadelphia's popular Historic District.

I double parked next to a white and yellow taxi outside the Eagle Inn's main entrance, out of which spilled a man and woman in baggy clothes. A green and blue banner with a golden eagle hung suspended from the inn's chocolate brown brick façade.

I turned off the engine. "I'll check us in. Be right back."

Derek craned his neck looking up and down the crowded little street. "Any idea where we are supposed to park?"

"I'll ask inside." I nodded to the burgundy and gold-liveried doorman as he toted a pair of large green and yellow-striped shopping bags for the taxi couple.

The best thing about the foyer was the black and white photo taken of a long-ago Philadelphia. The Eagle Inn might have been historic but the lobby floor looked like it hadn't been vacuumed in ages. Rich green and blue wall paper hung limply on the walls.

A slouching woman with a pair of oversized tortoiseshell glasses on her nose straightened her back and positioned a smile on her face as I approached the front desk. "Good evening," she said with a brilliant flash of teeth. "How can I help you?" Her accent said New Jersey.

I placed my purse on the counter. "Amy Simms." I glanced out toward the van. "And company. We're checking in."

"Wonderful." The woman's manicured fingers began clicking away at a black keyboard. "How many nights will you be with us?"

I did the mental math, which was harder to do than you might think given my state of mental fatigue. "Uh, four?"

Peggy, or the woman who'd pinched Peggy's silver and black nametag, replied with more keyboard clicking. "And how many are in your party?"

"Believe me, we're anything but a party."

Eyebrows went up, followed by a blank stare. "Excuse me?"

I did some more mental math. This was getting tiresome. I needed food and I needed sleep. Not necessarily in that order. I'd take them as I could get them. "Uh, five?"

"Five. I see. How many rooms will you be needing?"

"Actually, I guess I should have started with this. We're here for the American Birding Expo. Ms. Gates, Phoebe Gates," I added when Peggy or wannabe Peggy blinked without a sign of recognition, "she said that there were rooms reserved here for us."

Peggy frowned as she searched her reservations list.

"They might be under the name Hikers and Bikers Tours."

"Hmm." Her blue eyes scanned a computer screen that only she could see as her finger tapped out a measured beat on her lower lip. "I don't think so."

"Are you sure?"

"Yep."

I sighed. "Whatever. Okay, give me four rooms. The cheapest you've got." Floyd and Karl had already agreed to share a room.

"No can do."

"No can do?"

She wagged her head at me and clicked her very pink tongue. "I've got two rooms, double beds, fourth floor. Deluxe view."

"Two rooms?" I looked at her bleakly.

She held up two fingers, either to announce victory or demonstrate the math. Either way, I was stuck. It was too late to go driving around Philadelphia looking for better lodgings. Even then, we might not find any.

"There are five of us," I reminded the desk clerk.

"But you're related, right?"

"Well, sort of. It's not like we're family." The couple from the taxi disappeared behind the doors of a brass-faced elevator.

"But they aren't strangers," Peggy countered.

The woman was right. Some of them were strange but they were not strangers. Still, I couldn't see two of the guys snuggling up in one narrow, double bed. "Is there a convertible sofa in the rooms perchance?"

"Nope." She lit up. "I can have housekeeping send up a cot though. Although it is an extra twenty-five dollars per night." The phone beside her rang. I waited for her to pick up but she ignored it. She darted her eyes briefly at the phone. "That could be someone calling for a room."

"I'll take them," I said quickly. "And the cot." Derek, Floyd and Karl could work out their own sleeping arrangements.

"Great."

Sure, great for her. I handed over a credit card with a smidgen of space below its max threshold and couldn't help wincing as she named the price. And that wasn't counting the taxes. I couldn't ask the others to pay their own way. They were only in Philadelphia to help me.

So much for Mom's assurance that this trip was going to be cheap.

"Can you tell me where your parking garage is?"

"Sorry. The inn does not have a garage of its own. There is a public parking facility a mere two blocks from here."

"A mere two blocks? I guess that will have to do."

Shoulders sagging, feet dragging, I returned to the van. I waited until we'd unloaded everything necessary from the van and had piled everything onto a luggage trolley, and ridden the elevator to the fourth floor, before announcing our room assignments.

Derek was going down later to move the van.

I had put off the bad news as long as I could. "Karl, you and Floyd will be in 401. Derek…"

"Yes?" Derek floundered from foot to foot as he manhandled a pair of suitcases that hadn't fit on the trolley.

"You are with Karl and Floyd."

"You mean we are on the same floor?" Derek asked.

"I mean you are all in the same room."

Esther cackled.

"Oh?" Though he tried to mask it, the look on Derek's face was not a happy one.

"I could only get the two rooms."

"But—" Karl began.

"There's no sense standing around out here talking about this." A guest shouldered past us in the narrow hallway. "It's late and we're all tired. Two rooms is what we've got."

With a muffled groan, I turned to Esther, who had backed up to the wall. Her eyes were mere slits. "Esther, it looks like we are roomies."

There was nothing muffled about Esther's return groan.

* * * *

Thursday morning came too soon.

It took us forty-five minutes to reach the Greater Philadelphia Expo Center where the American Birding Expo was being held.

"Why on earth did the people that booked that hotel we're in pick a place so far away?" griped Esther, who insisted on riding shotgun that morning.

"I don't know." I didn't.

"Look on the bright side," Derek said from the backseat. "We'll be in the heart of the city after hours every day."

"Sure," said Floyd. "Restaurants, bars, shopping, sightseeing."

"Works for me," I said.

"Gambling." Karl rubbed his hands together greedily. "Where are those casinos Kim was telling us about?"

"We'll get some tourist information when we return to the inn later. I saw a bunch of racks filled with brochures off the lobby," I replied as we approached the sprawling exposition center.

Inside, a volunteer, Maury Bland, greeted us. I explained who we were and he showed us to our booth.

A number of folks moved about the exhibit hall making last minute preparations, others mingled in small groups chatting.

Most of the booths looked ready to go. The Expo started tomorrow. We had our work cut out for us.

Maury stopped at a smallish booth. "This is it." He picked up a tented cardboard sign bearing the name of the tour group.

"It says Hikers and Bikers Tours International." Karl pointed to the light blue at the rear of the booth. Similarly colored half curtains defined the sides of our space.

I dug my hands into my back pockets. "I suppose we can hang our store banner over it."

Our booth was positioned near the end of a long row. There was another row behind us and more vendors across the way. Most along this aisle seemed to be tour operators. Not surprising, considering we were taking over the spot of Hikers and Bikers, a tour outfit.

The space stage right of ours was completely empty. The booth stage left was the same size as ours. It held several TV displays and a long table covered with a black cloth. A sign on an easel stated that the booth represented a nonprofit bird sanctuary in Ecuador.

It took us several trips to unload the van with Maury pitching in.

Floyd and Karl got busy hanging the Birds & Bees sign using a roll of duct tape we had brought along for jobs such as that.

"Is Phoebe around?" I inquired.

The walkie-talkie attached to Maury's hip squawked and he answered. "Be right there," he said after listening a moment. He clipped the walkie-talkie to his belt once more and turned to me. "I gotta go. Ms. Gates' office is through that big set of doors, down the hall and then first door on your left."

Leaving my crew to finish setting up, I went around to the offices. Moving down a gray carpeted hall along which there were a number of doors, I slowed at the sound of a man's angry voice.

"I don't care." A paunchy, purple-faced man in a yellow polo shirt and khaki pants stepped out of a door on my left. He latched onto the doorframe as if he intended to rip it from the wall. "Keep away from Lorna or I walk."

He spun on his heels. I squawked as he barreled into me.

"Can't you watch where you're going?" Furious black eyes looked up at me. The sixtyish man was several inches smaller than me and that was in hiking boots.

"Sorry," I said, taken aback. Unnatural light thrown off from the fluorescent bulbs above reflected off the bald patch atop his gray head. He had wideset eyes, giving plenty of room to his fleshy nose. He needed a shave. And some manners.

On some men, a five o'clock shadow is sexy. On him, it looked like the Shadow of Death.

"You should be." Angry Guy narrowed his eyes and huffed. Did I smell alcohol on his breath? "Were you *eavesdropping?*" The word dripped out of his mouth like poison.

"Eavesdropping! What for?" I threw my shoulders back. "A dead sparrow could have heard you from the middle of the expo hall."

"You should learn to mind your own business." He flipped his hand, indicating that I was blocking his path.

"You should stop behaving like such an anachronistic jerk. If you did, you would see that this was a public hallway and that other people are using it."

Angry Guy, whose neck was now the burgundy shade of a Bolivian pompadour cotinga, stuck his arm out, nearly punching me in the chin.

Not wanting the situation to escalate out of control, I acquiesced, pushing my back up against the wall. He huffed as he surged past me. I watched him stomp off.

A blond head peeked around the corner of the doorway Angry Guy had vacated. It was Phoebe Gates.

I peeled myself off the wall and caught my breath. "Wow. Hi, Phoebe."

She grinned in recognition. "Hello, Amy. Good to see you again."

I moved closer and received a welcoming hug. "Who was that guy and what was his problem?"

Phoebe laughed and waved me inside. "It was nothing."

"Nothing?"

She cupped her right hand to her mouth. "I hear he's going through a divorce."

"My congratulations to his soon-to-be ex," I replied.

Phoebe looked smashing in a clingy black dress and matching heels. An American Birding Expo lanyard hung around her neck.

"I'm so glad you could make it." Phoebe took a seat at a well-ordered beige metal desk. "How's your mother?"

"Mom's minding the store." I took a chair opposite her when she indicated that I should sit. "She decided to stay behind. Health reasons."

"I'm sorry to hear that. Is Ms. Pilaster ill as well?"

"Esther? No, she's here. She's helping setup the booth with the others."

"Others?" Phoebe was scanning some documents on her desk as we spoke.

"Derek, Floyd and Karl. They'll be working the booth along with me."

Phoebe explained that I had some paperwork to fill out, which is normally sent out to exhibitors beforehand. I promised I'd get it back to her in good time.

"Bring it by at your convenience. If I'm not in, just drop it on the desk."

I stopped outside her door. "You never did tell me who Angry Guy is. I'd like to know so I can avoid him." At all costs, I might have added.

Phoebe's brow shot up. "You really didn't recognize him? I thought you were joking."

I played the brow game too, squeezing mine hard enough to show I was puzzled but not so hard as to leave permanent wrinkles. I had enough of those already. "Should I have?"

"That was James Jules Fuller."

I gaped. "*That* was JJ Fuller." I slapped my forehead. "Of course."

Phoebe grinned.

"It's just that in all his publicity photos he always looks so-so..."

"So jovial?"

I nodded agreement.

"So happy?"

My head kept bobbing. I was an Amy Simms bobble head.

Little wonder I hadn't recognized him.

Besides his Angry Guy disguise, I had never seen the man without a ball cap atop his head. The ball cap featured the embroidered image of *Campephilus principalis*, the ivory-billed woodpecker, a species thought by many to be extinct. An environmental group was offering fifty thousand dollars to the first person to lead one of their scientists to an actual living bird.

JJ Fuller had been boasting for years that the prize would be his. It was his Holy Grail.

Phoebe opened her arms. "Like I said, word on the street is marital problems."

"Are you sure it isn't mental problems? Maybe all that birding has made him cuckoo."

Phoebe laughed.

JJ Fuller was one of the rock stars of the birding world. He was a famed bird photographer and bird expert. His face had appeared on countless birding and wildlife magazine covers. He'd written for every major birding magazine.

JJ Fuller was this year's American Birding Expo's guest of honor and keynote speaker.

And I had insulted the guy. Bird poop.

At the registration desk, an officious young woman printed out American Birding Expo badges for each of us. I grabbed a handful of lanyards and some welcome swag bags and carried them to the booth.

Floyd lowered a bottle of water from his lips. "Derek ran out to the van."

"And Karl?"

"Tagging along."

"Okay. We should be done here soon. Here's your ID. You'll need to wear it the entire time we're working."

Floyd strung his lanyard around his neck.

"You, too, Esther."

Esther looked at her badge. "At least they spelled the name right."

"I suggest we head back to the hotel, freshen up and enjoy what Philadelphia has to offer."

"Karl's gonna like that. He brought a wad of cash."

I narrowed my eyes. "Define wad."

"Four grand."

"Cash?" I gasped.

"Sure."

"Floyd, I don't think it's a good idea for Karl to be wandering around town with four thousand dollars in his pocket. Pockets," I amended. How many pockets did one require to haul around four thousand dollars?

Floyd threw up his hands. "Tell him that."

"Karl is a stubborn old coot." Esther put in her two cents. The money kept piling up.

"Are you still planning on hitting the casino with us, Esther?"

"Yep."

"Well, you can count me and Derek out." I had no idea how much money Esther was intending to gamble and did not want to know.

"We weren't counting you in," Esther deadpanned.

"Floyd, why don't you—" I froze.

"You okay, Amy?" Floyd asked.

"What? Yes." JJ Fuller was strutting up the aisle. He was the last person I wanted to see. Nor did I want him to see me. I placed my hand on Floyd's shoulder and shielded myself behind him. "How about taking a look for Derek and Karl? They should have been back by now."

"Okay."

"Ask them if they can scrounge up an extra chair or two." We had been given three six-foot tables and three chairs. We had arranged one table in front and one on each side, leaving the drapery covering the rear.

Floyd saluted. "Sure, Chief."

I made myself busy unboxing and sorting Barbara's Bird Bars. We had several trays of the sample size bars to give away.

"What's this?" I heard a now all too familiar voice bark. I didn't dare turn around. It was Fuller.

"Those are special copies of *Hummingbirds and Their Habits*," Esther explained. "Each one personally autographed by the author himself, Dr. Mason Livingston."

Fuller harrumphed in reply.

"He's dead, you know," Esther said.

A small shiver went up my spine. Mason's death had been both untimely and unpleasant.

I heard the sound of pages turning and, figuring JJ Fuller was intent on the book, I dared a peek out of the corner of my eye. He flipped the heavy pages, making unflattering remarks and sounds as he did so.

Fuller read the inscription on the title page aloud. "To my friends at Birds and Bees. So." He slammed the cover on the coffee table-sized book. "This man was a friend of yours?"

"Not me. I barely knew the man," Esther replied as she straightened the book on the pile. "But Amy here, she and Mason were best friends."

I flinched.

"Isn't that right, Amy?"

"You!" Angry eyes flared at me. "I might have known." Fuller rolled his head side to side. "You were friends with that—that fraud, that plagiarist!" He aimed his finger accusingly at the cover of Mason's book.

I stormed to the front table and dumped a handful of bird bars in the woven basket on the table beside Esther. "Professor Livingston may have had his flaws," and then some, "but he was a brilliant man.

"And this," I said, grabbing the book and clutching it to my chest, "is a brilliant piece of work." The last work that Mason Livingston would ever do.

I had bought out the supply from our now defunct local bookstore. I thought I might be able to sell a few of the autographed copies at the Expo. I had a personally signed copy that I kept on my bookshelf at home.

"The only thing brilliant about that book is the coloring of that blue-throated goldentail." Fuller's chest puffed out like a greater sage-grouse at mating time. "And he probably photoshopped that."

Okay, so the man knew his hummingbirds. He was right, it was a blue-throated goldentail on the cover. Anybody with a bit of birding knowledge could have figured that out. The unique hummingbird boasted a long, sharp bill that was distinct for being red except for the dark tip and a golden fan for a tail. "Lucky guess."

Esther pressed her knuckles to the table and leaned toward Fuller. "Are you planning to buy anything?"

He looked at her with something between incredulity and amusement. "I do not *buy* anything. Do you see who I am?" He tugged at the lanyard now draped around his neck and jammed his thumb against his badge. "JJ Fuller, Guest of Honor."

"People give me things." He snatched a bar from the basket and began unwrapping it from its plastic covering quickly, his fingers moving deftly. "People *pay me* to endorse their products."

"Well, you aren't any guest of ours." Esther wrestled the bird bar from his fingers before he managed to sink his teeth into it. "If you want something here, buster, you are going to have to pay for it. Those bars are four dollars each!" She stuck her hand out, palm up.

Fuller sneered and reached for a fresh bar.

Esther slapped his hand. He drew back with a sick laugh.

"I admire your spirit, Ms. Pilaster." He shook his red fingers. "However, if you lay a hand on me again, I shall have you removed."

Esther's fist lashed out for Fuller's nose like a heat, or in this case, flesh-seeking missile. "Remove this from your—"

"Now, now, Esther." I clamped my hand over hers and forced her to lower her arm. "Esther gets a little cranky when she's off her meds. Don't you, Esther?"

"What?" Esther was seeing red. "I don't—"

Fuller snorted triumphantly but triumph turned to venom as a flash of light went off in his face. "What do you think you are doing?"

We spun sideways to see a photographer snapping pictures. An action shot of Esther taking a poke at the guest of honor.

The photographer, a lanky man in his early forties with short dark hair, brown eyes and a big smile, said, "Thanks for the shot, JJ. This will look great in the daily Expo blog." He lowered the fancy camera around his neck.

"I've warned you before, Lisbon," Fuller growled.

"Great," I sighed, feeling my world collapsing all around me. "Just what I need, a photograph of us fighting with the Expo's guest of honor."

"We might never get invited back," mumbled Esther. "Not that I care."

"We might not last the weekend," I whispered.

"If you post that, Lisbon," Fuller warned, "I'll walk. And then I'll sue."

"Okay, okay. It was just for fun." The photographer waved his hands in surrender then snatched up the camera once more. "How about a shot of the three of you standing in front of your booth?"

The man named Lisbon squinted at the sign. "Birds and Bees?" A lopsided grin formed on his face. "I love it. Come on, JJ. What do you say?"

JJ Fuller thrust his hands in his pockets and stomped past us, hopefully never to be seen again. A little voice inside my head told me it might be best to avoid the keynote speech he was scheduled to give tomorrow night.

The photographer smiled. "I guess that's a no, huh?"

"I'm afraid so," I answered.

"One shot of him probably would have shattered your lens." Esther grabbed the basket.

"What did you stop him from taking a bite for?" I asked.

"He's nasty." Esther rewrapped the bar and dropped it in the basket. She wiped her hands on her apron. "Somebody ought to give him an attitude adjustment. Preferably with a baseball bat."

Satisfied with her handiwork, she angled the basket so it would be within easy reach of passersby.

"It was bird food, Esther. I'd have paid to watch him eat it."

Esther chuckled. "Wish I'd thought of that. Next time I see him, I'll apologize and give him one as a peace offering."

"Let's get a shot of you ladies, anyway." Lisbon held up his camera. "Okay?"

"Great." We could use all the publicity we could get.

Esther ran from behind the table. She slipped between me and the photographer and marched off.

"Esther! Where are you going?"

"Bathroom break."

I shrugged for the photographer's sake. "Old people, right?"

The photographer extended his hand. "I'm Dennis Lisbon."

"Amy Simms. A pleasure meeting you. Are you with the local paper?"

"No." He shoved his camera to one side, revealing his badge. "Dennis Lisbon, freelance photographer for the ABE."

I posed in front of the booth while he took several pictures for the Expo's daily blog.

After his departure, I wandered the aisles, checking out the other exhibitors. The Expo was bigger than the one I'd attended previously. Founded by Bill Thompson, III, of *Bird Watcher's Digest* magazine and hosted with its partners, the American Birding Association, and the John James Audubon Center at Mill Grove, it really was a one-stop shop for all things bird with over a hundred vendors including conservation groups, clubs, nature and birding tour companies, optics firms, birding equipment and supply firms, booksellers, bird- and birdwatching-related clothing retailers, artists, photographers and more.

There was still no sign of Esther. I sat in our booth and stretched my legs. The next thing I knew, or didn't know, I'd dozed off.

"Wake up, sleepy head."

I opened my eyes to the sight, and lovely feel, of Derek planting a soft kiss on my forehead.

"You are back." I grinned and kissed him back.

"Ahem," Karl cleared his throat theatrically. "Sleeping on the job already, Chief?"

I jumped to my feet. "I was waiting for my deputies."

"We're here now. What do you need?" Floyd asked.

"How about rehanging the sign?" It had fallen to the floor not long after Dennis Lisbon snapped his pictures.

"What about me, Chief?" Derek slung his coat over his shoulder.

"Did Karl ask you about the chairs?"

"Yep. We talked to Maury. He said he would see what he could do."

"Would you mind running out to one of the stores and picking up some snacks and drinks? A number of the exhibitors have candies and drinks, that sort of thing, for people passing by. I thought we should do the same."

"No problem."

"Where's Esther?" Floyd eased himself into a chair as Derek headed off.

"I don't know. She's been gone quite a while."

A group of four, arms full and dressed in matching khaki shirts and olive pants, bustled into the booth next door like storm troopers. One of the two young women waved in our general direction after setting down a pair of bulging black duffel bags.

I set a business card holder on the front table. Esther had brought a stack of her own business cards as well: Esther Pilaster, Birds & Bees, Assistant Manager. I moved hers a little behind my own.

There was a sudden crash, and somebody shouted, "Heads up!" Another yelled, "Watch out!"

I spun around as a retractable aluminum stand crashed down on our front table. The drapery sagged.

"Sorry about that," an apologetic brunette with short locks said. "Be more careful, George," she added, turning her attention to an abashed young man clutching a five by eight-foot banner in his hands.

"Sorry. You okay over there?" George had a boyish face, made more so by the longish dirty blond hair dangling untidily around his head.

"I'm fine." I handed him the fallen stand. "Are you okay, Floyd?"

"Tiptop." Floyd looked a little flustered but otherwise uninjured.

The young woman thrust out her hand. "Robin Tork, Back to Nature Tours."

Strong fingers gave mine a squeeze. My hand felt like a dishrag in comparison. Robin had a pert nose, a tanned complexion and jungle green eyes.

"I'm Amy Simms. That's Floyd and that's Karl."

Robin pointed to her coworkers, who included clumsy George Dolenz, stunning Romena Jones with her bouncy brown locks in a ponytail, and an easy on the eyes young man with a swarthy complexion and charcoal eyes called Harry Nesmith. "We'll try to set up our booth without knocking your booth down. Won't we, people?"

George and the others pledged to be more careful in the future.

"I've got your extra chairs." Maury wheeled up with a handcart stacked with chairs.

"Thanks." I asked Floyd and Karl to hold down the booth until I got back.

"Will do," Karl had crossed over into neighbor territory and was lending the lovely Romena, who had a sultry Spanish accent, a hand unboxing postcards.

"Let's meet up here in an hour. We've done all we can today and we'll want to be here bright and early tomorrow."

"What about Esther?" Floyd looked forlorn.

"I'll tell you what, Floyd. Let's split up and look for her." I knew he'd been hoping for some Esther time. "I'll take this half of the hall." I indicated with my hands. "You take the other. Whoever finds her first, comes back here and waits for the other to return in an hour."

"You don't suppose anything has happened to her, do you, Amy?"

Floyd's wife had passed suddenly. And he hadn't been there to say goodbye. I knew that experience still left a hole in his heart.

"Of course not, Floyd. You know how Esther is."

Honestly, I didn't think any of us knew quite how Esther was. Though always more than willing to make her opinions known when it came to the rest of us, Esther was secretive in regard to her personal life and her past. "I'm sure she's only lost track of time."

"She never wanted to come in the first place." Floyd tugged his moustache. "You don't suppose she went home, do you?"

"To Ruby Lake?" I wasn't surprised at the idea but I was surprised that it had crossed Floyd's mind as it had mine. I hoped for his sake she wasn't right this minute standing at a freeway onramp trying to thumb a ride back to Ruby Lake.

"Can you keep a secret?"

Floyd nodded.

"Esther is playing hard to get."

Floyd wrinkled his brow. "Hard to get?"

"Sure, Floyd. Esther likes you. She really likes you. But…" I shrugged. "She doesn't want you to think she's being too easy."

"She doesn't?"

"Nooo. Esther is afraid that you will think badly of her if she comes on too strong."

"I'd never think anything bad about Esther, Amy."

"Of course, you wouldn't." I smiled broadly. "Let's find Esther and get out of here. I'm ready for some fun."

"Me, too."

"Remember, what I said?" I pressed my finger to my lips. "Our little secret, right?"

Floyd nodded then turned on his heels to begin the search for Esther.

I prayed Floyd could keep a secret because if he mentioned a single word of what I had said to Esther the Pester she would kill me.

3

I wandered slowly through the expo hall looking for signs of my missing assistant manager. Spotting a frizzy gray head bobbing in the distance, I squinted.

"Like to borrow a spotting scope?" a deep-voiced man asked.

"No, thanks. That won't be necessary. False alarm." The frizzy gray head belonged to a man in black suspenders.

The speaker looked down at his badge then held out his hand. "Irving Shipman, Ornitho Optics."

"Amy Simms, Birds and Bees." Ornitho Optics was a small, yet prestigious Zurich-based optics firm that had been around for a hundred years or more.

"Looking for a bird to add to your life list?" he teased.

"Looking for an employee who's already on my 'making life difficult' list. She appears to be missing in action. I don't suppose you've seen her?"

"What's she look like?"

I described Esther down to her orthopedic sneakers.

"Sorry, I can't say I have." He dutifully looked up and down the aisle. "I'm sure she'll turn up. Stay in one spot long enough and everybody passes by, a dozen times or more."

Irving Shipman reached for a business card from a modest stack on his front table and handed me one. "First timer?"

"Yes," I answered as I fingered the thick linen card with blue foil accents on a white background. "How did you know?"

"You've got that look. Like an owl caught in the glare of a spotlight."

"I hope my eyes don't look that big." I chuckled.

"Speaking of eyes, take a look over there." Irving Shipman chinned to his left.

I slowly turned. JJ Fuller stood arguing in the far corner. I might not have recognized JJ during our first confrontation but, even from a distance, I knew who the woman was. The statuesque blonde in the tight green slacks, hiking boots, and taut tan top was Ilsa Skoglund, a world-famous birder and filmmaker. Her production company was responsible for a number of bird-related adventure programs.

Apparently she and JJ Fuller had their differences.

"I wonder what those two are arguing about."

Irving sat on the edge of the table. "My guess is that JJ isn't happy to see Ilsa here."

"Oh? Isn't she one of the guests?"

"No. Generally speaking, organizers know not to schedule the two of them for the same event the same year. Ms. Skoglund must have decided on her own initiative to attend."

"She's either very brave or enjoys getting Fuller's goat." I watched as Fuller, the shorter of the two, poked his finger repeatedly in Ms. Skoglund's face.

"The remarkable young lady has traveled the world on birding and wildlife adventures. She's as tough as nails." Irving Shipman slipped a thick pair of reading glasses from his coat pocket and hung them on his nose after giving them a wipe with a lens cloth.

"If I were her," I said, "I might be using my fingernails right about now." Fuller was practically puffing like a dragon in the woman's chest.

"There's more than a little blood lost between them." He ran his eyes over a list of email contacts on a clipboard lying flat on the table. Shipman's Ornitho Optics booth was about the size of ours. The space contained a plethora of spotting scopes and binoculars of many sizes, tripods and other optic equipment of interest to birding enthusiasts.

"I'm not surprised."

"Is that the voice of experience?" Irving popped a lime green candy-coated piece of gum in his mouth and offered the pack to me.

I declined. "No. I ran into Mr. Fuller earlier and he was a bit cranky, you might say."

Remembering Phoebe's words about his pending divorce, I knew that JJ Fuller might be having a bad day. We all have our troubles. I vowed not to let my less than stellar first encounter with him color my impression too harshly.

"I won't be surprised if those two kill each other." Irving chewed slowly, and his breath came out peppermint scented.

"Do they hate one another that much?"

"And then some. Folks need to learn to let go. You live longer that way." Shipman was an ordinary looking fellow about Karl and Floyd's age, with slightly sunken cheeks, a pale complexion and dark brown hair, graying at the temples. His eyes were medium brown. His suit matched his eyes.

He picked up his box of gum and tipped another onto his tongue. "Have you ever seen two male robins fighting?"

I shook my head in the negative.

"Robins can be quite ferocious. They will do anything, stop at nothing, to defend their territory."

A man in a security uniform stepped into the fray, separating JJ Fuller and Ilsa Skoglund. JJ threw up his hands and stomped off.

Ilsa stayed behind, chatting with the anxious-looking security man. "Poor guy. The security man, I mean. I'm sure he didn't expect to have to worry about anything more than ruffled feathers and double-parked cars when he signed on to work a birding festival."

"I've seen that pair arguing at more of these birding festivals than you can imagine, young lady. It will never end."

"Unless they really do kill each other," I joked.

"Birders don't kill one another."

"Glad to hear it."

"They do far worse."

"What could be worse?"

"They set out to destroy their nemesis's reputation."

"Care to elaborate?"

"I've said enough."

"I understand."

Fuller was now chatting, a bit more civilly, or so it seemed, with another woman, a short black-haired woman in denim jeans and a red scoop-neck sweater. The two had settled at a small round table near an empty booth. "You seem to know all the players. Who is that woman that is with Fuller now?"

"JJ's wife, Lorna."

Lorna reached across the table and slapped her husband on the cheek.

"That was no love tap." I turned around to hear Irving Shipman's thoughts on the matter but he had moved a few steps away and was talking to Maury.

I nodded goodbye and resumed my hunt for my missing, self-proclaimed assistant manager.

I swung through the main entrance doors. The sun had broken through the morning clouds. A small flock of chimney swifts were enjoying the pleasant weather. There was no sign of Esther. I had been gone nearly an hour. Hopefully, Floyd had found Esther and I would find both of them waiting for me back at our booth along with the rest of my motley crew.

I decided to stop by Phoebe's office to ask if she'd seen Esther. As I started down the hall, a nondescript man in a dark suit turned the far corner.

The door to Phoebe's office was open so I went right in. The woman Irving had identified as JJ's wife was leaning over Phoebe's desk with her hand in a drawer on the right side. She straightened and slid the drawer shut with her knee.

"Can I help you?" she demanded.

"No." The small office contained two desks. The other sat laterally to Phoebe's. I hadn't seen anyone using it but it was piled with papers and folders. A jug water cooler stood in the corner near a door in the back.

"Then you'll excuse me." She hurried out in a cloud of perfume. I heard a cough and whipped my head around in time to see the back of Esther's head as she scurried up the hallway.

"Esther." I ran out the door. Esther was several yards away. "Esther!"

Esther turned in surprise. "Amy?" She squinted my way. "Here you are."

"Here *I* am?" I placed my hand firmly on Esther's upper arm to keep her from disappearing once again. "I've been looking all over for you. Where have you been?"

Esther's lips twisted into a deep frown. "Follow me." She turned and headed the way she had come.

I hurried after her. "Really, Esther. Everybody is waiting for us. It's time to leave."

"Not now," Esther said sternly. She kept marching.

"Come on, Esther." How could she walk so fast? I was half her age and struggling to match her stride. "Can't this wait?"

"Nope. Trust me. It can't."

"You're acting very strange," I huffed, holding my purse against my side to keep it from flopping against my ribs. "Even for you."

Esther jammed on the brakes and I slammed into her backside.

"Ouch." I rubbed my chin. "Be careful."

Esther eyeballed me. "You want strange?"

I couldn't come up with any better response, so I furrowed my brow.

What I wanted was a comfortable seat in a romantic restaurant overlooking the river. What I wanted was good food and a stiff drink.

"I'll give you strange." She spun around and resumed her walking.

"Where are we going?" I whispered as we passed an open office door through which I saw several figures seated at computer desks.

"Hold your horseflies. We're almost there."

I hoped so because I had no idea where we were. The Expo Center was humungous. I was hungry and I hadn't gotten much sleep. Esther's snoring and insisting on setting the thermostat to eighty-two degrees Fahrenheit had seen to that.

We came to a stop at a three-way intersection. Esther looked left then right. Maury jogged down the corridor to the right, keys jangling as they slapped against his hip.

How had he gotten there so quickly?

"I thought this was supposed to be a birding expo not a speed walkers convention."

"What are you talking about? Come on. This way." Esther motioned for me to follow her and took the hall to the left.

Several yards further, Esther mercifully came to a stop down a short empty hallway. There were several unremarkable doors, two on the right, one on the left. The corridor dead ended at a blank white wall just beyond the left-hand door. An overhead fluorescent light flickered on and off.

Esther held up her finger to indicate I shouldn't make a sound.

There had been no need. I was at a loss for words. Esther had always been puzzling to say the least. Now I wondered if she had completely lost her mind.

Esther placed her hand on the doorknob of a door marked Private, and turned it slowly. She stuck her nose in for a second then beckoned me to follow her as she slipped inside.

Stunned but more than a little curious, I did what every good horror film victim learns too late, if it seems like a scary bad idea...don't do it.

Unfortunately, instead of listening to those hushed, frightened voices in the audience urging me not to do it but rather to turn and run, I listened to Esther's impatient voice as she whispered harshly, "Get in here, Amy. Be quick. And shut the door behind you."

"This better be good."

"It's not," was Esther's ominous reply.

I tiptoed in and shut the door. Would they kick us out if they caught us sneaking around unauthorized? Would I get my money back for the booth?

The small room contained a small green sofa with sagging cushions, a mini fridge, a microwave and a wooden table holding several bottles of hard liquor and wine. There was a window covered with a metal blind behind the sofa. Light slanted through the blind over the sofa and onto the industrial carpet. An empty glass and a bottle of Grey Goose lay on the floor.

"You brought me here to see this hovel?" The claustrophobic room reeked of alcohol and sweat. I turned to leave.

"Not so fast." Esther moved to a small door and pushed it open. "I brought you here to see this."

I was presented with a partial view of a white porcelain bathroom sink. "A bathroom? Really, Esther. This is a complete waste of both our time."

Esther beckoned me closer with her finger.

I decided to take a look, if only to humor her before having her committed to an institution. This was Philadelphia. There had to be at least one mental hospital in the area with a vacancy.

JJ Fuller sat on the ground, his back against the wall, his knee against the toilet bowl.

"Please tell me he's passed out drunk."

Esther waited a beat before replying. "He's passed out dead is what he is."

Peeking further, eyes adjusting to the dark, my heart froze in my chest. "Are—are you sure?" Fuller's slack face fell to his chest. His clothing was rumpled. His eyes were hidden by the visor of his ball cap.

"He's got no pulse."

"Heart attack?" Please let it be a heart attack.

Esther shook her head side to side.

"Stroke?" Please please please let it be a stroke.

"My guess is that, first off, somebody clobbered him."

"Clobbered?" As in bludgeoned? As in murdered?

Esther flipped on the bathroom light. "It seems to me he got his head caved in by that pair of binoculars."

I peeked over Esther's shoulder. A pair of binoculars lay at JJ Fuller's side. The strap was broken at one end.

"Maybe he slipped and hit his head."

Esther turned off the light with the side of her finger. I didn't object. I'd seen too much already.

"And maybe I'm the tooth fairy."

I shuttered my eyes. I knew what tooth fairies looked like, at least in my imagination, and the woman before me was not it. I knew what a dead body looked like too, including ones who had met violent ends. The body in the bathroom was a perfect match.

"Besides," Esther's words seem to be coming at me from deep inside a tunnel with no end, "I don't think that's what killed him. Either the killer clobbered him first to incapacitate him and then slashed his neck or vice versa."

Esther turned her cold, hard eyes on me. "But what would be the point of clobbering a guy you've already killed?"

"Slashed his neck? Are—are you sure?"

"You want me to turn the light on again?"

"No!" I gasped.

JJ Fuller had been murdered.

As ironic as it sounded, it seemed I had another dead body to add to my life list.

4

I yanked the bathroom door shut and leaned against it.

To keep a vengeful spirit from getting out? Maybe.

Think, Amy. Think.

Okay, JJ Fuller was dead. Murdered.

My heart was slamming against my chest. Esther was stooped over, moving around the room like a northern bobwhite sniffing out a beetle.

I was stuck in a room with a dead man and a crazy woman. I should be home in Ruby Lake, selling birdseed to little old ladies who wore dainty white lace-trimmed gloves when they refilled their bird feeders after church on Sundays.

Finally, Esther straightened her spine, then her apron. "I don't see anything else."

I had no idea what she meant. What was she looking for? A second dead body? And would finding it have been a good or a bad thing?

I was chilled to the bone. I'd plunged into an ice-covered lake. Murder Lake. I vigorously rubbed my hands up and down my arms. "I feel like my body temperature has dropped twenty degrees since I stepped in here, Esther. More precisely, since you showed me JJ Fuller. Or what's left of him."

"We know why and we know where." Esther picked up the drinking glass from the floor with the sides of her fingers pressed to the inside of the rim. She sniffed.

"I understand that we know where. But we can't possibly know why."

"Sure we can," snapped Esther, carefully returning the glass to the ground where she'd found it. "The man was an arrogant pain in the patooty."

I frowned. "I'm not sure being a pain in the patooty qualifies as a reason to murder a man."

Esther seemed to consider my words. "Maybe. Maybe not."

"Trust me," I said. "It's not. I think we—"

"Hold on." Esther dropped slowly to her knees. "What's this?" She dropped down in front of the sofa.

I watched as Esther bent her nose to the carpet. "What is it?"

"Have you got a pair of tweezers?"

"A pair of tweezers?"

"Yeah. A pair of tweezers. In that capacious purse of yours."

"I—I don't think so." I began rummaging through my purse although I didn't know why I was humoring her. "This is crazy."

I dug all the way to the bottom of my bag and came up empty. "Sorry. No tweezers." Good thing. If I'd had a pair, I might have plucked my eyeballs out in an effort to expunge the ghastly sight I had seen.

Esther's eyes darted around the room. "Never mind. Hand me one of those flyers over there."

I turned to see where she was pointing.

"And be careful not to touch anything you don't have to."

I took two steps left to a stack of flyers lying atop an open cardboard box. The glossy full-color flyers advertised an upcoming coin show to be held at the Expo Center. I peeled off the top flyer and handed it to her. "Have you been drinking?"

Ignoring me, Esther slid the sheet under the sofa and moved it around.

"What on earth are you doing, Esther? Need I remind you? There's a dead man in the bathroom. We need to call the police, not be foraging around under a sofa." I lifted my cellphone.

"Not yet." Esther cursed, jiggled the paper, cursed some more and moved her hand slowly. A moment later, something whitish popped into view atop the flyer.

It was the white tip of a quill.

Moving delicately, Esther slid the paper back from beneath the sofa. A long, delicate feather lay atop the paper.

"Is that a feather?" I stepped around the table and angled for a closer look at the blackish-brown barred specimen. It appeared to be a tail feather. What I could see of the underside appeared white. "That looks like an osprey feather."

Esther let go of the flyer and fell back on her heels. "I was afraid of this. Oh, they are good. Real good."

"Who's good? Afraid of what? What does an osprey feather have to do with anything and how did it end up under the sofa?"

Esther lofted the feather gently, holding the quill in her pinched fingers. "This changes everything." It revolved slowly around as she manipulated it.

I was dumbstruck. What was going on with Esther and that feather? She appeared mesmerized.

The corner of Esther's mouth turned down. Far down. "I told you Philadelphia was a bad idea, Simms." She shook her head. "I said I don't do Philly. Didn't I say I don't do Philly?" She jammed the feather behind her left ear.

"You said you don't do Philly," I replied woodenly. Why, oh why hadn't I listened? I could be home in Ruby Lake selling bird feeders and mason bee houses. Enjoying the birds and the friendly faces that visited my store. Lying in bed with the sheet pulled up to my nose.

My big ideas had gotten me into a big mess. I was far from home at the American Birding Expo in Philadelphia, a town I didn't know at all, up to my neck in bird poop.

"I need another look." Before I could object, Esther threw open the bathroom door and hit the light switch.

Like a moth to the flame, I followed.

For the first time, I saw the knife in the open toilet bowl.

Esther moved closer to the body, straddling her legs over it. "Okay, here's what we're going to do."

"What do you mean *here's what we're going to do*? What we are going to do is call the police and security and Phoebe Gates and—"

"Get a hold of yourself, Amy." Esther pinched my left triceps.

"Ouch." I rubbed the underside of my arm. "That hurt."

"Sorry."

I didn't believe her for a minute.

"I don't suppose there's any way we could move him?"

Why was she looking at me when she said that?

"Move him?"

"You know, hide the body."

My mouth flew open but words refused to spill out. Not surprising because my brain had gone into lockdown.

"Sometimes you are completely useless." Esther planted her fists on her knobby hips as she looked at the fresh corpse. "Looks like the work of the Osprey."

I knew Esther was no bird expert but still, an osprey? "Osprey? Nonsense." I found my voice if not my sanity. "An osprey couldn't do that. The man's throat has been slashed. With that." I pointed to the knife jutting pointy end up in the toilet bowl.

Esther nodded. "That's the MO of the Osprey, all right."

My stomach lurched. "Uh, Esther." I pointed at the murder weapon. "Is that the knife you were using to slice the bird bars?" I recognized the nick on the handle, like someone had dropped it in a garbage disposal.

"Guess so."

"Where did you get it?"

"I borrowed it from the bagel stand in the food court."

I frowned. "Do they know you borrowed it?"

"Not yet."

"What is it doing here? More to the point, what is it doing there?" Who tries to flush a knife down a toilet? I'd had enough and said so. "I've seen enough. Let's go."

Esther followed me out of the bathroom. It hadn't been designed to hold three people even if one of the three was dead.

I plucked the feather from Esther's hair.

"Hey, what are you doing?" Her hand flew to her head.

"This is evidence, Esther."

She snatched it back. Sometimes her reflexes were scary fast. Fast enough to bash a so-called "pain in the patooty" on the noggin and then slash his neck?

"You can't do that." I reached for her hand. "That feather is evidence. You must turn it over to the police."

"Not a chance." Esther backed up to the wall. "Not yet, anyway."

"Why?"

"Because I need time to think. We have to figure this out first. Our killer probably hit him over here by the door. See that?"

There was a purplish spot behind the door.

"That's blood. Hit him. Dragged him to the toilet. Then slit his throat."

"Esther," I pleaded. "You are not making sense."

Esther the Pester had once accused me of murder. To be honest, she had seen me standing over a dead man with a bloody bird feeder hook in my hand. Still, I had been offended at the time. I had always hoped to turn the tables on her.

Now that I had, it wasn't half as satisfying as I had dreamed it would be. In fact, it wasn't satisfying at all.

"None of this makes sense," Esther replied. "And I don't like it." She carefully placed the feather inside the pocket of her apron. "I don't like it at all."

"You can't do that," I protested for the umpteenth time.

"Trust me."

Trust her? I hadn't trusted Esther since the day I'd met her.

Next, Esther bent and scooped up the flyer she had used. She balled it up and tossed it to me. "Put that in your purse," she ordered. "We'll get rid of it later."

"Why don't I just throw it in the trash can?" There was one beside the sofa, another in the bathroom.

"Not here." Esther was adamant. "Fingerprints."

"Okay." My fingers shook as I dropped the crumpled flyer in my purse.

Esther extracted a lace-edged hankie from the folds of her dress. She used it to wipe the light switch inside the bathroom and the door knob.

"Esther, would you mind telling me—"

"Check outside and see if the coast is clear." Esther peered through the blinds and muttered something unintelligible.

I eased the door open a crack and looked down the hall. "Silent as a tomb." Poor choice of words.

"Good." Esther gave me a soft shove. "Let's go."

"Not until you tell me what's going on." I planted my feet and pushed back.

Esther snarled at me. "Not now, Amy."

"But Esther."

Esther pushed me through the doorway. The Pester was stronger than she looked. "I said not now." Using the same hankie she'd used on the bathroom light switch, she rubbed all trace of fingerprints from the exterior door knob too.

"Esther, the killer's fingerprints could have been on that knob."

"I doubt it," was her reply. "But ours? Definitely."

Esther grabbed my arm and started pulling me down the hall. "I told you I don't do Philadelphia," Esther repeated. "But would you listen?" Her head shook side to side. "No, none of you would listen. Now look what you've gotten us into."

"What *I've* gotten us into!" I found myself shouting, then lowered my voice to a whisper as we scurried down one hall then up another. "What I've gotten us into? I didn't murder anyone."

I suddenly came to a halt, forcing Esther to do the same. "Did you?"

"Of course, not." She thrust out her hands, her bony wrists extending past the sleeves of her dress. "Do these look like the hands of a killer?"

I grabbed Esther's hand. "Is—is that blood?" I whispered. There were dark red, almost black stains under the tips of her fingernails.

"Huh?" Esther pulled her hand away and held her curled fingers under her nose. "I must have cut myself shaving." Esther shoved her hand in one of the hidden pockets of her dress.

"Cut yourself shaving?"

"Shh." Esther cocked her head in the direction of two women moving into an office a dozen yards up the hall. "Let's go this way."

Before I could complain that she was about to set off an emergency alarm, Esther pushed her hands and hip against the metal bar of an exterior door that read *Fire Exit Only.*

There was a flash of light followed by a rush of cool air. We had come out on the side of the Expo Center, a sea of blacktop covered with a school of cars.

Surprisingly, no alarms went off.

"How did you know the alarm wouldn't go off?"

The door slammed tight behind us.

"You ask too many questions."

"That's because you do too many puzzling things," I retorted. Curious faces peered at us out the tall narrow window of an expo office.

A minute later, we arrived at the Expo Center's front entrance. Everything appeared normal—well, except Esther. People were calmly going about their business. Which I assumed did not include murder for all but one of the attendees.

"Esther, did you see anyone? Anyone else at all?"

"Just a dead guy."

"I mean besides JJ Fuller."

"I'm telling you. The dead guy."

I clamped my hands over her scrawny shoulders. "Esther, you aren't making any sense."

She pushed my hands away. "Yes, I am. I'm making perfect sense. I saw a guy. He looked dead."

Before I could open my mouth to complain that she was talking about Fuller again she pinched my mouth shut. "Ouch."

"Let me finish."

I glared at her but kept my jaw firmly clenched. That pinch hurt.

"There was this guy. I saw him sort of stumbling along in the hallway."

"A dead guy?"

"That's right. Baggy gray trousers, a long-sleeved gray cotton shirt that was too big for him." Esther waved to a passing taxi. "Anyway, he must have heard me coming because he turned and looked over his shoulder. That's when I noticed he looked dead. He had a limp."

"I'd limp too, if I was dead. At the very least."

The cab hurled to the curb. The cabbie lowered his window. "Where to?"

Esther opened the back door and climbed in. I had no choice but to follow. "Just drive," she instructed the cabbie.

The taxi was warm, humid and smelled of tandoori chicken. Our driver, a dark-skinned, heavily bearded fellow in sunglasses with a red and black Ukraine Soccer Club hat steered for the main road.

I leaned toward Esther. "About this dead guy—"

Esther held up a finger and looked pointedly at the driver.

He was busy and happy. The meter was running with no particular destination in sight and somebody was crooning through the taxi speakers in a language that might have been Ukrainian, Russian or even Venusian.

I thought I understood the sentiment but the tune's lyrics could have been calling for a revolution rather than a kiss. The music was interrupted only sporadically by the crackling of the driver's connection to his dispatcher.

Satisfied, Esther whispered, "His hair was all gray and tangled. His face was ashen and his eyes were pink."

I pushed my hands through my hair. It was either that or start pulling it out. And I didn't think I had any to spare. "Esther," I began, as the cab lurched over a speedbump and out into traffic, "I don't know who or what you saw but what, if anything, does it have to do with—"

I stole a look at the driver who sat directly in front of me. "You know what."

"That's hard to say," Esther admitted. "But he looked like he'd seen a ghost."

"A minute ago you practically said he was a ghost."

"I think he was in that room."

"The one where we saw the…"

"Yep."

"You think he's the person responsible for, uh…" Trying to have a conversation about a dead body in the back of a taxi with the driver a foot in front of us was absurd. "I think we should continue this conversation back at the hotel."

Esther chewed her lip. "I have a better idea."

"I rather doubt it."

Esther leaned toward the front seat and tapped our driver on the shoulder. He jerked, sending the taxi veering wildly to the right. There was a screech of brakes, both ours and those of the two cars on the right we almost slammed into.

Our driver was the jumpy sort.

Neither he nor Esther seemed to mind our near-death experience. The two drivers shooting us hand signs that I was sure they did not teach in any American Sign Language course seemed to have taken umbrage, however.

I ducked my head and waved an apology.

"Take us to Laurel Hill," Esther ordered.

The driver glanced at her in the rearview mirror. "Laurel Hill?"

Esther nodded.

"You got it."

"What's Laurel Hill?"

"A cemetery."

5

"A cemetery?" I was sorry I had asked.

We drove southeast, the skyscrapers of Philadelphia growing taller until we were in the midst of them.

The car stopped outside the cemetery entrance. Esther hopped out quickly. "Pay the nice man."

I staggered out my side and paid the nice man a not very nice lump of money. He was gone before I could request a receipt for tax purposes.

The historic cemetery sat along the scenic Schuylkill River. I'd been hoping to see it, just not from between rows of ancient tombstones.

A massive white building in the Roman Doric style, with four columns on each side, created an imposing entrance. I barely had time to read the plaque at the street as Esther moved through the tall archway in the center of the building, grabbed a map and unfolded it. All I caught was that the cemetery had been founded in 1836 by a Scotsman.

Esther studied the map then thrust it in her pocket. I stuck to her side as we snaked our way quietly past one remarkable ancient headstone after the other.

To maintain my sanity, I did some birdwatching. I spotted a hairy woodpecker, a northern flicker, a white-breasted nuthatch and a Carolina wren that made me homesick. "I wish I'd brought my binoculars."

Esther paid me no attention.

Near the river's edge, we came to a halt beside a fairly unremarkable stone, pressed closely between two taller ones. A simple cross decorated the weathered granite grave.

The sky had grown overcast. The greenish waters of the Schuylkill moved sluggishly. The sounds of the river mingled with the rasp of Esther's heavy breathing.

Esther ran her fingers along the stone cross.

"Who was Martin Ritter?" I read the name on the tombstone. "Ex-husband?" I joked.

I sat to give my feet a rest. I had one eye on the grave, the other on a pair of purplish European starlings crisscrossing the river. Mr. Ritter had been dead about forty years.

"Ex-lover," Esther answered.

If I had been standing I would have tipped over. While I did have hopes for a relationship between Floyd and Esther, I never thought I would hear the word *Esther* and *ex-lover* in the same sentence.

"I-I'm sorry," I said, regretting my insensitivity. Once again, I realized just how much I did not know about my tenant and business partner.

"Hand me my apron, would you, Amy?" Esther sounded different from her usual ornery self. I detected a weary sadness, perhaps even a broken heart.

My purse lay on the ground beside me. I unclasped it and pulled out her apron. She had given it to me in the taxi. I stood and handed it to her.

Esther carefully extracted the osprey feather from the pocket and held it by the tip of its quill.

I held my tongue, fascinated, as Esther hitched up her dress and knelt to the close-cropped grass. Dropping to one knee, she ran her tongue over her pale pink lips. Whispering some words I could not catch, she planted the osprey feather in the ground at the foot of Martin Ritter's gravestone.

Mission accomplished, Esther extended her hand toward me. I helped her to her feet.

"Esther," I said, emotions tugging at my heart, "please, help me to understand what's going on." First, she had led me to a dead body, then she'd stolen possible evidence from the crime scene. Finally, she had planted that evidence at a grave—the grave of an ex-lover, no less.

Esther narrowed her eyes, studying the scattered people wandering the cemetery. "We have to go."

"But, Esther—"

She silenced me with a shake of the head. "We have to go. He won't come if we're here. If we're watching."

"Huh?" I peered around. "Watching what? Who won't come?"

"Marty," she whispered.

"Marty?" Nothing Esther was saying or doing was making any sense at all. "Who the devil is Marty?"

I followed her eyes to the grave marker. "Oh. Marty." Martin Ritter. I fell silent. Whatever was going on was well beyond my comprehension.

Do ghosts appear in the daytime? What was I thinking? There was no such thing as ghosts.

Walking arm in arm, we left the cemetery.

My cellphone jangled as we sat on a bench beside the Schuylkill River Trail. People moved past us in both directions. It all seemed so normal.

"It's Derek," I announced, looking at the screen as the ringing went on and on.

"Aren't you going to answer it?" Esther was short-tempered and snappish.

I quickly answered. "Derek, hi."

"Amy, where are you? I've been trying to reach you. Me, Floyd and Karl have been looking everywhere. Where did you disappear to?"

"That's a long story." I sighed.

"Really? Wait till I tell you what's happening here at the birding expo."

"Oh?" I braced myself. I was no mind reader but I knew what Derek was about to say.

"They found the guest of honor dead. The police aren't saying much but the whispers I've been hearing say it was murder."

"Do—do they have any suspects?" I squeaked. Like a little old lady and the scared to death owner of a store for bird lovers?

"Rumor has it that they've arrested his wife."

"Thank goodness."

"What?"

"I mean. That's too bad. I mean—" What did I mean?

Derek cut me off. "I think I know what you mean. Murder is never fun but it's good to know the police have the perp in custody."

"Yes, that's exactly what I meant." Close enough.

"You're lucky you weren't around when it happened. Who knew a birding expo could be dangerous? I'm glad you are safe." Derek was talking a mile a minute. "What about Esther? Have you seen her? The guys and I can't find her anywhere."

"She is here with me."

There was silence on the other end. "Where is *here* exactly?"

"Hold on a sec." I muffled the phone with my palm. "Derek wants to know where we are, Esther. What should I tell him?"

Esther blinked at me. "Tell him we're at the cemetery. You want to sit here all day?" She rose, rubbed her rump and sat again. "This bench is hard."

"Don't you think he's going to want to know why we're at a cemetery?"

"Tell him we're window shopping."

I pulled my hand away from the speaker. "Derek? We're at Laurel Hill."

"Who is Laurel Hill?"

"It's not a who. I mean, she's not a who. She's a cemetery. That is, it is a cemetery."

"A cemetery?" Floyd was making noises in the background as Derek conveyed my words to him.

"Ask her what she's doing in a cemetery," Floyd urged.

Derek came back on the line. "Floyd wants to know—"

"I heard him," I interrupted. "Tell Floyd everything is fine. Esther and I only came to—"

I muted the phone once again and turned to Esther. "Derek and Floyd want to know what we're doing at a cemetery. What do I tell them, Esther? I cannot tell them we're shopping for our graves."

Esther extended her hand palm up. "Give me the phone."

I did.

Esther put my phone to her mouth. "I'm tired and I'm hungry. Come get us." She hit the red button ending the call and handed me back the phone. "He'll be right here."

Esther leaned against the bench and shut her eyes. Fifteen minutes later, she stood and we worked our way back to the main entrance, skirting Martin Ritter's grave as we did.

Derek arrived with the van. He had lots of questions but since I had none of the answers and whatever answers Esther had she was not willing to share with either him or me, not much was said.

Back at the booth, Floyd took a step in Esther's direction to hug her but stopped midway. Her look said *hands off.* Floyd thrust his hands in his pockets.

"Glad you ladies made it back," said Karl. "You missed all the excitement."

Esther scooped up her purse from under the table.

"So I heard. Derek was telling us all about it. So Lorna Fuller murdered her husband?"

"I'm not so sure. The police took her in. Then they released her." Karl's eyes shot around the Expo Center. "The killer could still be among us."

Was it my imagination or did his gaze stop on Esther for a tiny moment too long?

"Let's call it a day. The expo starts bright and early tomorrow," I suggested. "What do you say?"

"Suits me." Derek handed me my jacket.

A beefy gentleman in a brown suit, yellow shirt and blue necktie approached our booth. With him was a young man with a limp dressed like a zombie.

They made an odd couple.

Esther turned her back.

"That's her," pointed the zombie. "That's the lady I saw."

"Ma'am?" said the brown suit.

"Me?" I said.

"No. The other one, in the flowery dress." The gentleman pointed his finger at Esther. A heavy gold watch dangled from his wrist. "Ma'am?"

Esther turned. "Yes?"

The zombie turned eager eyes on his human escort. "She was in the hall, detective. Ask her. Go ahead, ask her."

"Detective?" Derek shot me a look of concern.

The detective looked at the young man with unmasked disdain. Maybe he didn't like the young fellow telling him his job. Maybe he simply did not like zombies.

I wasn't a big fan myself.

"Ma'am. I need to ask you a couple of questions."

Derek and the guys were flummoxed. I was less so.

"Shoot." Esther folded her arms across her chest.

"First, let me introduce myself, Detective Simon Locke." The detective had thin blond hair with a trace of blond fuzz under his lower lip. He pulled out his ID and presented it to us.

"If you say so." Esther was playing it cool.

"Can you tell me your name, please?"

"Esther Pilaster." She pulled her badge from her purse and flashed it at the detective.

We had removed our lanyards in the taxi.

"Thank you, Ms. Pilaster. I'm afraid there's been an unfortunate incident. A murder."

"You don't say?"

"Yes." Detective Locke cleared his throat. "A JJ Fuller. Did you know the deceased?"

"We only arrived in Philadelphia last night. We're from North Carolina."

I interrupted. Lots of people had seen Fuller at our booth. It was only a matter of time until someone Locke interviewed pointed this out. "Mr. Fuller stopped by our booth this morning while we were setting up, don't you remember, Esther? He wanted to introduce himself."

"I remember now." She smiled apologetically. "I'm afraid the memory isn't what it used to be, young man."

"Of course." The detective stuck a finger under his collar and tugged. "This man here," Detective Locke said, indicating the zombie, "Mr. Peter Porter, reported seeing you, Ms. Pilaster, roaming the halls in the vicinity of the murder."

Esther said nothing.

Detective Locke continued. "Is that true?"

"I don't know," Esther said, sounding suddenly feeble. "I was wandering around. This is a big place, isn't it? I was looking for the ladies' powder room." She stared at the zombie. "Where did this horrible murder take place?"

"A small dressing room that doubles as a storage room," explained Locke.

"If you like, I can retrace my steps maybe," Esther offered. "It is time for my heart medication though. Could you give me a minute? Amy, be a dear and fetch me my pills, would you?"

Good grief. She was really playing up the little old lady routine.

Detective Locke slipped his notepad into his shirt pocket. "I don't think that it will be necessary to trouble you right now." He read our banner. "I suppose you'll be here all weekend?"

"Yes," I said. "Ms. Pilaster is with Birds and Bees. Like me. We're exhibitors."

"A murder at a birding expo seems highly improbable," Derek noted. "Do you have any idea, detective, what the motive might have been?"

"I really couldn't say. We're still looking into that, sir. It's early days." He helped himself to a handful of tiny wrapped chocolate kisses from the bowl Derek had set out earlier.

"Robbery?" I suggested. "I mean, what else could it be?"

"It may have been robbery." Detective Locke allowed. "There was approximately two hundred in cash in Mr. Fuller's wallet but a very expensive camera is missing. Worth thousands, according to his wife, that is."

I wanted to ask why the thief hadn't taken the binoculars I had seen near JJ Fuller's body. Those were worth a couple grand too. But how could I ask without tipping my hand that I had seen them?

Detective Locke departed, taking his zombie with him, after telling us that if he had any further questions, he'd stop by.

"Do you want me to see if I can pry any more information out of him, Amy?" Karl asked. He looked itching to go after the cop. As an ex-lawman, he was always at the ready.

"No, that won't be necessary." I buttoned my coat. "We're here to promote Birds and Bees, not investigate crimes."

"That's right." Derek trained his eyes on me.

"And to have fun," Floyd put in.

Esther took Floyd's arm and a smile took over his face. "What do you say we hit the casino? I could use a little excitement."

"Sure thing, Esther." Floyd grew about twelve inches before my eyes. "You coming, Karl?"

Karl dipped his hand into his pocket. "Got my cash money right here."

6

With the others gambling, Derek and I had had the evening to ourselves, settling on an Italian restaurant in the historic district where we shared pasta primavera, a bottle of wine and the pleasure of each other's company. After a late night, we had returned to the Eagle Inn on foot.

That was when I discovered Esther hadn't returned.

Not that I had been worried. Esther was a grown woman. Karl and Floyd were keeping her company. And Karl was an ex-lawman. He might even be carrying a gun despite my admonishing him not to.

I'd gone to bed, sleeping fitfully as the events of the past day replayed themselves over and over in my mind. Nothing made sense. The only thing that remained a certainty—unless the whole day had been a nightmare—was that JJ Fuller was dead.

Throwing off the covers, I looked at Esther's bed. There was no sign of her or that her bed had been slept in.

Now I was beginning to worry.

I decided to shower and investigate. I was reaching for the blow dryer when there was a knock on the door. "Esther, is that you?" I ran to the door barefoot, pushing a bath towel through my damp hair.

"Hello, Floyd." I looked over his shoulder, up and down the hall. No sign of Esther. "I thought you were Esther."

"Not even in one of her best Sunday dresses could I look like Esther," Floyd joked. "Where is she? Getting ready in the bathroom?"

I cleared my throat. "She's not here, Floyd."

"What do you mean Esther's not here?" Floyd peered past me into the room. "Is she downstairs getting breakfast?"

"No, I don't think so."

"Where is she?"

"Actually, I'm not sure where she is, Floyd."

"I don't understand." Floyd poked his nose in. "Esther? Are you here?"

"I'm telling you. I haven't seen her. She never came back to the inn. At least, not to our room," I added as Floyd swept past me, took a look at Esther's crisply made bed then poked his nose in the still steaming bathroom.

Floyd fell onto the corner of Esther's bed. He ran his hand over the duvet. "Her bed doesn't look slept in."

"Uh…" I didn't have a clue where Esther could be and I didn't know how to explain her absence.

Floyd looked sharp in a brown and black houndstooth sport coat, brown slacks, a white shirt and a tie. He smelled of lime cologne and was freshly shaven. "I don't understand."

I draped my towel over the chair at the desk and sat next to him. "What happened last night, Floyd?"

"What do you mean?"

"You, Esther, and Karl went gambling at one of the casinos, right?"

"We went to SugarLand Casino in the north part of town. Karl won ten thousand dollars."

I fell from the bed. "Ten thousand dollars? That's great."

Floyd shrugged. "He lost it all again. Plus another three."

"Oh." I sat back down and draped a friendly arm over Floyd's back. "Tell me about Esther."

"How do you mean?"

"When did you see her last?"

Floyd eyed me curiously. "What kind of question is that? Didn't she return at all last night? What aren't you telling me, Amy?"

"Calm down, Floyd," I found myself saying, although I was feeling anything but calm myself. JJ Fuller ends up dead and Esther was the one pointing him out to me in an obscure out of the way bathroom, then she acts all bizarre and takes me to a cemetery where she proceeds to plant an osprey feather on a grave and tell me about her ex-lover.

Next, she goes to a gambling casino and disappears.

I stood and paced, my feet trying to keep up with my racing thoughts. I couldn't possibly tell Floyd any of it.

I pulled back the drapes and looked out at Philadelphia. People were walking, cars and buses were moving. Everything appeared so normal.

So ordinary.

So why was I living in the Twilight Zone?

Floyd interrupted my thoughts. "Did Esther come back to the inn or not? Tell me, Amy."

"No," I answered. "She didn't. At least, not to our room. She wasn't here when I went to bed. Once, in the middle of the night, I woke up and noticed she wasn't in her bed. I just assumed..."

"Assumed what?"

"Well, that maybe she was, you know..."

"Huh?"

"With you." I averted my eyes.

"With me?" Floyd's face blew up a bright red. "You think Esther and I—" Floyd stopped mid-sentence. We both knew where he was going.

I nodded.

"How could you think such a thing? Esther is a lady. I would never. Besides, I'm sharing a room with Derek and Karl."

"Philadelphia is full of hotel rooms."

"No, Amy. The last time I saw Esther was at the casino. She said she was tired and wanted to come back to the inn. I offered to accompany her but she insisted I stay and keep an eye on Karl. So that's what I did."

"And she definitely said she was coming back to the Eagle Inn? You are sure?"

"Sure, I'm sure. I saw her get in the cab myself."

I had a sudden thought. "Let's call her." I grabbed my cellphone from the night table and punched in Esther's number. "It went straight to voicemail."

Floyd frowned. "Let's telephone the police."

"No, no police." Whatever Esther was up to and whatever had happened to her, I didn't want to call the police. At least, not yet. Whatever was going on had to have something to do with JJ Fuller.

And Esther appeared to be up to her pestering little eyeballs in it. I had to find out just what sort of trouble she was in before dragging the police into the matter.

I had to hear Esther's side of the story, as ominous as I feared it might be. It had been crazy enough already.

Besides, I wasn't sure if calling the local authorities would do much good. If Esther wanted to stay out all night, there was nothing to be done about it. "It is too early to report her missing."

"I suppose..."

"Let's get the guys and see what they think. Karl might have some ideas. Maybe he even has some local contacts. Don't worry, Floyd. I'm sure Esther is perfectly fine."

* * * *

It was a long, subdued trip to the American Birding Expo. I filled Derek and Karl in on Esther's escapades and disappearance. Well, up to a point.

There were some things that I wasn't sure if I should mention just yet. Like our connection to JJ Fuller's corpse.

Floyd said little on the drive. Karl worked hard to try and cheer him up. It was the first full day of the Expo and the hall was filling quickly. Workshops and bird walks were on the schedule each morning. I was hoping to take part in some once things got back to normal and we settled into our routine.

If it wasn't for the murder and Esther being missing in action, I might have been happy.

Floyd and Karl roamed the aisles searching for a sign of Esther. Derek was handing out sample bird bars.

"Did you hear about the murder, Amy?" Robin leaned over the curtain divider.

"Yes," I said. "Terrible, isn't it? I hope it doesn't put a pall on the birding Expo."

"Me, too. We came all the way from South Carolina for this."

"First time?"

"No, we've been doing the Expo since the inaugural a few years back. You?"

"First time. I'm hoping to drum up some interest in my store. Mostly coming to the Expo would give me some ideas about how to expand my business."

"I get that. Have you been in business long?"

"No, a year or so. I've been toying with the idea of developing an online storefront."

"You know what you should do?"

"What's that?"

"Offer birding tours."

I furrowed my brow. "Me? Birding tours?"

"Sure, like we do."

"No, I don't think so."

"It's a growing business. Ecotourism. Trust me."

"I believe you but I don't know anything about running tours."

"Maybe not but I'm guessing you know about birds."

"Yes, but—"

"And I'm guessing there are probably plenty of folks in your town—where were you from?"

"Ruby Lake, North Carolina."

"In Ruby Lake, North Carolina, I bet there are folks who would love to go on a birding tour. It doesn't have to be anything fancy or extended. You could start with a long weekend."

"Where would we go?"

"I'm sure if you put your mind to it, you can come up with something that will appeal to your customer base."

"You know, I think you might be on to something."

"I think so, too." Derek had been listening in. "In fact, I think it is a terrific idea." He gave me a squeeze. "You can count me in."

"We're talking birding, not golfing," I teased.

"Okay. I'll leave the clubs at home and bring the binoculars." He frowned. "Have you got a spare pair of binoculars I can borrow?"

"Very funny." I gave Derek a gentle shove. "I'll give it some thought, Robin." I was intrigued. Running the occasional tour could prove lucrative. Lucrative enough to make covering Birds & Bees ever-increasing payroll less challenging.

"Good." Robin smiled. "If you need any help or want to brainstorm, just ask me or one of the others. Except Harry, here," she said, nodding at the young man who'd joined us. "His ideas have a way of going amuck."

"Ha-ha," Harry said.

"I'll keep that in mind."

George Dolenz came from the food court. He dumped a bunch of wrapped sandwiches on their table. "Guess what." Before anyone could, he said, "I heard that Skoglund volunteered to take over for Fuller and deliver the keynote address tonight."

"Interesting," I said. "I heard the two of them hated one another."

"Where did you hear that?" George wanted to know.

"From one of the other exhibitors."

"It's true." Robin grabbed a sandwich from the pile and peeled back the wrapper. She held it to her nose and took a whiff. "I've never known them to have a civil word to say to one another. Tonight ought to prove interesting."

And it did.

7

I felt a tap on the shoulder and turned. "Esther!"

"Sorry, I'm late." Esther set her purse under the table. Somewhere along the way, she had managed to change clothes. Yesterday's dress had been replaced by a pair of comfy heather slacks and a black Birds & Bees sweatshirt. "What's new?"

Did she seriously just ask me what was new after being MIA since last night?

"Where have you been?" I demanded.

"I had to freshen up. Then we stopped for a bite." Her hands were busy pointlessly rearranging a stack of store brochures.

I bit my tongue and turned to Esther's unknown companion. "I'm afraid we have not met, Mister..."

"This is my friend, Marty," explained Esther.

"Martin Ritter," said the gentleman with a tip of his head.

"Marty?" I squeaked. "The one who—"

"That's right," Esther said.

"In the—" I blubbered.

I stuck out my hand and introduced myself. I'd never shaken hands with a dead man before but there was a first for everything. "Hello, Mr. Ritter."

The merest of smiles welcomed me. "Please, call me Marty," Martin Ritter insisted in a booming basso voice. "It is my dear pleasure to meet you."

"Your *friend*?" Floyd looked the fellow up and down.

I couldn't blame Floyd. How did Esther have a friend in Philadelphia? She'd never mentioned one.

She didn't do Philadelphia.

Derek introduced himself. "Thanks for bringing Esther to us. We've been very concerned about her."

"I'm sorry. I can assure you"—he patted Esther's hand—"she is well taken care of."

"Who is this guy, Esther?" Floyd snapped uncharacteristically. He puffed out his chest like a gray catbird.

"Calm down, buddy." Karl dragged Floyd to the rear of the booth and plopped him into a chair.

Marty plucked a worn brown fedora from his head. His face was long. His chiseled features had begun to erode, a patch of black hair had begun to recede but his hazel eyes seemed as sharp as any hawk's. A small, jagged white scar ran along the right side of his nose.

All in all, he looked pretty good for a dead guy.

"Esther has told me so much about you. She tells me you work for her in her store."

"She did, did she?"

Funny, she'd told me nothing about him except for the fact that he was living six feet underground at the Laurel Hill Cemetery.

"Yes, it sounds quite charming."

I forced my lips to turn up when they most definitely wanted to turn down. "Charming doesn't begin to describe it, Marty."

Floyd and Karl were whispering loudly in the far corner of the booth. Though Karl tried to hold him back, Floyd surged forward once more. "Esther." She stiffened as he wrapped his arms around her in an awkward embrace. "We were very worried about you, Esther."

"Whatever for?" Esther pulled free and tugged at a string of big pearls around her neck. She had eschewed her usual ponytail and her gray hair hung loose.

"You were out all night." Floyd looked up at Marty who stood an inch or two taller.

"I'm afraid I am to blame." Marty held a pair of black leather gloves in his left hand. He wore a nice but ancient black wool coat and dark trousers. Beneath the coat, bits of a rumpled gray cable-knit sweater were visible.

I detected a slight accent in his speech but couldn't place it.

Plastering a big phony smile on my face, I turned to Esther and said, "Esther, dear. Can I speak with you for a minute? Alone, please?"

"What for?" Esther tugged to free herself from the grip I had placed on her left hand.

"Thanks. Would you all excuse us, please?"

"Hey—" Esther swore up a storm as I dragged her to the food court for some relative privacy. We passed Mr. Shipman manning his booth with a young assistant in a matching purple polo shirt. He waved hello.

I propelled Esther into the nearest empty plastic chair at the farthest empty table. "Let's start with the obvious. Wait. Is that makeup you're wearing, Esther?" The Pester wasn't big on what she called face paint.

Esther's fingers went to her cheek. "What of it?"

"Nothing." I shook myself, trying to jumpstart my brain, get my thoughts back on track. "What about the knife?"

"What knife?"

"The knife that was used to slit JJ Fuller's throat," I whispered. Esther could be exasperating at the best of times.

"It was in the toilet bowl, remember?"

"That won't have stopped the police from fishing it out." Though it might have stopped me. "It is the knife you were using in the booth yesterday. It's only a matter of time until they find your fingerprints on it."

"It was in the bowl butt down."

I ignored the poorly timed pun. "That doesn't mean the police won't find any fingerprints." I had watched enough TV to know that.

"Even if they do, so what? I used the knife to slice bird bars, not JJ Fuller's throat. Are we about done here? I could use a bagel."

I placed my hands flat on the small round table. Were we moving? Why did it feel like we were in a dinghy in rough swells? I don't do well on boats.

I was wishing that I didn't do Philadelphia.

I was feeling seasick. I clasped her hands. "Listen to me, Esther. We're going with the insanity defense. I'll have to ask Derek what the laws are in Pennsylvania. He might know."

I could hear myself rambling. "They don't execute crazy little old ladies here, do they?" I shook my head. "No, no. They wouldn't do that. Too cruel."

"You're babbling, Amy." Esther lashed out across the table and slapped me across the cheek.

"Ouch!"

"Feel better now?"

I massaged my jaw. "Hardly."

"Listen," Esther planted her elbows on the table. I kept my eyes on her hands. If she went to hit me again, I'd be prepared. "I did not murder JJ Fuller. And I don't know who did. What I do know is that whoever is responsible is trying to make it look like the work of the Osprey."

I sighed. Esther hadn't only lost her marbles, she'd lost the bag they had come in. "The osprey?"

"That's right." Esther nodded firmly.

As much as I knew I was leaving myself vulnerable, I took my eyes off her slap-happy hands to look in her eyes. They didn't look any crazier than usual. "So this osprey got in the Expo center and murdered the guest of honor in the bathroom of his dressing room? With a knife? Shouldn't it have used its talons at least?"

"You aren't listening," Esther said with exaggerated patience. "Somebody wants us, the authorities, I should say, to think that the Osprey is responsible."

I braced my hands on the sides of my chair, closed my eyes and took a deep breath. I made a wish but when I opened my eyes I was still in the food court with the Pester looking at me like I was the one who was crazy.

"I'd like to see this osprey."

"You already have."

"I have?"

"Sure, you met him."

"I met the osprey?" I pinched my brows together. There was going to be a raptor show on Sunday, the closing day of the American Birding Expo, but I hadn't seen any live birds anywhere. Not yet.

"Yeah, Marty."

This time I did fall out of my chair. Esther stuck out her hand and I took it. "Thanks," I said, red-faced, as I dusted myself off.

"Let me get this straight." I returned to my chair and waved to the million eyes staring at us to show that everything was okay—which it most definitely was not. "Marty. Martin Ritter is the osprey?"

"That's right. With a capital O."

"The same Martin Ritter whose tombstone you showed me yesterday at the cemetery?"

"He isn't really dead, Amy."

That was one thing we could at least agree on.

"You're wasting a lot of time going over the obvious, Amy."

I gave her a deadly look. "Humor me. Explain how Marty can be an osprey."

Esther beckoned me forward with her finger. I leaned closer. "That's his code name: the Osprey. At least it was his code name."

"Code name, right." I ran my fingers through my hair. "And somebody wants us, wants the police, to think that Marty slit JJ Fuller's throat?"

"That's what I've been trying to tell you. The Osprey always leaves behind a feather. That's his thing."

Was slitting throats his thing too?

"Why would somebody want to pin JJ's murder on your friend? Did he have a motive?"

"No."

"Were the two men enemies?"

"Nope. Marty says they never met."

"So why in heaven's name would somebody be trying to frame Marty?"

"You don't get it. They aren't exactly trying to pin the blame on Marty. They're trying to pin the blame on the Osprey."

I hooded my eyes. "You said Marty was the Osprey!"

"Shh." Esther flapped her hands. "Lower your voice. You want the whole world to know what's going on, Amy?"

"The whole world?" I hissed in disbelief. "The whole world? How could I possibly tell the whole world what's going on when I don't have a clue what's going on myself?"

Esther cleared her throat and stood.

"Where are you going?"

"It's a long story and I'm thirsty." She pulled a small wad of cash from her pocket. "You want anything?"

"Only if it's one hundred proof," I shot back, not caring who heard me now. I folded my arms across my chest as I watched Esther toddle off to the refreshment stand as if she had all the time in the world.

By the time she'd returned with her frozen lemonade, I was fuming and had a migraine the size of a quasar.

She sat, sucked noisily at her straw. "Marty and I go way back."

"Right, you were lovers." Even as I said the words, I had a hard time getting my head around them. "And then he died. Well, he didn't die exactly..."

A rumble came from Esther's throat. "Are you gonna let me tell this or are you going to keep interrupting?"

We glared at one another.

I caved first. "Fine. Please, continue."

"Marty is a retired agent."

"You bought a house from the guy? Is that how you met?"

"Not a real estate agent. He's what you might call an agent of a foreign country."

"I don't get it."

Esther rattled the tabletop with her fingers. "A spy, Amy. Boy you are dense. Marty used to be a spy."

"A spy?" I spluttered.

"A spy."

I grabbed Esther's frozen lemonade and pressed the side of the cup to my temple.

Out of the corner of my eye, I noticed Detective Locke striding into the food court. There was a uniformed officer with him. The officer had one of those medical walking boots on his left leg. Kim had worn a similar one when she'd broken her foot when it connected with a submerged rock on a Breckenridge, Colorado ski slope.

The two representatives of the law headed for the bagel stand.

"Marty and I go way back," Esther began, oblivious to the detective and his companion. "We met for the first time here in Philadelphia."

"You said you don't do Philadelphia."

"It was the seventies. I did Philadelphia in the seventies."

I set the frozen drink on the table and Esther sucked noisily for a minute, rattling my brain. I was afraid to ask the next question, the one that was slamming like a sledgehammer behind my skull dying to get out. And it did. "Are you, that is, were you a spy, too, Esther?"

There was a moment's hesitation. Then she nodded.

"You and Marty? What, like a team?"

I couldn't imagine Esther and Marty as a far less glamorous version of Robert Wagner and Stefanie Powers in *Hart to Hart*, let alone spies. It was near impossible to imagine Esther during the seventies. She would have been what? About my age now—maybe younger.

"Marty and I were what you might say working opposite sides of the fence."

Another question shot out of some far corner of my mind and slipped through my lips. "Dare I ask whose side you were on?" I was sweating profusely. Which was weird considering I felt like I was sitting on a block of ice. I could no longer feel my toes.

"What kind of question is that?" Esther squeezed her cup. Lemon slush gushed over the sides. "I was—"

Detective Locke interrupted. "Ms. Pilaster?"

"Yes, dear?"

Good grief. The woman was sounding like a doddering old woman again. She'd probably studied acting in How to Be a Spy 101.

"I'd like you to accompany me down to police headquarters."

Esther's brow creased. "What for?"

I stood. Esther remained seated and silent.

The uniformed officer took a clumsy step in my direction. He halted when Detective Locke raised his hand. "Take it easy, Clark."

"Yes, sir." The officer frowned and took a bite of his untoasted bagel.

"Ms. Pilaster, if you would, please." The detective stepped back as Esther stood.

"Detective Locke," I began, "surely you can ask Esther whatever questions you want right here. There's no need to take her down to the station. Is there? It's the middle of the Expo. I need her."

"Sorry, this can't wait."

Officer Clark laid his fingers over her elbow.

"Let go of me." Esther jumped aside, crashing into the detective.

Officer Clark hobbled towards her.

Detective Locke narrowed his eyes. "Esther Pilaster, I am placing you under arrest for the murder of James Jules Fuller."

"That's ridiculous," I squeaked.

"The knife used in the commission of the murder has been traced to that bagel stand." The detective pointed. The woman behind the counter glared at us. "She is prepared to testify that Ms. Pilaster stole that knife from the bagel stand and—"

"Borrowed," interrupted Esther. "I only *borrowed* the knife." She snatched her purse from the table.

"For heaven's sake, be quiet, Esther," I admonished.

"And I believe Ms. Pilaster used it to slit Mr. Fuller's throat." Detective Locke waved at Officer Clarke. "Let's go."

Esther appeared tiny as I watched her being marched away.

8

I ran to the booth, dodging startled attendees left and right. "Esther has been arrested!"

Robin and George turned to stare at me.

Karl and Floyd were playing cards at the back table. Karl looked up from his hand. Floyd threw his cards on the table.

"What's this?"

"Esther. She's been arrested." I latched onto Derek's arm.

"Very funny."

"I'm serious."

Karl cleared his throat. "I know the two of you have had your differences but I never thought you'd have the woman arrested, Amy. You've got guts, I'll hand you that."

Floyd leapt to his feet, jarring the table. "You had Esther arrested?"

"No, no, Floyd. I had nothing to do with it. It was that detective—"

"Locke?" Derek inquired. "So you are serious?"

"Yes. He came to the food court with another officer."

Floyd wrung his hands. "And they just took her away?"

"What for?" Karl demanded. "Littering or just plain orneriness?"

"This is serious, Karl." I motioned for the three of them to huddle with me in the corner of the booth.

"Detective Locke seems to think that Esther killed JJ Fuller," I whispered.

"No." Floyd backed into the curtain and thrashed about. Karl extracted him.

"I'm afraid so."

"What evidence do they have?" asked Derek.

I explained how Esther had been using the knife that killed him right here in our booth. "It doesn't help that she was witnessed arguing with the man here earlier either."

"Esther wouldn't harm a fly," Floyd vowed.

I wasn't sure if that was true but I knew Esther was no killer. At least not in this case. Had she been a spy? If so, had she ever...no, I wasn't even going to go there.

"Where's the Osprey?"

"The what?" Karl asked.

"I mean, Marty. Where did he go?"

"Don't ask me," said Karl. "The guy flew out of here like something or someone was after him."

Karl didn't know how right he might be.

Floyd shoved his arms into his jacket.

"Where are you going, Floyd?" I asked.

"To the police station to check on Esther."

"Wait for me, Floyd." Derek brushed his lips across my cheek and grabbed his jacket.

"Let me know what you find out."

That left Karl and me alone in the booth.

"Everything okay?" Robin leaned over the low curtain between us.

"Personnel issues," I said lamely.

Karl tapped me on the shoulder. "If you don't mind, I think I'll do a little snooping."

"Good idea. Me, too."

"What about the booth?"

I thought a moment. "Keep an eye on our booth for a bit?"

"No problem," Robin agreed.

We agreed to meet up at the booth in an hour. He was going to check with the Expo Center's security folk. I wanted a word with Phoebe Gates. Maybe she had some information on JJ Fuller's murder that she might be willing to share.

Phoebe looked up and smiled when I poked my head in her office. "Hi, Phoebe. Got a minute?"

Phoebe waved me in. A woman sat across from Phoebe with her back to me.

"I'm not interrupting, am I?"

The seated visitor turned. It was Ilsa Skoglund.

"I was just leaving. Remember," Ilsa Skoglund said, clutching the canvas bag at her side, "not a word until my announcement."

"Of course." Phoebe motioned for me to sit. "What can I do for you?"

"You heard about the murder, of course."

The corners of Phoebe's mouth turned down. "Who hasn't? It's bad for business."

It had been pretty bad for JJ Fuller too. "The police seem to think that Esther had something to do with it."

"Esther?" Phoebe scooped up a pile of mail and shoved it into her desk drawer. "That's ridiculous. She's a dear."

The phone rattled and Phoebe motioned for me to hold for a second while she answered. She frowned with the receiver to her ear. "I told you the end of the week." Silence. "Yes, well, you will simply have to wait until then. Promise." She hung up and smiled at me. "Where were we?"

I pressed my knees together. "You were about to tell me who might have wanted to see JJ Fuller dead."

"Was I?" Phoebe picked up a pencil and beat out a pattern on her desktop. "Take your pick. There's his wife, of course. The shrew."

"You mentioned he was getting a divorce? Is it acrimonious?"

"I couldn't say."

"Do you think JJ could have been seeing another woman?"

"Amy, there is always another woman."

"Care to elaborate?"

"No." Phoebe stood. "I really should be going." Phoebe wiggled her butt as she moved, looking much like her namesake, the phoebe, which was known for its tail flicking behavior.

"Before you go, is there anyone else you can think of in attendance who might have wanted JJ dead?"

"JJ was a man of grand ambitions, Amy. He ruffled the feathers of more than one man—and woman—over the course of his career."

Phoebe paused in the doorway. "Then again, perhaps it is for the best that JJ is dead."

"Why do you say that?"

"Because Ilsa's announcement tonight would have absolutely killed him."

9

After a stop at the hotel, Derek and I returned to the Expo Center alone. Floyd and Karl had opted out, claiming they were too tired. I made them promise to stay out of trouble.

And gambling casinos.

"That's JJ Fuller's widow," I indicated as we shouldered our way through the crowd toward the main hall where Ilsa Skoglund was now set to speak in place of JJ Fuller.

"Let's go pay our condolences," I suggested. It would be a good excuse to see if Lorna Fuller could provide any insight as to who really murdered her husband.

Derek brushed his lips over my cheek. "You do that. I see one of the onsite security guys. Karl struck out earlier but I'd like to see if he remembers seeing or hearing anything or anyone else this morning that might shed some light on things. Maybe we can get Esther released."

"Is that really a good idea?" I half joked.

"What do you mean?"

"Maybe Esther is better off in police custody until this whole thing gets sorted out."

"Do you think somebody might be out to harm her next?"

"No, I think being behind bars will keep her out of mischief."

"Trust me, being led away by the police on suspicion of murder will have set her straight."

"If only I could believe that."

Derek disappeared into the throng. I scanned the moving crowd until my eyes alit on Lorna Fuller several yards away, nodding as passersby whispered their sympathies. Her face was pale.

I pushed my way through. "Excuse me, Mrs. Fuller."

"Yes?" Lorna Fuller said wearily. Her mascara was smeared and her lavender lipstick poorly applied.

"I'm Amy Simms."

She looked me up and down with a pair of very judgmental blue eyes. "Another of JJ's little conquests?"

"Excuse me?"

"Another bird in a gilded cage?"

"No, I never actually knew your husband. Not personally. In fact, I only met him yesterday."

Lorna Fuller pressed her pinkie against the corner of her mouth. "I'm sorry. I didn't realize. It has been a difficult couple of days."

"I can imagine."

"A difficult week really." She sniffed.

"Oh?"

"It's the traveling. JJ loves—loved it. Myself, I'd rather stay home." Her lip moved down. "However, I thought it best to come this time." Something danced across her eyes as she added, "Make sure JJ was taken care of."

"I suppose that what with all the birding your husband must have been away from home a great deal."

"I told him time and time again that there were plenty of birds to be seen at home. Why, the golf course in our neighborhood is simply filled with the things."

"I see." I had a feeling JJ Fuller was a seeker of far more adventure than mere golf course birding. Derek, on the other hand, would have loved it.

"Just last week he was in some forsaken corner of the world in the middle of nowhere."

I pictured exotic locations like Spain or Portugal or maybe Patagonia. "It must be nice to have the opportunity to explore the world."

"The Pearl River, that was it." Lorna's eyes glazed over. "Near the Louisiana border with Mississippi. I assumed it was all a lie and that he was going to New Orleans, probably to meet up with some floozy."

"I've heard there is a lot of excellent birding in that part of the country," I said in defense of her now dead husband. Why, I didn't know.

"JJ telephoned me. He was quite excited. He said he couldn't wait to tell me all about his trip. He said he couldn't wait to share with everyone."

"You mean at the Expo?"

"I guess. I told him he should just tweet it like everybody else seems to do these days." Lorna rolled her eyes. "JJ liked to make as big a splash as he possibly could."

I refrained from saying what I was thinking, which was that JJ Fuller had made the biggest splash of his career at the American Birding Expo. One he would never top. Unless he returned from the dead—which apparently was not impossible. After all, Marty had managed it.

"What was it that he was so excited about?"

"He wouldn't tell me. That's how my husband was. Always making big secrets out of little ones." She chuckled. "He probably found a dodo bird feather or something."

I was pretty sure there was no such things in existence.

Derek was waving his arm to get my attention.

"If you don't mind me asking, do you have any idea who might have wanted your husband dead?"

Lorna Fuller's manicured eyebrows rose but her forehead remained smooth as glass. "In fact, I do mind, Ms. Simms. I mind very much. Excuse me."

"You're not staying to hear Ilsa Skoglund?"

"Not a chance." Mrs. Fuller swayed on her feet. "That should have been me up there." I smelled alcohol on her breath.

"Really?" I couldn't imagine that JJ's wife would have had many kind words to say about her dearly departed husband if rumors of the divorce were true. Not to mention the vicious swing I'd seen her take at him mere hours before his demise.

"My husband may not have been perfect but he deserves a proper eulogy, not this circus."

"Of course." I nodded solemnly.

Lorna scowled at me. "Please, you're just like the rest of them."

"What do you mean?" I pushed away from the door as the remaining stragglers filed passed us to get into the room where Ilsa Skoglund would soon be speaking.

"Do you think I haven't heard the whispers? The rumors?"

My blood grew cold. "I'm not sure I—"

"JJ might not have been a perfect man or an ideal husband." She sipped the remains of her wine. "But I loved him. He did not deserve to be murdered."

"I saw you arguing with your husband yesterday morning, Lorna."

JJ's widow smiled. "I hit him, didn't I?"

"That you did."

She shrugged. "We had our ups and downs. That doesn't mean that I wanted him dead."

"Someone did."

"I heard the police have taken a suspect into custody. Some old woman. Can you imagine?"

"No, I can't. I heard JJ tell Phoebe to stay away from you. Why?"

"You must have heard wrong. You want to know who killed him, Ms. Simms?" I nodded, and she continued. "Let me tell you. If it wasn't the woman in custody and it wasn't one of his little birdies who'd gotten angry because he'd dumped her and moved on to another, then it was Skoggie."

"Skoggie? Do you mean Ilsa Skoglund?"

"The two loathed one another."

"Why?" Shipman had told me pretty much the same thing.

"They were competitive to a fault. Both preferred the spotlight on themselves. Neither was happy when the light of the birding world fell on the other."

"And now your husband, JJ, is dead..."

"And the spotlight falls only on Skoggie." With those final and potentially significant words, Lorna Fuller tottered off, disappearing out the entrance and into the darkness.

By the time Derek and I entered the hall, Ilsa Skoglund was standing behind the lectern.

"Did we miss anything?" I asked Shipman as we squeezed in beside him.

"No. Ilsa is only warming up."

The younger man to his left in a matching slate polo shirt bearing the Ornitho Optics logo giggled.

"Not so loud, Travis." Irving Shipman tugged at his associate's arm. "This is my replacement, Travis Stevens."

Travis had short dark hair and a prominent nose. I found something about him a little off-putting. Maybe it was the fact that he was skinnier than me.

"Replacement?"

"I'm retiring shortly."

"Irv's showing me the ropes," Travis added.

The force of angry eyes prompted us to shut our yaps and return our attention to the speaker.

"JJ was a rock star," Ilsa boomed. "A true star in the cosmos of birding."

"Oh, brother," a svelte young woman near the edge of the podium whispered rather too loudly.

"Who is that?" I muttered.

"Nikki Nilsson. JJ's assistant."

"I hadn't noticed her before." Nikki Nilsson was a knockout. Half JJ's age but from what I'd learned so far, JJ did not discriminate on the basis of age.

"Nikki arrived today." Shipman tugged at the lanyard around his neck. "She flew up from Miami."

I inched forward. "I think I'll go introduce myself."

"What for?" Derek asked.

"Shame on you!" Nikki Nilsson tilted her head toward Ilsa in anger. "You are a fraud!"

Anonymous voices shouted her down.

Ilsa's fingers turned white as she gripped the edge of the lectern. "We are all going to miss dear, sweet, brilliant JJ," she said, defiantly staring down at the distraught former assistant.

A security guard led Nikki away. I pushed after them but by the time I pushed through the crowd, she and the guard had disappeared.

"And that is why it is with mixed emotions that I announce to you all the discovery of a lifetime." Ilsa turned to the side of the podium. "Phoebe, if you would, please."

Seated at a table on the right side of the stage, Phoebe punched some keys on her laptop. The big white screen behind Ilsa came alive.

The crowd gasped.

"What's going on?" Derek appeared at my side.

"I'm not sure." The photograph on the screen was blurry and dark. It showed a bird of some sort on the branch of a thick tree.

"Yes," Ilsa said. "The elusive and long-thought dead ivory-billed woodpecker, ladies and gentlemen." She nodded to Phoebe who showed two more pictures, each clearer than the previous.

I jolted.

"What is it?" Derek asked.

"Could it be? Are those really shots of an ivory-billed woodpecker?"

"I don't see what the big deal is. We see woodpeckers all the time."

"Yes, but not the ivory-billed woodpecker. It's been thought that the bird is extinct."

"It looks like Ms. Skoglund has proven that theory wrong."

"Yes. And she's fifty thousand dollars richer for it."

Derek let loose a low whistle. "How do you figure?"

I explained about the reward being offered.

"Maybe I haven't been taking bird-watching seriously enough."

"You'll get no argument from me over that." I pulled at Derek's arm. "Come on. I've seen and heard enough."

"Did you learn anything from security?" I asked as Derek steered the van back to the Eagle Inn.

"Nope."

"So nobody saw or heard anything unusual." My hands fiddled with the A/C vent, blowing warm air my way.

"Not until Esther found JJ Fuller's body in that bathroom." Derek pulled into the parking garage. "Say, you don't suppose for even one minute that Esther actually..."

"Actually what?"

"You know." Derek ran a finger along his neck.

"Not for even one second."

Derek parked and we started down the dark street toward the inn. I locked my arm through his.

"What about this spy business?" Derek asked.

"What about it?" I had shared a bit with Derek what little Esther had shared with me about her past.

"Do you believe our Esther was actually a spy?"

We marched on as I considered the question. It was a question I had been asking myself over and over. I still had no good answer. "No. I don't think so." I stopped on the sidewalk forcing passersby to skirt around us. "How could she be? It's impossible, right?"

"What's that line about believing six impossible things before breakfast?"

"That's something the queen says to Alice in *Through the Looking Glass, and What Alice Found There.*"

"Think about it, Amy," Derek said, pulling me along once more. "You are always saying how mysterious Esther is."

"And annoying. And pushy."

"Yeah, that too."

I forced Derek to a halt once more. "But a spy? Really?"

"What do you really know about her?"

"Well, I—"

Derek cut me off. "Face it. You say it yourself. You don't know anything about her past. She lives in the same house as you and you don't even know for sure if she has a cat."

"I suppose but—"

"Maybe she was like a Mata Hari." Derek wriggled his brow in reference to the notorious WWI courtesan and reputed German spy.

"This Mata Hari needs a drink." I angled into a noisy brewpub on Market Street.

"Yes, ma'am." Derek didn't put up any resistance.

A jazz trio wailed away on a squat raised stage in the front window. We found a tiny table near the bar and sat.

"If Esther was a spy," I said once our beers arrived, "how did she end up in Ruby Lake?"

"She's no spring chicken. Her sister lives in Ruby Lake. She probably retired there. Maybe Ruby Lake is where old spies go to end their years. Maybe Floyd and Karl are ex-spies too. Maybe—"

"Maybe you've had too much to drink." I pushed my mug across the table. "A spy, huh?"

"Stranger things have been known to be true."

"I can't picture Esther as a spy or a coldblooded killer."

Derek took a long drink before answering. "Maybe it wasn't so coldblooded."

"Now what do you mean?"

Derek leaned his elbows on the table. "What if JJ Fuller was a spy too?"

I narrowed my eyes at him.

"And what if Esther was sent to, you know, eliminate him?"

I held my breath. "Derek, you don't think—"

He broke out in a deep laugh and tossed back his beer. "Of course not, Amy. I'm only teasing."

But was he teasing?

And could there be any truth to his theory?

Six impossible things before breakfast. An extinct bird had come back from the dead.

Was Esther a professional assassin?

10

The next morning, we met in the lobby of the inn.

Derek handed me a large cup of coffee. He raised another to his lips and sipped tentatively as the steam spilled from the tiny hole in the lid.

"Thanks. This is just what I need." The coffee was strong and bitter.

I could see trouble written on his face. "What's wrong?"

"Floyd and Karl never got back last night." Derek rubbed his free hand over his cheek. He wore a pair of nice-fitting blue jeans, hiking shoes and the heather gray Birds & Bees sweatshirt I had gifted him. He smelled of fresh lime. The ends of his hair were damp.

"You're joking?"

"I wish I was."

"And they didn't call?"

"Nope. I tried both of their cells. Floyd and Karl are incommunicado. I hope nothing has happened to them."

"I'm sure they are fine." I yanked up the zipper of my jacket. According to the local weather forecast, it was going to be a chilly forty degrees. "Something is going to happen to those two when I get a hold of them."

I took a moment to consider what two crazy old men would do in Philadelphia. It didn't take me long to reach a likely conclusion. "I bet they spent the night gambling."

"Probably." Derek wasn't convinced. "Do you want to wait here while I go fetch the van?" He started for the door. It was five-thirty. There was no doorman in sight. The front desk was unattended.

"I'll walk with you." I grabbed his arm. "I could use the fresh air. Besides, I have a feeling you are not telling me everything."

We marched up the dark quiet street for several minutes before Derek replied. "There is one little thing."

"So spill it, already." My breath came out in a cloud of vapor mingling with the steam from my coffee.

"Esther's out."

"Esther's out." I paused outside the parking deck. "You mean out of jail?"

"That's right."

"Then why don't you sound happy about it? That's good news, right?"

Derek pulled the van's keyring from his pocket and bounced it in the palm of his free hand. "It's not that simple."

I couldn't help but roll my eyes. "Believe me, with Esther the Pester *nothing* is ever simple!"

We walked up to the van and climbed inside. "So where is she? Do we have to pick her up at the station or is she meeting us out at the Audubon Center?"

We were on our way to the John James Audubon Center at Mill Grove. Derek and I had signed up for one of the birding walks.

The original home on the property had been built in 1762. The house sat on a hill overlooking Perkiomen Creek, a tributary of the Schuylkill—the very same Schuylkill along which the Laurel Hill Cemetery was located.

As a young man, John James Audubon had spent several years living in the house at Mill Grove, which was now only a mile or so from the Greater Philadelphia Expo Center.

I'd been looking forward to visiting. Now, my excitement was dulled by current events.

Derek cranked up the engine and pulled onto the street. "She's MIA."

"MIA?"

"Missing in action."

I turned to stare at him. "What do you mean missing in action? When did the police release her?"

"Last night."

"She never came to our room. Didn't they give her a ride back to the Eagle Inn?"

"Detective Locke says they offered."

"And?"

"And Esther declined."

"Declined." I shut my eyes as Derek sped up. "Are you telling me the police let an old woman loose on the streets in a strange town, late at night to walk home alone?"

"She left in the company of a friend."

"Floyd and Karl?"

"Marty."

I bit my lip.

"The Osprey." I clenched my fist. "What are those two up to?"

"I wish I knew." Derek stomped on the gas and passed a wide gray sanitation truck. "Do you really believe all this Osprey stuff?"

"With Esther, I never know what to believe." Knowing it was probably futile, I dug my phone from my purse. "I'm calling her." I dialed and pressed my ear to my phone.

"Well?"

"I got a recording." I tried Floyd and Karl next. Ditto. "Do you think we should telephone Detective Locke and tell him Karl and Floyd are missing now?"

Derek exited the highway. "Philadelphia isn't his jurisdiction. Not to mention, we have no idea where they are. Two grown men, one of whom is a former police chief. I don't think the locals are going to get too worked up over them spending a night on the town."

"I suppose you're right."

Derek smiled. "I always am. You said it yourself, they probably gambled all night."

"Considering how much money Karl lost the first night, the two of them will end up penniless and homeless."

Derek's smile turned to a big fat smirk. "They could always move into your house."

"Oh, no. I've got two boarders too many already."

"Understood." Derek's phone spat out some directions and he complied. "Besides, we'll probably find all three of them huddled together sipping coffee and eating jelly doughnuts down by the creek."

My stomach growled as we pulled down a twisting rural road. Derek found a parking space in the nearly full lot. I tipped the remainder of my bitter black coffee down my gullet. Another gallon of coffee and a dozen warm donuts and I'd be good to go.

Irving Shipman was to be our guide. We found him and about a dozen others huddled near the small compound that housed some permanently injured birds, including a great horned owl and two eastern screech owls.

Irving said hello and looked at his watch. "Let's get started, shall we?"

We followed John's Trail, a steep, lovely path along which we managed to see and hear several species including chimney swifts, crows, several great crested flycatchers and even an adult female northern parula.

Trailing behind the others, I trained my binoculars on a common yellowthroat as it bounded through the vegetation.

Derek tapped my shoulder. "Who is that down there?"

I reluctantly lowered my binoculars. The male common yellowthroat was a rare sighting for me. The bird has a black mask like Zorro.

Far off the trail, a man and woman stood in close quarters.

"I wish I had thought to bring my camera. Something about that man looks familiar."

Derek pulled me sideways until we were half hidden by a black walnut tree. "I don't know about the kid. The woman definitely looks familiar."

"She should." I trained my binoculars on the pair as they stood near the water's edge amongst a tangle of shrubbery far below us. "That's Ilsa Skoglund." She was dressed in olive pants and a tan coat with a knit cap over her long tresses. The young man wore rumpled jeans and a black hoodie.

I watched in silence. The two were gesticulating in hard, rapid movements. "I wish I knew what they were saying."

"I don't think they're talking about birds." Derek leaned heavily against the tree.

"Neither do I."

Ilsa Skoglund glanced up. She must have said something to the man because he looked up too.

I smiled and waved my binoculars in the air. "Nice morning for bird watching, isn't it?"

The young man limped off. Ilsa stared at us a moment longer then left in the opposite direction.

"That was interesting." Derek brushed himself off. "Until I met you, I didn't realize birding was so much like a soap opera."

"Neither did I."

We quickened our steps in search of Irving and our group. We found them gathered on the expansive lawn below the big stone house.

"What's going on?" I whispered to Irving.

"Phoebe has arranged for a sunrise memorial for our JJ."

"I see." Derek and I had left in the middle of the keynote speech last night and were unaware.

I heard whispers discussing Ilsa's surprise declaration. In terms of gossip and newsworthiness among my fellow birders, the discovery of the lingering existence of the long-thought extinct ivory-billed woodpecker was on par with the sudden demise of JJ Fuller.

Phoebe stood shoulder to shoulder with Lorna Fuller. The widow was dressed for the occasion in dark slacks and a long black coat. Her hair sparkled in the rising sun. Phoebe was more casual, in faded blue jeans, hiking boots and a navy parka. A half dozen candles had been placed in the earth. Their tiny flames flickered as Lorna said a few words.

Nikki Nilsson stood off to one side, alone. Her eyes appeared puffy. Whether it was from grief or too much drinking and lack of sleep, I couldn't say.

There was no sign of Ilsa or the mystery man in the woods.

Derek dropped me off back at the Expo Center. He was going to check in with Detective Locke at the sheriff's office. Despite telling ourselves that there was nothing to worry about, we were both concerned about the disappearance of all three of our friends.

"Don't you disappear next." I leaned through the window and kissed Derek goodbye. "Next thing you know, I'll be driving back to Ruby Lake alone."

"Not a chance." Derek kissed me back, hard. I watched breathlessly as he disappeared from sight.

A man and woman were arguing in the parking lot next to a tow truck. The truck had an old silver Honda sedan hooked to the back of its winch like a bluntnose shark at the end of a fishing line.

The woman doing the yelling was Phoebe Gates. She shook her fist and stamped her feet. The man dressed in baggy green shorts and a tank top despite the cold folded his arms as if he'd heard it all before. He probably had.

The beefy man glanced my way as I moved closer but showed no interest in me. Phoebe had her back to me.

"Please," she begged. "I told them I would pay them at the end of the week."

"Sorry, lady," the man sounded weary.

"But you can't take my car. I need it."

"Lady." Beefy Man jerked his thumb at the car and truck. "I've already taken your car. You want my advice?" He didn't wait for her to answer. "Pay your bills on time like everybody else and this won't happen again."

Phoebe let loose a string of invectives. The driver shrugged and climbed inside the cab of the tow truck. Phoebe, I had to give her credit for guts, jumped in his path as he started moving.

She leaped just as quickly out of his way when he honked twice and surged forward with what seemed every intention of running her down.

Phoebe stood in the middle of the parking lot cursing as her car was towed off.

I began moving in the opposite direction.

"Amy, wait!"

I stopped and reluctantly turned.

Phoebe slowly approached. Her face was blotchy and her eyes damp. "You don't have to run away. I saw you." She frowned. "I suppose you saw everything."

"I don't know what to say."

"Can I buy you a cup of coffee?"

"Well…"

"Hey, I can still afford coffee. Come on."

We went to the food court and took a table in the middle of the room with our snack.

I waited for Phoebe to speak and it didn't take long.

"Money's been tight lately." She carefully peeled the paper from the side of her oversized muffin with long, painted nails.

"I'm sorry." I turned my muffin on its head and pinched off a chunk of the bottom. "Things must be extra hard for you right now. On top of everything else, you've got the Expo to manage. JJ Fuller's death must have hit you hard too."

She narrowed her eyes at me. "Why do you say that?"

"I couldn't help notice your tears at the memorial this morning."

"Don't read anything into it, Amy." Her voice had changed like water from a tap going hot to cold. "I cry over everything, including spilt milk."

"Sorry." I was taken aback. "I didn't mean to imply anything."

Phoebe chomped down on her apple-granola muffin and chewed. "I know." She ripped open two packs of sweetener and dumped them in her coffee. "Frankly, I can't wait until this Expo is over."

"Speaking of the Expo, I never really thanked you for thinking of Birds and Bees when the other exhibitor dropped out."

She waved her hand dismissively. A ring decorated each of her fingers. "Think nothing of it. In fact, it wasn't really my idea. I mean, when Hikers and Bikers dropped out, we had to have someone to fill in. It doesn't look good having an empty booth."

"Why us?"

"I had a waiting list of exhibitors," Phoebe explained. "I was going to start working my way down it when I got a call from JJ's office saying it would be a good idea to include you."

"Why? I mean, I never even met the man. He's never been to the store. Not that I recall, anyway." My mind was racing. Why would JJ Fuller suggest that Birds & Bees fill in for an exhibitor who had cancelled at the American Birding Expo? It was hard to believe he had even known I and the store existed prior to the Expo.

Phoebe was frowning now too. "I remember. You didn't even recognize each other in the hallway." Her fingernails played a tune on the table. "That is odd."

"I'll say." Silence filled the space between as we both tried to come up with an explanation for JJ's odd recommendation.

"We'll never know now." Phoebe patted my hand. "I'm glad you came. I hope you're managing to have a good time and making some good connections."

I didn't want to make the woman feel any worse than she already did. "It has been wonderful. It's inspiring. I've got lots of new ideas for the business."

Phoebe drank then ran her tongue over her lower lip. "Such as?"

"We may start offering some birding trips."

"Tours?"

"One of the exhibitors gave me the idea."

"It's a good one. Birding tours are popular. If you decide to give it a go, give me a call. Maybe I can help."

"Thanks, I'd appreciate that."

"In fact, if you need any help at all with the business, I'm available."

"Oh?"

Noting my confusion, Phoebe explained. "Working with the ABE is only a part-time gig. That's what I do, help bird festivals and tours with their organization, logistics and long-term planning."

Phoebe stuffed a crumpled, lipstick-stained napkin into her empty cup. "I could probably help you. Maybe scout some possible locations."

"That's very kind." She handed me her personal business card. "I'm not sure how I could afford to pay you."

"Don't worry," Phoebe said, quickly. "We can work something out. Anything is better than going home."

It was an odd thing to say but I let the remark slide. I placed her card in my purse. "Where is home? Do you live in the area?"

"No. Cleveland. Not that it's much of a home any longer. Nor do I have a car to get back there with even if I wanted to."

"No family or friends there?"

"My husband and I divorced and my children aren't speaking to me."

"I'm sorry."

"He was a cheating bastard."

"I know how you feel. I had a boyfriend once who cheated too."

"Never trust a man." Phoebe shoved the remaining half of her muffin in her mouth and forced it down her throat. "You're single, right?"

I nodded.

"Never married?"

"No."

"Count your blessings."

I waited as she swallowed. It was like watching a python swallow a small rabbit. "You mentioned the other day that JJ was going through a divorce."

"So?"

"I've met Lorna. She didn't mention it."

Phoebe's brow lifted in surprise. "Did you ask her?"

"No."

Her face fell. "I see. Not that it matters now."

"What do you mean?"

Irving Shipman interrupted. "Excuse me, ladies. I was wondering if I might have a word with you, Phoebe."

"Is there a problem, Irv?"

"No. I was only wondering if it would be possible to move up the time of my workshop."

Phoebe stood from the table. "Let's go check the schedule. It's in my office."

I finished my snack and stood to leave, noticing the daypack under the table. It was Phoebe's. I picked it up. A keycard to the Mill Grove Lodge had spilled out. I slipped it inside and walked to Phoebe's office to return the pack.

But the office was empty.

Peeking inside the daypack, I spotted a wallet and other personal items. Rather than carry it around or leave it out in the open where anyone could steal it, I slipped it into the bottom drawer of her desk. I'd call her later if I didn't run into her on the floor to let her know where she could find it.

Returning to the booth, I wrapped my arms around Derek. "Thank goodness you are back."

"Sorry. I didn't expect to be gone so long." Derek pulled off his jacket.

"Did the police have anything to say?"

"Only that they still consider Esther a 'person of interest'," Derek said, wrapping his words in finger quotes.

"She's interesting, all right. I wish I knew where to find Marty."

"Besides six feet under at Laurel Hill, you mean?"

"Yeah." I sighed. "I wonder what we'd find if we took a shovel and started digging there."

"Maybe we don't want to know."

"You could be right. Who knows what skeletons, figurative or literal, might be buried there."

"Have you eaten?" I asked. "Can I bring you anything from the food court?"

"I wouldn't say no to a cold drink and a hot sandwich."

"You've got it. Anything in particular?"

"Surprise me."

But I was the one who got the surprise as I angled out of the exhibit hall and discovered Floyd and Karl slipping through a door clearly marked *Employees Only.*

11

"Stop right there, you two."

Karl and Floyd froze. Karl's left palm rested against the door.

Karl shot a look at me over his shoulder, then pushed.

"Don't even think about it," I warned.

Karl slumped. His arms fell to his sides. Neither Floyd nor Karl had changed out of the clothes they had on the day before. Both were bleary-eyed.

Karl smiled weakly. "Hi, Amy."

I glared and crossed my arms over my chest. "Don't *Hi, Amy*, me. And that's Chief, to you."

Floyd gave his friend a troubled look.

"Yes, Chief," Karl replied meekly. "We were just looking for you."

"I'll bet."

I moved closer and focused on the weakest link. "Talk to me, Floyd."

"We're on the case." Rather than look at me, Floyd seemed to be enjoying looking at his feet. What he found so fascinating about a pair of clunky brown orthopedic penny loafers with half-inch rubber soles, I couldn't imagine.

"The case, Floyd?" Of all the people in the world I thought I could trust, that I thought I could count on to be stable, to be reliable, to be…normal, Floyd Withers was that person.

Had he gone over to the dark side? Crossed over to the crazy side?

Floyd seemed to be turning to stone. "What case?" I prodded before he reached total transformation and I lost him for good.

"Well…" Floyd chewed his lip and snuck a peek at Karl.

"May as well tell her." Karl plucked a half-smoked cigar from inside his windbreaker and popped it in his mouth.

"Spy stuff," mumbled Floyd.

I narrowed my eyes at him. "Spy stuff?" I was too late. Floyd had gone over the edge. Next he'd be telling me that Esther had been kidnapped by aliens.

"You know, the Mysterious Esther case." Floyd found an itch to scratch at the back of his gray head.

"The Mysterious Esther case?" I looked from one to the other.

"We can't just let her rot in jail, Amy." Floyd sounded pleading.

"Of course, not, Floyd. Nobody wants that." Two men stepped out from behind the closed hall door. I motioned for Karl and Floyd to follow me to a quiet corner. "The truth is, Esther isn't in jail anymore. But she is missing."

"We know that." Karl poked me with his cigar.

"She isn't missing," Floyd piped in.

"Not exactly," refined Karl.

I wiped a mix of damp spittle and tobacco from the middle of my sweater. A wet, brown spot remained.

"Sorry about that, Chief." Karl smiled weakly.

"You know about Esther being out of jail?"

Both men nodded.

"How?"

"I have my sources." The ex-lawman puffed out his chest.

"Yeah," repeated Floyd, "Karl has his sources."

"Do any of these sources happen to know where Esther is now?"

Detective Locke and a second uniformed officer were moving down the hall. I turned my back to them.

"No," admitted Karl. "But we do."

"You do?"

Floyd nodded enthusiastically. "Me and Karl rented a car and we've been sleuthing."

"*Investigating*," Karl said.

"Investigating," Floyd agreed. "We want to help Esther."

I wasn't sure if Esther needed or wanted our help but it seemed she was getting it anyway. "Is that why the two of you never returned to the inn last night?"

"We were on a stakeout," boasted Karl.

"Who and what were you staking out?" I squeezed my eyes shut a moment to still the dizzy spell coming on. "And where were you conducting this so-called stakeout?"

"It's like this," Karl explained. "We were looking for Esther."

"We went to see her at the police station." Floyd interrupted. "We watched her leave."

"Who's telling this, me or you?" Karl snarled.

"I don't care who tells the story, just spit it out all ready." Detective Locke was watching us from afar, like we were specimens under the microscope. It was making me nervous.

Floyd motioned for Karl to take over.

The ex-chief of police cleared his throat. "I had my feelers out. I got to hand it to the Pester. She leaves little trace."

"Don't call her that," interrupted Floyd.

"Right. Sorry," Karl replied sheepishly. "The lovely Ms. Pilaster." He rolled his eyes at me.

"I saw that!" said Floyd.

"Anyway, at the police station," Karl continued, "I went in to talk to the officer at the desk."

"Did he tell you anything?"

"Sure. He was giving me a hard time at first, but when I showed him my badge, he opened right up."

"Did you talk to Esther?"

"Yep. She told us to get lost."

"Why would she do that?"

"I don't know," moaned Floyd. "We only wanted to help."

"She acted like she wasn't happy to see us at all." Karl shot a look at his friend that was full of pity. "After, we went out to the car and sat for a while, pondering our next move. That's when we saw Esther come out."

"Alone?"

Karl nodded. "She came out alone but she climbed into a car with that fella Marty."

Floyd's face darkened, whether it was at hearing Marty's name or knowing that Esther had left the police station with him, I couldn't tell. Probably both.

"Do you know where they went?"

"Sure, we followed them."

"And? Where is she?"

"Holed up in some small apartment house in Philly. I got the address right here." Karl pulled out a mangled notepad bearing the inn's name.

"With him," Floyd added with a pang of jealousy.

"Show me."

As we moved towards the exit, Detective Locke stepped into our path. "Hello, Ms. Simms. I'd like a word with you."

I turned to Karl and Floyd. "Why don't I meet you two outside? We'll find someplace nice for lunch." I smiled at the detective. "You are a local. Any recommendations?"

The detective named a spot down the road and Floyd and Karl bustled out.

"What can I do for you, detective?"

"I'm looking for Phoebe Gates. I was told you were with her in the food court earlier."

"I was but she went to her office. I haven't seen her since."

"So you have no idea where she is?"

"None at all. What's this all about?"

Detective Locke blinked, his face betraying no emotion. "We received an anonymous phone tip that Ms. Gates had been having an affair with the deceased. Did she say anything to you about that?"

"I had no idea."

"Rumor has it, she abandoned her husband and children to be with Mr. Fuller."

"You consider her a suspect in his murder?"

"I do. Because, according to Lorna Fuller, JJ had been known to have a fling or two but would never, under any circumstances, leave his wife."

"What makes you, and her, so sure of that?"

"Lorna Fuller comes from a very wealthy family. The widow claims, and our background check confirms, that JJ Fuller liked the good things in life. The best things in life. All that world traveling he was so fond of did not come cheaply. If he left his wife, his world would crumble."

"I don't know where Phoebe is. She left the food court with one of the exhibitors, Irving Shipman, to check on something. That's the last I saw of her."

"Thanks. She is not in her office. She may have gone offsite."

I left the detective to his own devices. Phoebe had had an affair with JJ Fuller? If that was true, had the cad promised to leave his wife for her?

If so, Phoebe had been duped. She had left her husband and children, abandoned her home, to be with a man who had had no intention of being in a committed relationship with her.

When she had found out the truth, it must have crushed her, knowing what she had done and what she had given up to be with him. Her family, her entire life, ripped apart, torn asunder.

She must have been furious too. Had JJ's betrayal made her angry enough to kill?

12

I climbed into the back seat of Karl and Floyd's rental and settled back for the ride. Some minutes later, we were driving along an all too familiar sight.

I leaned forward in my seat. "That's Laurel Hill."

"What's that?" Karl eyed me in the rearview mirror.

"The cemetery the deceased Martin Ritter calls home."

"I don't get it," said Floyd.

"Neither do I," I admitted.

Karl squeezed up to the curb outside a six-story brown brick apartment complex. I pressed my nose to the car's rear side window. "This is it?"

"Yep." Karl killed the engine.

"I wonder what apartment they are in."

"I wonder what sort of hanky-panky they are up to." Karl chuckled.

Floyd shot him a death ray look.

"They are in 3C," Floyd said stiffly.

"How do you know that?"

"We saw them." Karl lifted an expensive pair of binoculars.

"Until somebody pulled the curtains."

"Where did you get those?" I demanded. "That's a two-thousand-dollar pair of optics."

"We borrowed them." Karl laid the binoculars at his feet.

"Yeah," Floyd said. "Borrowed them."

"From who?"

That was a top-of-the line pair of Ornitho Optics glasses.

"It's not important," Karl said. "What's important is what do we do next."

"Yes, but a pair of binoculars like that—"

Floyd turned around to face me. "We took them from the exhibit hall late last night. It's okay."

"It's okay? Are you telling me that you broke into the Expo Center after hours and stole a pair of expensive binoculars?"

"Not stole," Karl countered, stuffing his damp cigar between his lips. "Commandeered."

"Stole." I gaped at the two men. "You could both be arrested for burglary, grand theft maybe." What were the laws in Pennsylvania regarding crazy old coots who *commandeer* pricy binoculars from a locked facility?

Derek might have to do some more fact-checking.

I scolded them with my finger. "You could both end up in jail. Isn't it enough that Esther's there?"

"Uh, Amy." Floyd tapped my shaking knee. "Esther's out now, remember?"

"Yeah," said Karl. "She's up there with spy guy." He rolled down the driver's side window and spat his cigar out on the sidewalk. "The question is do you want to talk about what's been done or about what we are going to do next?"

I fell back against the seat and blew out a breath.

"And we are going to give them back," Floyd said patiently.

"Fine. You two wait here." I slammed the door shut behind me. "I'm coming right back."

I picked up Karl's cigar stub and handed it to him. "No littering."

Floyd leaned across the seat. "We checked in the lobby. The unit is registered to a K. Bergdorf."

I thanked him and climbed the concrete stoop. The front entrance was unlocked and the door hung loosely. The entryway was dark and dreary. There was a well-worn track in the olive green carpet which laid lifelessly on the floor. A bank of brass mail slots was built into the wall on the right.

Sure enough, K. Bergdorf was listed as the occupant of 3C of the Laurel Cove Apartments. I climbed the narrow steps to the third floor and knocked. I waited, breathing in years of mold that was probably sucking years off my life. There was no answer.

I tried again. "Esther?" I knocked harder. "Marty? Mr. Bergdorf?"

An old woman popped her head out of 3B. "Nobody's home."

"Hello. I'm looking for my friends. Esther and Marty." I glanced at the door of 3C. "Are you sure nobody is home?"

"I said so, didn't I?"

"Yes, yes, you did. Sorry. I guess I missed them."

"Left more than an hour ago. Maybe two."

"Do you know when they'll be back?"

"Nope." She sniffed as if testing the air. Not a good idea, under the present toxic conditions. Her hair was silver and her skin white and age-lined. She wore a long black dress and slippers.

"I don't suppose you know where they went?"

"Try the cemetery."

"The cemetery? You mean Laurel Hill?"

"It's the man's favorite spot. He practically lives there."

If she was talking about Marty Ritter, she didn't know how meaningful those words were. "Do you know Marty?"

She eyed me blankly.

"Martin Ritter?"

"Never heard of him."

I gave as good a description as I could manage.

"Sounds like an old fart," the woman replied, rolling her tongue across her upper lip. "This building is full of them. And when it's done with them, they end up across the street."

I was stumped for a minute, then realized she meant the cemetery. "Well, thank you for your help."

"Be careful when you leave," the old woman admonished me. "Don't talk to strangers."

I smiled at her. "Don't worry. I am not planning to."

"See that you don't. There's been two weirdos hanging around downstairs."

My brow went up. "Oh?"

"Yep. They were here for a spell then drove off. That's when I heard 3C go out."

"I see." Though I wasn't sure that I did.

"They're back now."

"Who's back?" I was confused all over again. Had Esther and Marty and this Bergdorf character snuck in behind me. I glanced at the door of Bergdorf's apartment.

"The weirdos." She wrapped her hands in the folds of her expansive dress.

"They are?"

"Perverts, if you ask me." Her eyes bounced around the foyer. "I called the police. When I heard the knocking out here, I thought you was them."

"Perverts?"

"Parked in that dark sedan at the curb. Peeping in the windows."

"You mean—" I had a feeling I knew exactly which perverts she was talking about. I needed to warn them. We needed to get out of there before the police showed up and arrested them for peeping.

"Thanks for your time. It was a pleasure meeting you."

I bounded down the stairs and flung myself in the backseat of the car.

"Hey, Chief," Floyd said. "Where's Esther? Did you talk to her? Is she coming?"

I banged my fist twice on the back of Karl's seat. Was that a police siren I heard in the distance? "Drive."

Karl switched on the engine and floored the gas pedal. The car lurched forward, missing the truck in front of us by mere inches.

Karl threw the transmission into reverse and, after backing and twisting the wheel hard, managed to gain the road.

"Turn here," I directed.

"Sure." We slid around the corner butt first.

"Left!" I shouted next.

A police car, lights flashing, was coming on fast. I swiveled my head in every direction. "The cemetery," I shouted. "There's the entrance."

The ornate Laurel Hill entrance was ahead on our right. Thankfully, no cars were coming our way down the narrow road bifurcating the main complex.

I hoped that Karl could negotiate through it without mishap.

"Slow down, you old fool!" Floyd said what I was thinking.

Karl cursed and lifted his foot. With a screech of brakes and a lurch, we turned off the main street. We dashed through the entrance. Karl was forced to slam on the brakes as an unfortunate groundskeeper in a slow-moving golf cart crossed our path.

He looked at us in surprise and angrily waved a rake at us. "This is a no wake zone! Slow it down!"

Karl waved back. We moved slowly up the hill to the right. I looked out the rear window. The police car had not followed us.

"Stop here," I said finally.

Karl pulled the car over to the side of the lawn. He lit a fresh cigar with a shaky hand.

"Where to now, Amy?" Floyd asked. "Back to the Expo?"

I pushed open my door. "I want to show you something first. Follow me."

After a little trial and error, I found what I was looking for.

"What does it mean?" Karl scratched the back of his neck.

Floyd stood with his hands folded. "According to his headstone, Marty died nearly forty years ago."

"Maybe he's one of those zombie guys." Karl chuckled.

"Zombie guys. Why didn't I think of that earlier?" I spun around. "Back to the Expo."

We hurried back to the sedan as quickly as we could.

"There's a piece of paper stuck under the windshield." Floyd pointed.

Karl puffed out a cloud of foul smelling smoke as I plucked the paper from behind the wiper blade and unfolded it.

"What's it say?" demanded Karl.

"Probably a ticket for parking on the grass," Floyd said.

"No." I reread the note then scanned the horizon. There were few people about and didn't recognize any of them. Between the trees, the shrubbery and the tombstones, a body—a living body, that is—could hide just about anywhere, even near at hand, and not be seen. "It's from Esther."

"Esther?" Floyd pressed against me. "What does she say?"

I handed Floyd the note. "She wants me to meet her at some bar later."

Floyd read the note. "I don't like this."

"Neither do I." I slid inside the car. "Let's ride."

13

"There you are." Derek leaned across the display table and planted a kiss on my lips.

"Sorry." I threw my purse on the rear table. "Something came up."

"No problem." He reached under the table and pulled out a book. "I got you a present."

"The latest *Crossley ID Guide*!" I flipped through the photos. "Where did you get this?" Richard Crossley was a noted photographer and authored a unique series of birding guides.

"The author was signing books a couple booths down. Look." Derek turned to the frontispiece. "He autographed it."

I read the inscription and smiled. "We carry his books in Birds and Bees."

"I know. I told him."

"You, sir, are too sweet." I pushed up on my toes and kissed him hard on the lips, and I didn't care who saw me.

"Thanks. Right now, I'm too hungry. Where's my sandwich?"

I groaned. "I am so sorry—"

"No problem. I'll go get something in the food court."

"No. I feel awful." I fished my wallet out of my purse. "I'll go. You stay here. Karl and Floyd should be along in a minute."

"They're back?" Surprise showed on his face. "Where did you find them?"

"Long story." I hurried across the crowded floor. "I'll explain when I return."

The food court was filled with zombies. Tall ones, short ones, fat ones, thin ones. The only thing they had in common was that they were all recognizably undead.

The invasion had begun.

ZombieFest was going on at the other end of the Expo Center and was clearly in full Saturday swing. I studied the gray, ashen faces as I stood at the back of the long line leading to the sandwich counter.

Did one of these pasty faces belong to Peter Porter, the zombie who had reported to the police that he had seen Esther in the vicinity of JJ Fuller's dressing room at the time of the murder?

I glanced at my watch as I inched my way further up the line.

"Hey, Peter. Wait up." A young woman with double ponytails, severe black lips and hollow-looking eyes bounded up to a young man of average build. And average looks, for a zombie, that is. He limped towards her.

It was my Mr. Peter Porter. I jumped out of line. "Hold my place for me?" I smiled sweetly at the gentleman behind me and barged between Peter Porter and his friend. "Hi, Mr. Porter. Amy Simms, remember me?"

"No."

"Who's she?" Her dark blue eyes seemed to scour my flesh. Was she sizing me up? Wondering how I'd taste?

The skin was peeling from her face and her teeth were yellow. Then again, what zombies weren't?

"I never saw her before, babe." Porter removed the young woman's hand from his forearm. He balanced a plastic food tray in his hands. On it sat a roast beef sandwich, fries and a soda. Hardly flesh-eating zombie food. "Can I help you?"

"We met the other day. You were with Detective Locke."

"Who?" The girl was determined to stick her nose in.

"Nobody," Porter said to the girl.

Porter was squirming. He looked repulsive too. His face was covered in icky pustules where it wasn't marked by bruised, dead-looking flesh. More wounds covered his body. His charcoal trousers were torn at the knees and tattered at the cuffs. Loose dirty bandages crisscrossed his torso over a camel-colored shirt. An open pack of cigarettes stuck out of his shirt pocket.

I didn't bother to tell him those things could kill him. After all, he was dead, or undead, already. What would be the point?

"You told the detective you saw my friend, Esther Pilaster, in the vicinity of the murder."

The young woman gasped. "You mean that dead bird guy?"

I nodded. "JJ Fuller."

"What's this all about, Peter?" pressed his companion.

Porter scowled, looking suddenly very zombielike.

"Nothing, Suze."

He stepped around me. "I've gotta go."

I jumped in his path. "Please, my friend is in trouble. The police seem to think she may be involved in JJ Fuller's killing."

"Isn't she?"

"No." I stuck my chin out at him. "She isn't."

"Whatever." Porter stepped to the left.

"What were you and Ilsa Skoglund doing in the woods together?"

Porter froze.

"Alone." I added that bit knowing it would get a rise out of his maybe girlfriend. It did. She was looking daggers at him now.

Definitely a girlfriend.

"None of your business," he snapped.

"She didn't look happy. In fact, neither of you looked particularly happy."

"Who is Ilsa Skoglund?" Suze's eyes were on Porter. I detected a flash of jealousy. A big flash.

Peter looked around and set his plastic tray on the nearest empty table. "Give me a minute, Suze."

"But—"

He raised his hand. "I'll meet you inside."

Suze frowned but tromped off.

"Listen, lady. I don't know what your game is but I don't want any trouble."

"Neither do I. All I want is the truth."

Peter Porter looked at the crowded space filled with inquisitive ears, then clenched his jaw. "Not here. Not now."

"Fine. But I want to talk to you. When and where?"

Noting his hesitation, I added, "You may as well get it over with. I'm not going to stop badgering you until you do."

He pulled back the fake grey bandages that wrapped up his spindly arm and studied his watch—the face of which portrayed a zombified Albert Einstein.

And I thought bird lovers were eccentric. The zombie-loving crowd had it all over us.

"One hour." He pushed down his sleeve.

"Where?"

This seemed to require more thought.

Finally, he said, "The fashion show. Backstage."

"What fashion show?"

"The ZombieFest Runway Show," he replied as if it was obvious, which it obviously wasn't. "I'm the emcee. I'll meet you before the show."

Peter Porter scooped up his tray and melted into the crowd. Not an easy thing to do dressed as a zombie, but he somehow managed.

* * * *

"You're alone?" I handed Derek a tuna on whole wheat, a bag of potato chips, coleslaw, and the largest root beer I could buy. Derek is a nut for root beer soda. "Where are Floyd and Karl?"

"I have no idea. They never showed up."

"That's funny." I looked around again as if they might suddenly appear. They didn't. "How long can it take to park a car?"

"You missed all the excitement though."

"What excitement?"

"That assistant of JJ Fuller's, Nikki Nilsson, showed up. She looked pretty—"

"Pretty?"

"You didn't let me finish. Pretty smashed. She caused quite a scene."

"I don't see any sign of her now."

"No." Derek tore open the bag of chips and dug inside. "Irv Shipman intercepted her."

Irving Shipman. I wondered if he'd noticed all his missing gear. Expensive missing gear. I'd look for him later and try to explain, sort things out. Before he had a chance to file a report with the police, if he hadn't done so already.

My checkbook couldn't handle having to provide bail for both Floyd and Karl.

As Derek wolfed his meal, I explained about my run in with Peter Porter. "I'm supposed to meet him soon."

"Go ahead." Derek wiped his mouth with a paper napkin. "I can handle things here."

"Are you sure?" I wrung my hands. "I feel terrible sticking you at the booth for hours and hours."

"Mostly I've been collecting business cards and handing out yours. Talking up the store." Derek shrugged off my concern and extended his arms. "Besides, what else have I got to do?" he asked with a grin. "You wouldn't let me bring my golf clubs." He took an imaginary swing.

"Nice shot," I commented. "Now kiss me."

He did.

"Next time," I said, feeling all weak in the knees, "I promise, you can bring your clubs. I wish I had one of them now. I could use your nine iron to keep Floyd, Karl and Esther in line."

Leaving Derek alone once again, I hurried to the opposite end of the Expo Center. A man guarding the entrance to that hall had a harried look on his face as I tried brushing past him. "Hold on," he ordered, grabbing hold of my lanyard. "This says American Birding Expo."

"Yes." I snatched my badge back.

"This is ZombieFest, ma'am." A fat finger pointed back the way I had come. "You want the other end of the Expo Center."

"No. This is the right place. I'm here to see someone."

The burly security guard wore a long-sleeved black t-shirt which stated in block letters that he was SECURITY. The shirt fell over a generous stomach. "You don't have a ZombieFest badge. No badge, no admittance."

"I'll only be a minute. I'm supposed to meet Peter Porter." I checked the time on my phone. "I'm running late as it is."

"Sounds like you better hightail it over to registration."

The man, with a face that was too small for his nose, made a gun of his right hand and shot a round of blanks toward a row of portable six-foot tables set up along the wall opposite. Each was manned by a ZombieFest volunteer.

I approached one with more rings on and in her face than I had in my entire jewelry box. Hers were silver. Mine were a mixed bag.

After some negotiation and the exchanging of money, mine, I was given a badge that gave me one-day admittance to ZombieFest.

Oh, joy.

But that wasn't the end of my troubles. The registration police guarding entrance to ZombieFest had refused admittance unless I dressed what they called *appropriately* for the occasion.

Suitable dress, per their standards, included an over-sized, over-priced gray and black ZombieFest t-shirt with a frayed collar, featuring a flesh-eating ghoul slurping up the brains of her unwitting victim. That set me back thirty dollars cash. Add that to the hair and makeup session that set me back another fifty and my little talk with Peter Porter was costing me big bucks.

I hoped the venture paid off.

Now I was late for my meeting with Peter Porter.

"Excuse me." I began pushing people aside as I cleared the entrance and entered the large exhibition hall. Well, I thought they were people.

Who was to say some real zombies hadn't infiltrated into the wannabe zombie crowd?

"I'm looking for Peter Porter. Have you seen him?" I asked one undead woman pushing a stroller. She was no help. Neither were the skeletal remains she was hauling in the stroller.

A nasty looking zombie with dark red blood—or something that I prayed only very much resembled it—dripping from an open wound on his cheek answered. "I saw him having a beer in back."

"Where's back?"

A heavily made-up hand ending in a ragged black fingernail pointed to my right. "He's probably still there."

I didn't want to know what was under his fingernails. Dead brain cells?

"Thanks," I shouted over the noise of the loud zombie four-piece band, which appropriately screeched out some nearly incomprehensible death metal tune.

Well, tune was a charitable description of the noise coming from the left side of the low stage. The keyboard player, in particular, seemed more intent on smashing keys than playing any specific notes in any predetermined order.

Across the room, I spotted Porter's friend, Suze, in black lingerie, covered in oozing abscesses. Two men in torn and blood-streaked bridal gowns flanked her.

"Such a waste of tulle and satin," I mumbled.

I waved to Suze. She ignored the gesture.

I spied Porter behind the black curtains.

He scowled at me. "You're late."

"Sorry. I had trouble getting in."

He nodded in understanding. "You look good."

I pulled at my dyed gray hair, glancing at my pasty complexion in a backstage mirror. I hoped I didn't end up looking like this in my old age. "Thanks."

"Let's cut to the chase," I began. "What were you and Ilsa Skoglund arguing about?"

"Nothing. We were having a little conversation, that's all."

"Why the secrecy?"

"Who says there was any secrecy?" he scoffed, tossing back a beer.

Porter dropped the empty can to the ground and stomped it underfoot. "You one of those conspiracy nuts?" He ripped another can from the yoke of the six-pack atop the wooden stool at his side.

I was getting angry. All the zombie music was giving me a headache. The veins in my temples throbbed in synch with the beat. Plus, I was having a reaction to the heavy makeup the woman had used on me. My face felt like it was being eaten by fire ants.

"You met Ms. Skoglund in the middle of the woods," I asserted. "You don't strike me as being the bird-walking type." If there was ever a zombie walk, Peter Porter would probably be at the top of the signup list.

I wondered if zombies kept life lists...or was that undead lists?

"You want the truth?"

"That's why I'm here."

"I never saw your friend anywhere near that dead guy's room." He glared at me with bloodshot eyes. Was it alcohol or special effects?

"You didn't?" I bristled. "Why did you tell the police you did? Don't you realize the trouble you caused?"

"Somebody paid me."

"You threw my friend under the bus for a few dollars? She could go to prison."

He stiffened. "I needed the money. Being a zombie doesn't exactly pay the bills."

"No, I don't suppose it does. Who paid you? Was it Ms. Skoglund?"

"I can't tell you that. And if you tell anybody what I said, I'll deny it."

"Hey, Porter." A corpulent, corpse-like giant zombie waved. "You're on. Get your rotting carcass on stage."

"Gotta go."

I scurried after Porter. "But you haven't answered all my questions. Who paid you?"

Peter Porter's face darkened. He looked frightened. And frightening. "After the show." He tipped his beer and chugged thirstily. "But, like I said, whatever I tell you stays between us. Tell anybody else and I'll call you a liar."

He handed me the can, turned and left. Suze stood watching us closely.

I tossed the can in an open trash barrel and squeezed my way to the middle of the audience to watch the runway show. I was there anyway and had paid for the privilege. Why not make the best of it?

Zombies of the male, female, and canine persuasions paraded the runway, lurching awkwardly like only zombies could or should. Some were in lingerie, others bandages, bikinis, bridal gowns and tuxedos.

One zombie man wore a giant diaper. That was just gross.

Peter Porter provided color commentary for each contestant.

At the end of the show, three of the undead were awarded gold zombie statuettes. A man and woman dressed as zombie bride and groom handed out the trophies to much applause and the occasional boo from a disgruntled fan who thought their favorite should have won.

I realized then there was no sign of Peter Porter.

I pushed my way through the crowd in search of him. I was afraid he would try to get away before he could tell me everything he knew.

And I had a feeling that was plenty.

14

Suze and a gathering of buzzing zombies loitered behind the curtain at the back of the stage near the exit door.

"Have you seen Peter?" I laid a hand on Suze's clammy arm.

She looked disturbed. And disturbing. But I figured that was normal. What zombie doesn't?

She pulled away. "Leave him alone. You've caused enough trouble."

"Wait. What trouble?"

But Suze no-last-name was gone.

I pushed through the tight-packed crowd, feeling squeamish. It was unnerving to be jostled by a pack of swarming zombies. I felt like I'd unwittingly stepped onto the set of a George Romero movie or, worse yet, into a very real zombie apocalypse.

I only hoped that these zombies had had their fill of human brains for the day because I wasn't in a mood to share mine.

A young man grabbed my wrist in a not unfriendly fashion. "Nice outfit, lady." His smile, meant no doubt to be suave and come hither, was spoiled by the dark brown caps over his teeth. "Who are you supposed to be?"

At least I hoped those were caps.

I blurted out the first thing I could think of, the name of a character from *Z: A Zombie Musical*, an obscure musical film from the early 2000s about a zombie pug who zombifies a trio of skinny-dipping nuns.

"Cool." My suitor nodded appreciatively. He wasn't bad looking actually. Under all that makeup, I imagined an olive-skinned Greek god with longish black hair and smoldering eyes, and a body that spent more time working in the gym than it did at a day job. "I'm Stalker. Can I buy you a drink?"

"Sorry, Stalker." I smiled. Stalker? I could only hope that wasn't the name on his birth certificate.

And I really hoped he hadn't gotten the moniker due to a predilection for following single women like me around. "One pint of blood a day is my limit." I tugged and he readily released his grip on my wrist. "Actually, maybe you can help me."

"Yeah? Happy to."

"I'm looking for Peter. Peter Porter."

"Oh." He appeared about as crestfallen as a zombie possibly could. That's a hard look to pull off when you are already looking like death warmed over.

"Have you seen him?"

After a moment's hesitation, my Adonis in zombie clothing reluctantly answered. "Yeah. I saw him go outside." He jerked his thumb over his right shoulder indicating the exit door. "Probably getting stoned or getting smashed." He chuckled. "Maybe both."

I rolled my eyes. It was going to be hard getting answers out of Porter if he was stoned out of his mind and drunk to boot, let alone meaningful answers.

"Thanks." I turned to go.

"I'll come with you." Making himself useful, he carved a path through his zombie cohorts and threw open the exit door.

Peter Porter sat on the ground, his back against the wall. His feet were tucked under one of the big garbage bins lining the rear.

Near at hand, a dented beer can lay on its side in a puddle of suds.

"Hey, Porter. Wake up. You've got company." Stalker gave him a toe kick. "Drunk again. What a lush." He turned to me with a look filled with distaste. "Disgusting isn't it?"

"Sort of," I could only reply. This was my first experience with a drunken zombie. Hopefully it would be my last. "Maybe we should let him sleep it off."

I was more frustrated than disgusted. A comatose zombie was a useless zombie.

"Are you kidding?" Stalker leaned forward and yanked hard on Porter's right arm.

I couldn't help thinking that if Porter had been a proper zombie, it probably would have come off in his hands.

"Hey, Porter!" Stalker yelled again as he tugged a second time.

That was when I noticed there was one more bleeding wound on Peter Porter than there had been earlier. A slow drip was coming from the region of Porter's left kidney.

It looked fresh and it looked like real blood, not movie magic or catsup. That purple bruise on his jaw looked new too. I tapped Stalker on the shoulder. "I'm thinking maybe you should stop now, Stalker," I suggested.

"Why?"

"Because I don't think it's going to do much good."

"How's that?"

"I think Peter Porter is dead."

Stalker promptly let go of Porter's arm. It slapped sickeningly against the blacktop.

I was feeling more than a little sick myself.

15

The police came and I was forced to tell my story. Detective Locke showed up nearly an hour later and I was forced to tell it again. One bit of news was that a camera was found in a dumpster near the body. The make and model matched that of JJ Fuller's missing camera.

Interesting.

Nothing changed in the telling. Peter Porter was still very much dead. As I overheard one of the EMTs put it, "Mr. Porter has gone from undead to dead." How the men had been able to joke about the situation was beyond me. Maybe you needed a morbid sense of humor in their line of work.

Now I was telling my story to Derek.

"Peter Porter lied about seeing Esther. He claimed somebody paid him." We were in a local coffee shop.

"Here. You're shivering." Derek wrapped my coat over my shoulders.

"Thanks. But he wouldn't tell me who. At least not then. Maybe he didn't want to say who it was in front of the others. I don't know."

"Ilsa Skoglund?"

"Maybe. I was supposed to meet him after the runway show. He promised he would tell me who had paid him to lie."

"I'm surprised."

"Me, too. Although he warned me he'd deny it if I told anyone else."

"I wonder what game Mr. Porter was playing." Derek handed me a cup of coffee. "Did he ask you for money in exchange for the information?"

"No."

"Maybe he was planning to."

"You may be right." If that had been his plan, it was a bad one. I didn't have any money in my budget set aside for paying informants. I barely had funds for utilities, food and gas.

"Whatever Porter was up to, it was a deadly game."

I agreed. "He was killed before we had a chance to talk. It must be connected to his murder somehow. Don't you think it must be connected to his murder, Derek?"

"I suppose so." Derek was drinking lemon tea. "What do you know about this Peter Porter?"

"Not a thing. I mean, only that he's into cosplay."

"Cosplay?"

"Costume play. There's a whole world of people out there who like to get dressed up as their favorite superhero or some other fantasy character. Though, in Porter's case, maybe it's only a zombie that he likes to play at."

"I guess everybody needs a hobby." Derek stirred a spoon around in his china cup. "I'll stick to golf. What?"

He'd caught me smirking. "I was just picturing you in dark tights like Batman."

"Please, if anything, I'd be Superman. At least that way I could fly like a bird."

"That I'd like to see."

"Getting back to Peter Porter." Derek cleared his throat. I had a feeling he wasn't as comfortable picturing himself in tights as I was. "You really have no idea who he was going to finger?"

"Not a clue." I broke off the corner of the peach scone we were sharing.

"And then he is killed before he gets a chance to tell you who."

"Who would want JJ Fuller and Peter Porter dead?"

Derek nodded. "You are forgetting one other thing."

"What's that?"

"Why would someone want to bribe your zombie to say he saw Esther leaving the vicinity at the time of the murder?"

"Good point." I ripped off a hunk of scone and made it disappear.

"You say Porter admitted he needed money. Who supplied it and why finger Esther?" Derek talked like a well-trained lawyer, which he was. "Mere chance? Because she happened to have been in the vicinity?"

"You mean the wrong place at the wrong time?"

"That's exactly what I mean."

"Somebody might have seen Esther and JJ Fuller arguing and decided she would make a good patsy."

Derek had a good theory. "They did argue on the middle of the Expo floor. There could have been a dozen witnesses to their little dust up."

"Meaning a dozen potential suspects," I said with a troubled sigh.

"And thank you." I leaned over and kissed him hard and long.

After catching his breath, Derek said, "What was that for?"

"For not remarking how ghastly I look." I was still made up like something from *The Walking Dead*. The lady working the counter had recoiled in horror when we'd entered the coffee shop. The poor woman probably thought the diner was under zombie attack.

"I've never been kissed by a zombie before." Derek smirked. "I've got to say. I kind of like it."

"I'll bet you do." I kissed him again.

"How long do I have before I become one of you?"

"I think the transformation has already begun," I said slyly.

A loud, shrill whistle cut through the air. It was Karl. "Boy, we could see you two necking like a couple of teenagers all the way out in the parking lot."

Karl looked amused. Floyd looked embarrassed.

"Hello, Amy." Floyd could barely make eye contact.

"Looking good, Amy." That was Karl. Nothing phased him.

"Never better." Derek patted my knee and I stuck my tongue out at him. Derek was unperturbed. "How did you find us?"

"Were you following us?" I asked.

"No," explained Floyd. "We were following her. She was following you."

Derek looked out the window in the direction of Floyd's gaze. Karl had tromped up to the counter and was ordering coffee and donuts. "Who is she?"

"We're not sure. Looks like a woman."

"She's wearing a hat and a scarf," added Floyd. "Must be a woman."

"Who would be following us?" I stood and peered outside. It was dark but I could make out a figure sitting alone in a car. Phoebe's silver car had been towed. This was a dark coupe with a sloping roofline. Whose car was this?

Karl tossed a bag of sugar donuts on the table between us. "Help yourselves." He handed Floyd a coffee and dumped sugar and powdered cream in his own cup.

"Phoebe and JJ Fuller were having an affair."

"Are you sure, Amy?" Floyd picked through the paper sack in search of the perfect donut.

"They are all the same, you old coot." Karl grabbed the bag, dropped one on Floyd's napkin. He then reached into the bag and took the first one his fingers landed on. He stuffed it neatly in his mouth, chewed and swallowed. "They all taste the same too."

Ignoring the shenanigans, I continued for Derek's benefit. "Phoebe as much as admitted it. She left her husband. Then JJ dumped her."

Derek whistled. "There's your motive."

The car's headlights popped on.

"She's leaving." I stuck out my hand. "Karl, give me your keys!"

"What?" Karl fumbled in his pockets.

"What are you up to?" Derek demanded.

"I'm going to follow her. See where she goes. The van's too noticeable."

"I'll come with you." Derek rose.

"Okay. You two take the van and go back to the Eagle Inn and wait for us."

"But Amy, this could be dangerous." Karl was itching to go.

"We'll be fine. I only want to get a close enough look to see who she is and where she goes." I held out my hand. "The keys, Karl. Quickly."

Karl grumbled as he dropped the key to the rental in my open palm. "Careful with it. I didn't pay for any extra insurance. I'm the only registered driver."

"I promise."

"What are we supposed to do?" complained Karl. He may have been retired but he still had a yearning for action. "Waiting in the hotel is boring."

"Maybe you could stake out the apartment again."

"What apartment?" Derek asked.

"I'll fill you in as we go." I grabbed my purse.

"Stake out the apartment. Yeah, good idea, Chief," agreed Karl.

"We can do that." Floyd helped himself to a second donut. "One for the road."

"Fine. But stay out of trouble. Be discreet." I pictured the woman next-door calling the police on them. Then I pictured them behind bars.

"Don't worry," boasted Karl. "I am the master of the stakeout."

The brake lights blinked as the car turned onto the main street behind a delivery van.

"We'd better run." I pushed my arms into the sleeves of my jacket. Derek reluctantly followed.

A light rain fell as we trailed the unknown driver at a distance. In the rain and in the dark, I was reasonably certain they wouldn't know we were tailing them.

"Did you get a good look at her yet?" I asked Derek as he peered through the window.

"No, nothing identifiable. I think the guys are right about it being a woman though. You could pull upside them at the next light."

"Too chancy. They might spot us."

After nearly ten minutes of driving, the dark coupe pulled up outside a chain hotel with a No Vacancy sign. I got stuck behind a shuttle bus that slowly disgorged a group of travelers at the entrance. When we were finally able to move, there was no sign of the other vehicle. "Did you see which way they went?"

"I think they went up there." He pointed to a gated parking garage. "We need a keycard to get in."

"Rats." I slid into a visitor parking space and cut the engine. "Let's check inside the hotel."

"Okay."

There was a big sign inside the door stating the hotel was the official hotel of the American Birding Expo. I wiped my feet at the mat at the entrance then brushed the rain off my damp coat.

"I don't see anybody suspicious." Derek peered through the window.

"I'll bet Phoebe is staying here. Ilsa Skoglund too. Let's see if we can talk to one of them."

"You do that," Derek suggested. "I'm going to walk up in the parking garage and see if I can spot that car." He rubbed his hands together. "I would love to learn who is so interested in us."

"Good idea."

Derek slipped off. I approached the front desk with a smile on my face and asked for Phoebe and Ilsa's room numbers.

And was promptly rebuked.

"We do not give out the room assignments of our guests," the gold-jacketed man behind the check-in counter informed me. A woman in a crisp white shirt running some papers through a copy machine behind him nodded her agreement.

It was two against one.

"Ms. Gates and Ms. Skoglund are with the American Birding Expo. Me, too." I fished around in my purse, yanked on my lanyard, releasing it from the twisted bowels of my handbag and displayed my nametag proudly on the counter. "I am supposed to be meeting them. They won't be happy if I'm late."

His eyes fell to his computer screen and his fingers got busy. "Sorry." He pushed the badge an inch in my direction with a shiny, manicured fingernail. "Both guests have requested that they not be disturbed."

"Fine. It will be on your head when they complain."

"Yes, ma'am. Will there be anything else?"

My attempt at intimidation failed. I stuffed the badge back in my purse. "How about the bar? Am I allowed to have a drink in there? Or is it for guests only?"

Without waiting for an answer, I proceeded to the dimly lit lounge to wait for Derek. I took a seat at the bar in the corner facing away from the annoying overhead television screens. My stool gave me a perfect shot of the lobby.

Businessmen nursing drinks watched avidly as grown men in oversized shorts bounced a ball around and tried desperately to get it through each other's hoop. I felt like I was jumping through hoops myself.

The men smiled at me. I smiled back.

A young couple at a nearby table was trying to contain their two cranky children, a boy and a girl, with generous baskets of French fries and large glasses of soda.

The boy had his eyes fixed on me.

"Don't stare at the nice lady," scolded the boy's father.

I wriggled my fingers and smiled to show I didn't mind. Dad scooted the boy's chair so he was facing the wall, not me.

What was that all about?

I ordered a glass of white wine from a bartender with a big smile on his face and nursed it while considering my options. I really needed to talk to Phoebe. She was my only lead.

I pulled out my phone and called Derek. "Hi, Derek. Any luck?"

"No. I've been up and down all four decks. Plenty of dark coupes but I couldn't swear which one is the right one. And there's an exit on the other side. The driver could be gone."

"Sounds like a dead end."

"I'm afraid so. But give me a few more minutes. Then I'll meet you inside."

"I'll be in the lounge."

"Great, order me a beer."

"I will. Be careful," I urged.

"Don't worry. I have no desire or intention of putting myself in danger. I expect you to do the same."

"Count on it."

"Good. Listen, I've been thinking that we should find out more about Peter Porter."

"I agree. Maybe the police will be willing to share some info on him. We can put Karl on it. He's chummy with them. I wonder if Porter was local."

"If he is, maybe we can talk to his family or friends, or…"

"What?"

"I just remembered. Suze."

"Who is Suze?"

"His girlfriend, I think."

"Do you have a last name?"

"No," I admitted. "The police might have it on file. Although I didn't see her around after the police showed up this afternoon." I explained how I'd met her and how she had been a hostile presence at ZombieFest, at least when it came to my presence there.

Had her hostility and subsequent disappearance after Peter Porter's death been connected?

"Hey, here comes a dark coupe. Gotta run."

"Derek?"

I frowned at the phone. He'd hung up. I ordered Derek a local dark ale and a plate of sesame-glazed hot pretzel nibs.

"Sure. Going to a party?" said the bartender.

"What? No," I replied.

The bartender rang a brass bell beside the register. A young waitress in a tight-fitting black shirt and slacks approached him.

"This is for 407, Gates."

"Sure." She snapped a wad of gum as he handed across a tray on which sat a bottle of champagne on ice and two glasses.

"It's been charged to the room."

"Back in a jiff."

"See that you are," replied the bartender who appeared several years her senior. He wore a black vest over a white shirt with black slacks. "And lose the gum."

She turned on her heel with a sexy strut that even the annoyed bartender couldn't help admiring. Her reply to his last words was to shoot him the bird.

The bartender chuckled good-naturedly. "She's a piece of work." He had aimed his words at me.

"You're very patient. If I were you, I'd—" Gates? I opened my purse and threw some money at him.

"If you were me you'd what?"

"Gotta run," I said, stealing Derek's line. I hurried to the elevator.

The blond waitress grinned at me as I walked toward room 407. She was walking away from it. Her hands were free, having delivered the champagne, but her mouth was still full and she chewed gleefully. "Love your outfit."

"Thanks." It was an automatic response. I wasn't wearing anything special.

"Have a nice evening," she chirped.

I wished her the same. Settling my purse strap over my shoulder, I knocked at 407.

The door popped open. "Did you forget something?" Phoebe's eyes narrowed then grew wide. "Amy, it's you."

16

Phoebe didn't look too happy to see me. She wrung her hands.

Since I had last seen her, she had switched to a thick white sweater and a slinky red skirt that fell to just below her knees. Her feet were bare.

"Can I come in?" Okay, so I was breaking all the rules and probably my promise to Derek to stay out of harm's way. I was asking to enter the room of a woman who very possibly could be responsible for the deaths of two men.

Had she been following us? Had we been following her?

"I suppose." She cast a nervous look over her shoulder then stepped aside. "Come on in."

The room held a king-size bed, night table and leather chair along one wall. Across from the bed was a black desk. A TV sat on a dresser beside the desk. The striped curtains were closed.

"Can I get you something to drink?" Phoebe pulled open the door to the mini-fridge and poked her nose inside. "I've got orange juice, beer, wine and 7Up."

"No, thank you."

"Have a seat." Phoebe waved to a brown leather chair. She helped herself to a bottle of light beer then sat at the edge of the bed to face me. "What's up? Are you staying here at the hotel?"

"No. I'm staying in Philadelphia, remember?" She looked puzzled. "The inn that Hikers and Bikers had booked?"

"Right. I guess I forgot." She took a small sip. "How are the rooms?"

"Fine." There was no point explaining the mix-up and how there were only two rooms and how I'd had to pay top dollar for them. It would only sidetrack me from my reason for being there: murder.

"So what brings you here?"

"I suppose you heard about Peter Porter's stabbing?"

"Who?"

Her hands had become very still in her lap. She held the beer tightly.

"The unfortunate man who was murdered at ZombieFest."

"Oh, sure. Him. Thank goodness the incident happened at ZombieFest and not at the birding expo. I mean, I'm sorry it happened at all but I'm not sure the Expo could have survived a second murder." She raised her beer and drank quickly. "You know what I mean?"

"I suppose." Was that why she had murdered Porter at the other end of the exhibition center? Because she was worried that a second dead body in the space of a couple of days would have dire consequences for the American Birding Expo?

"Were you a friend of Porter's, Phoebe?"

"Me?" Her free hand flew to her chest. "Not at all. Why would you even ask that?"

"No reason. I was just wondering. Someone mentioned they had seen the two of you talking." I was lying but wanted to see how she'd react.

"That's weird. I don't even know what he looked like," Phoebe was quick to reply. "Whoever told you that is mistaken."

"I guess so. Did you know it was Porter who told Detective Locke that he'd seen Esther in the vicinity of JJ's dressing room before he was killed?"

"No. Wow." Phoebe rose, turned her back on me and dropped her empty bottle into the trashcan beneath the desk. It hit with a very loud thud. "Are you sure I can't get you something?" She reached into the fridge and pulled out a fresh beer.

"I'm good, thanks."

"So why are you here exactly?"

It was time to lay all my cards on the table. "I'm worried about Esther. If the police can't find JJ's killer, she could go to prison."

"I doubt that. They don't really have enough evidence to convict, do they? I mean, wasn't she released? I thought I saw her wandering around the Expo Center this afternoon."

That got my attention. "You saw Esther this afternoon?"

"Yes. I mean, I believe it was her. She was with a man."

"Can you describe him?"

"No, not really. I only saw them from a distance. He looked to be about her age. He had on a long dark coat." She ran her thumb over the lip of the beer bottle. "I could be mistaken. It may not have been Esther."

I let this latest news sink in for a moment. If Esther had been at the Expo Center this afternoon, why had she kept it a secret from the rest of us? And who was with her?

It could only be Marty. She didn't know anybody else. At least, I didn't think she did.

And if the two of them were at the Expo Center, it meant that they could somehow be mixed up in the murder of Peter Porter.

Did the police know they had been at the Expo Center around the time of the second murder? If so, Esther could find herself back behind bars faster than a dive-bombing peregrine falcon hits its unsuspecting target.

"Are you okay, Amy?"

I opened my eyes. I probably shouldn't have shut them whilst alone in a room with a possible murderess anyway. "Yes, I was just thinking." At least I was still breathing and had no obvious wounds lethal or otherwise.

"If there's anything you can think of that can help Esther, help to find JJ's real killer, I'd appreciate it. We both would," I added. "Even if Esther is never actually tried and convicted, there will be a cloud of suspicion hanging over her head for the rest of her life. I'd like to clear her name."

"She's a dear. You know I'll do anything I can to help, Amy." Phoebe sat moving rhythmically side to side in the swivel desk chair. The motion was accompanied by the tiniest of squeaks. It was like listening to a mouse with asthma.

"I'm glad you feel that way. Tell me about your relationship with JJ."

Phoebe froze, the cold bottle an inch from her lips. Finally, she took a drink and set the bottle on the desk. "I'm not sure what you mean. Relationship?"

I clamped my hands over my knees. "I heard that you and JJ were having an affair."

"*Me* and JJ?" Phoebe appeared genuinely amused. "Is that what you thought, Amy?"

"I heard all about your personal troubles," I said, feeling awkward yet determined to hammer her for the truth even if I had to throw out a few little lies along the way to getting there.

Phoebe shook her head then turned and looked to the bathroom. "Lorna, you should come out now."

"Lorna?" I pushed out of my chair so I could see past Phoebe to the bathroom door. It had been shut the entire time. A familiar face appeared.

"Hello, Amy." JJ Fuller's widow stepped out of the bathroom in a cloud of condensation. Her hair was damp and she had wrapped herself in a short terry robe and slippers. She crossed the room silently and kissed Phoebe on the mouth. "This is a surprise."

I was plenty surprised myself. I fell onto the ottoman.

"Call me Lorna." She tugged at the belt around her waist. "Phoebe and I were about to make plans for dinner. Would you care to join us?" Her eyes danced with amusement. "Or do you have other plans?"

"Uh, no." Why did it feel like I was sitting on a rowboat bouncing in rough seas rather than an ottoman anchored to the carpet?

"I came by to see how Phoebe was doing. I mean, after her car was repossessed and the two murders..." I left my thoughts hanging because I really couldn't think of what to say next.

"And because you thought dear Phoebe might have had something to do with my husband's murder?" Lorna sat on the bed and crossed her legs, fluffing a pillow between herself and the headboard.

"Amy thought I was having an affair with JJ," Phoebe said without a trace of malice.

I colored. "Sorry. I heard a rumor."

"Never listen to rumors," advised Lorna. "I never do."

"Look..." I stood. "I'm sorry I came. Forgive me for barging in on you. I don't know what I was thinking, Phoebe. I thought you were having an affair with JJ and that you might have paid Peter Porter to cast suspicion on Esther.

"Again, I apologize. You've been so kind. After all, Birds and Bees wouldn't even be attending the expo if it wasn't for you."

Phoebe waved my words away. "Consider it forgotten."

Lorna frowned. "Who is Esther?"

"A friend of mine."

"I can't believe that you thought I paid someone to lie for me." Phoebe pulled at her hair. "Where would I get the money to pay anybody? I can barely afford my rent."

"That's okay," Lorna replied. "I've got enough for both of us."

They smiled at one another. I bolted for the door. If there was ever a time to feel like a third wheel, this was it.

My fingers latched onto the stainless steel handle and I froze as the thought popped into my head that Lorna might have murdered JJ herself, after all.

Lorna and Phoebe were standing shoulder to shoulder. Had they stood shoulder to shoulder in murder? Were these two harmless looking women responsible for the murders of JJ Fuller and Peter Porter?

If the two of them were having an affair, wouldn't it be far simpler to continue if JJ was out of the way? Permanently.

"Is something wrong?" Phoebe blinked at me.

"I do believe Ms. Simms thinks we might have conspired to murder JJ." Lorna picked Phoebe's beer from the table, took a sip and frowned.

"Did you?" My heart pounded against my chest. Did I really just ask that? If the answer was yes, was I about to be overpowered and stabbed or throttled to my death? Despite a woeful lack of exercise beyond hiking, I was reasonably sure I could hold my own against one of them. But what if they double-teamed me?

Derek couldn't come to my rescue because he didn't know where to find me. I told him I'd be in the lounge.

I inched my arm backward, my fingers desperately exploring for the door handle I knew was back there somewhere.

"Don't be crazy."

Did Lorna mean crazy to try to get away or crazy to think they were cold-blooded killers?

"Where were you at the time your husband was murdered?" I blurted in cop fashion.

A look of amusement danced across Lorna's face. "The police have already asked me that question. After all, isn't the wife always a suspect?"

"And what did you tell them?"

"That I was here at the hotel."

"Can you prove it?"

"The police seem satisfied with my answer. As you can see, I'm not under arrest." She jutted her arms out from the robe.

She had me there. Her pale wrists were free of handcuffs.

"Did Porter know your husband, Lorna?"

"As far as I know, the two were unacquainted. He was into flying birds, not walking dead." Lorna laughed at her little joke.

"And yet the two of them are dead. Both killed at the Expo Center."

"Do you really believe there's a connection, Amy?" Phoebe asked.

"There has to be. I only wish I had some idea what it was."

"Isn't it obvious?" Lorna said with a devilish grin. "If Mr. Porter was paid to point the finger at somebody other than the true murderer of my husband—"

I picked up the thread. "Then it stands to reason that Porter might have been blackmailing the killer."

"And JJ's killer would not have taken too kindly to that." Lorna tugged at the gold necklace around her neck.

"Which brings us back to who killed your husband." I sighed.

We had come full circle. Who knew going in a circle could lead to a dead end? It seemed impossible and contrary to all the laws of physics that I knew, yet it had.

"If anybody wanted JJ dead it was probably that annoying Ms. Skoglund," Lorna said rather coldly.

"Ilsa? Why would she want your husband dead? I heard there was bad blood between the two of them but, still, murder?"

"She's not the goody-two-shoes she pretends to be." Lorna removed herself from Phoebe's side and retrieved an open bottle of Riesling from the fridge. She poured a small amount into a plastic cup and drank.

"I realize there was a certain competitiveness between your husband and Ilsa but was there so much animosity that she'd want him dead?"

"JJ used to call her a she-devil in birder's clothing," Lorna snapped.

"Skoggie is ruthless," Phoebe put in.

"It wouldn't be the first time one of them tried to kill the other." Lorna raised a brow pointedly.

"What?"

Both women nodded briskly.

"There have been accidents." Phoebe pulled at her fingers.

Lorna handed her the glass of wine. Phoebe sipped gratefully.

"Accidents, incidents. Either way, whenever the two of them got together, they clashed. Sometimes with verbal clashes, other times things got physical."

"JJ physically attacked Ilsa?"

"More the other way around." Lorna threw back her head and laughed. "JJ was not the biggest or fittest of men. Ilsa is more than capable of holding her own against any man. I don't think she considered my husband much of a threat at all."

Maybe. Or maybe she considered him a big threat and decided to do away with him once and for all. Now that Lorna had mentioned it, I could imagine Ilsa quite capable of overpowering JJ.

And it wouldn't take much strength to poke a knife into a zombie. A certain cold mental capacity, yes, but not much muscle power.

"Have you told the police this?"

"What's to tell?" Lorna took back her lipstick-stained cup and drank. "Two egomaniacs at each other's throats. It was old news."

"I'll say." The cell phone sitting on the night table vibrated. Phoebe looked at it. "One of the exhibitors. Another *crisis*, I imagine." She put air quotes around the word.

I couldn't help wondering how much of what the two women was telling me was the unadulterated truth and how much was exaggeration.

Or misdirection.

"I can tell you this," Lorna began. "JJ was being paid to take pictures."

"Of birds?" That was hardly newsworthy. Bird photography was a big part of what made JJ Fuller who he had been.

"Yes, there was always that. But I'm not talking about birds."

"What then?"

"I don't know. The most innocuous stuff really." Lorna pulled a pack of cigarettes from a shiny black leather purse and lit up. I was sure the hotel had a nonsmoking policy but that was her problem.

"More innocuous than birds?"

"Buildings and things. Airports. Waste treatment facilities. The most mundane things, really. I mean, it's not like birds are all that exciting but compared to this other stuff, well…" She flicked a quarter inch of ash into her empty wine cup.

I wondered what had brought JJ and Lorna together. It certainly hadn't been a shared love of birds.

"I caught him in his office one afternoon at the computer with his back to me. He was downloading pictures off his camera onto his PC. He wasn't happy to see me. When I asked him about the photographs, he told me it was none of my business. I didn't know what the fuss was for. All I saw were birds and people. Perfectly ordinary people."

"Naked?" I wondered aloud.

"Completely clothed."

Okay, so JJ Fuller wasn't into anything kinky. I scratched my head. "What's wrong with that?"

"Nothing, right?" She sucked on her cigarette. "Yet when I questioned him about it, he flew off the handle. He told me to forget what I had seen. I didn't even know what I had seen. Crazy, right?"

Phoebe moved to the thermostat and cranked up the A/C, waving her hand in front of her nose. No fan of smoking, I guessed.

"I'll say." Or was it? JJ traveled the world as a birder. But had he been something more? And was that why he'd been murdered? If so, I knew just the man who could be involved up to his eyeballs in things: Marty.

And, if that was the case, Esther could be in even bigger trouble.

17

I fled the room but there was no escaping my thoughts.

Was there anything to the idea that JJ Fuller had been a spy? Or was I merely becoming a victim of my own overactive imagination?

Esther. It was all her fault. Trips to cemeteries. Talk of spies. Crazy, unexplained behavior.

Murder. No, make that two murders.

Now she had me seeing spies everywhere.

This whole thing, this whole ugly weekend of murder and mayhem was probably nothing more than a couple of random muggings gone awry.

Probably.

And Esther being off her medications. She'd probably forgotten her prescriptions at home.

Yes, that would explain everything.

Again, probably.

Speaking of Esther, I was supposed to meet her and it was time I did. She might not be happy that I was bringing Derek along, but I was beyond caring what she wanted at this point.

I rode down in the hotel elevator with an elderly gentleman and his wife, both of whom I remembered from the morning birding walk. I said hello. They looked at me blankly.

I popped into the lobby restroom to freshen up before hooking back up with Derek.

I screamed.

"What's going on out there?" demanded a voice from behind one of the stainless steel stall doors. "Is everything okay?" I heard heels scraping the tile floor.

"Y-yes, everything is fine." Not. I sobbed and ran my fingers through my hair. My gray, straggly dead looking hair. Staring back at me, looking every bit as aghast and ghastly as I felt, was Zombie Amy.

I had forgotten to remove my undead makeup.

Bird poop.

To make matters worse, the rain had smeared my zombie makeup in every direction. I now looked completely grotesque, from my pallid skin to my blotchy black lips. I was a hot mess. A dead hot mess.

What must Phoebe and Lorna have thought when I showed up at their door made up like a freaking zombie?

And I hadn't even made mention of it. They hadn't either. Probably because they were too uncomfortable or embarrassed to do so.

I groaned.

Because then there was the desk clerk earlier. And the bartender. And the waitress. What had she said? Nice outfit?

Plus the businessmen who'd been smiling at me so nicely in the bar. And those parents with their children...

Bird poop bird poop bird poop.

I grabbed both faucets and turned them on full blast.

"What are you doing out there?" the woman demanded again. I heard the sounds of flushing.

"Just washing up." I squirted a mountain of soap into my palms and smeared it over my face. I next grabbed a length of paper towel from the wall dispenser, cupped my hand under the running water and started scrubbing.

"Do you mind?" A woman in a navy dress and pearls glared at me in the mirror.

"Sorry." I stepped aside so she could wash up.

She did so very quickly—using a fraction of the cleaning supplies I'd needed—and stormed out, shooting me one last look of disapproval that I wouldn't soon forget before she did so.

Several minutes of hard scrubbing later, I didn't look any better but at least I didn't look like I had just stepped off the set of a George Romero zombie flick.

My cheeks and forehead glistened pink from the scouring and my hair was dripping wet. I dried the ends with more paper towels and tossed the lot in the trash.

There was nothing I could do about the ZombieFest t-shirt but hide it beneath my jacket, which I did.

There was no sign of Derek in the bar.

I zipped up my coat and headed outside to the parking garage. I roamed through the aisles, calling his name.

On the third floor, I found him. He sat on the cold hard ground, leaning against a concrete support column.

"Derek. Are you all right?"

I raced to his side.

"Yeah." He rubbed the back of his head. When he drew his hand around I saw blood.

"You're hurt."

"It's nothing."

I helped him to his feet. "What happened? Did you slip?"

"Only after somebody hit me in the back of the head."

He winced as I palpated the back of his head.

"It doesn't look too bad," I said.

"It's not."

"Who did this?"

"I don't know. It was right after we talked. I spotted a car coming down the ramp fast. I stepped back and then I felt a sharp pain."

"Did you see who was driving the car? Was it the same vehicle as before?"

"Sorry. I have no idea. It happened too fast. The driver slammed on the brakes. Then I heard the sound of running footsteps."

"So whoever hit you must have been an accomplice of the driver. We should call the police."

"No, no police. Not yet," suggested Derek. "What could we tell them? We don't know who hit me or even if this is related to the murders."

"But you could have been killed."

"I wasn't even mugged." He patted his back pocket. "Still got my wallet. Besides, you are supposed to meet Esther. If we involve the police, we could get tied up for hours." He grabbed my hand. "Let's go."

He had a point. "Okay, I'll meet Esther. You need to get checked out in the ER."

"It's not that bad, Amy."

"What is it with men?" I asked as we reached our car. "You could bleed to death and still say it's not that bad."

Derek chuckled. He moved tipsily to the driver's side but I vetoed the move. "I'll drive. You rest. In fact, if you won't go to the ER, at least go back to the room and wash that wound out."

We argued about it for a couple of minutes. He finally broke down and agreed. Which was a good thing because I was already headed to the Eagle Inn.

After seeing Derek safely to his room and promising that I would be back soon to take up nursing duties, I guided Karl's rental car to the address written on the sheet of paper she had slipped under the windshield wiper of the car while I and the guys were at the cemetery.

It led me to a bar called Missing Persons.

Her idea of a joke?

Esther occupied a small table next to a rowdy group of college boys. "What happened to you?" were the first words out of her mouth. "You look a hot mess," were the second.

I flopped into the empty chair beside hers.

"Thanks," I snapped. "If you think I look bad, you should see Derek."

I was out of breath. The closest parking spot was a block and a half away. I had run to the pub, fearing I'd miss Esther.

I was also in a bad mood. Not enough food, not enough rest, not even fun and too much murder had taken its toll on my weary bones and aching skull. "I had a beauty treatment."

"If I was you, I'd ask for my money back." Esther was drinking something glowing pink with an unnaturally red cherry bobbing around at the surface. A small triangle of red-tinted pineapple kept it company.

"And if I was you, I'd start talking." I wiggled my fingers in a come-hither fashion. "And fast."

Instead, she leaned forward and sucked at her lime green straw. I watched the ice cubes swirl and counted to ten.

"Well?" I folded my arms across my chest and stared at the Pester.

"Not yet."

"Not yet? What do you mean, not yet?"

Esther reached for her drink. I snatched it away. I caught an inadvertent whiff of her drink and reeled. It was potent.

The waitress came by balancing a tray on her upturned hand. She asked if I'd like a drink. I told her no.

"Wait," I called as she pushed toward the bar.

"Yeah?"

"Give me one of these." I hoisted Esther's pink poisonous concoction. If it killed me, so be it.

I tugged off my coat and dropped it on the empty chair. People could think what they wanted of my ZombieFest attire.

The five guys squeezed around a table for three beside us burst into happy shouts at something on the sports channel. College football.

Personally, I always thought football fields were a waste of green space. Why not turn that big, flat field into a garden? Fill it with wildlife-supporting flowers and shrubbery rather than dozens of sweating men in uniforms chasing a pigskin.

I had yet to win Derek, or anybody else for that matter, over to my way of thinking. Yet.

Which brought my thoughts back to Esther.

"Don't you think Marty could be responsible, Esther?"

"No," she was quick to respond.

"Surely it must have crossed your mind?"

"He's been set up."

"Who would want to set Marty up for murder?"

"Once a spy, always a spy," Esther said rather enigmatically.

"Esther." I tugged my hair until my eyes watered. "Would you please stop talking in riddles and tell me once and for all what's going on?"

"I said not yet."

"What do you mean not yet?" I repeated sternly. What was the boiling temperature of blood? Because I could practically feel my blood boiling under my skin. "Two men are dead and there's all kinds of crazy going on. I want to know what's going on and I want to know now."

I slapped my hand on the table. Hard.

It stung. I felt tears spring up in the corners of my eyes.

The waitress showed up in the nick of time with my drink. I took a slug.

Purely for medicinal purposes. Sure enough, it took the edge off my pain. And probably the enamel off my teeth and the plaque off the sides of my arteries.

Esther grabbed her own drink back and held it tight in both hands. "I'm waiting for someone."

"Who?" I clamped my eyes shut because for a second there I was seeing double. One Esther was plenty. Two was unthinkable. I opened my eyes. "Marty?" I looked forward to laying eyes on him again. Maybe, just maybe, he could give me some straight answers.

"No." Esther's stern look melted into a smile. "Her."

I turned toward the entrance. It was Ilsa Skoglund.

18

If looks could kill, we would have all been dead.

Ilsa Skoglund shoved a man the size of a refrigerator out of her way with a well-executed stiff arm to the chest. He bellowed, she barked, and he stumbled out to the sidewalk.

There was no doubt in my mind that Lorna Fuller was right. Skoggie could handle any man, up to and including Lorna's late husband.

Ilsa Skoglund's eyes scoured the room and landed on us. She threw back the hood of a lavender parka and walked purposefully to our table.

Esther removed her voluminous purse and my coat from the chair between us. Ilsa Skoglund sat. Esther slipped the strap of her purse over the back of one side of her chair and my jacket on the other side.

"Amy Simms, yes?" Ilsa unzipped her coat and shook out her hair. I noticed several men in the bar checking her out including the guys at the table next to us. She took it in stride. I was sure she was used to being the center of attention. And for all the right reasons.

"That's right, Ms. Skoglund."

"I wasn't expecting to see you here."

"Nor I you." I turned to Esther.

So did Skoggie, as she said, "What's this all about?"

"My question exactly." I took an ill-advised second sip of my drink and my cheeks puckered. Whatever was in that drink, and I tasted pomegranate and strawberry, the concoction had to be at least eighty proof.

I snatched a bowl of pretzels from the waitress as she passed. I set it down between us, but not before helping myself to a handful. I needed something bland to counter the alcohol.

Was it my imagination or did the bartender look like Ben Franklin?

The old post office where Ben used to work was just a few steps up the street. Maybe the old guy was moonlighting. Maybe he was a two hundred-year-old zombie.

Maybe I'd had too much to drink.

"I want to know why you set me up, Skoglund." Esther was down to the last dregs of her own pink poison and it didn't seem to be having any untoward effects on her at all.

"I don't know what you're talking about." Ilsa's jaw jutted out as if begging the Pester to give it a punch or at least dare to contradict her.

Esther chose option two. "I have a reliable eyewitness who saw you hanging around at the Birds and Bees booth."

"You're bluffing." Ilsa folded her arms and stared at the space between us.

"Who?" I wanted to know.

"Nikki Nilsson," answered Esther.

I saw a flash of recognition pass across Skoggie's face. "The woman's a drunk and a pothead. I wouldn't trust a word she says. If you were smart, you wouldn't either."

"JJ's assistant? When was this?" I interrupted. It wasn't like we had any state secrets or valuable merchandise lying around but I still didn't like the idea of a virtual stranger poking around our booth.

"Don't interrupt me, Amy," Esther was quick to complain. "I'm working here."

I scooped up some pretzel wreckage and dropped it back in the basket.

Skoglund wasn't making a sign or a peep. Nor was she enjoying the pretzels. I didn't mind. That left more for me.

"You planted something in my purse." Esther thumped her purse on the table, spilling half the contents.

Skoggie finally spoke up. "And what is it you think that I planted?"

"An SD card. And not just any SD card. The blank SD card that the police speculate is the SD card that was missing from JJ Fuller's camera when he was found dead in that makeshift storeroom slash dressing room."

"Why would I want to plant a memory card in your purse?"

Esther narrowed her eyes at the accused. "I don't know. That part doesn't make sense. Why me? And why was the SD card empty?"

I cleared my throat of pretzel dust. "That's a good question. I'd seen JJ taking plenty of pictures at the expo."

"That was a sixty-four-gig card," Esther said. "Yet there was nothing on it." She pointed a finger at Skoggie. "Could it be that there was nothing on it because you erased it?"

Ilsa Skoglund rolled her sexy eyes. "Why would I do such a thing? Is this why you asked me to meet you here? So you could hurl wild and ridiculous accusations?" She swung on me. "Really, Ms. Simms, you should control your employees better."

Little did Ilsa Skoglund know just how much I wished that were possible but just how utterly impossible that was when it came to Esther.

Skoglund rose suddenly, banging her chair into that of the person at the table behind us. "I've had enough. I'm a very busy woman."

"I'll bet you are." Esther was standing now too. "Especially since you discovered that—" She looked at me for guidance. "What was that bird, Amy?"

"Huh?" I was busy polishing off my drink.

"The one Ms. Skoglund *discovered*." Esther added a dose of sarcasm to the word. "The one that I hear is gonna get her fifty thousand dollars."

"Oh. The ivory-billed woodpecker." My eyes snapped to Ilsa Skoglund. "Oh!"

"Oh is right," said Esther. "What if the lovely Ms. Skoglund here didn't take those pictures of that bird? What if JJ Fuller did?"

I gasped. "And what if you killed him to get those pictures?"

Skoggie fell back in her seat. "It's not true." Her words sounded hollow.

"You killed him to get your hands on these photos he took. Then you planted the SD card in my purse to throw suspicion off you and onto somebody else."

Esther cackled. "My luck, you picked me. What was it? Was I just convenient?" Esther shook her head side to side. "Shame on you picking on a poor, defenseless old woman."

I couldn't help looking dubiously at Esther. I wasn't so sure about that *defenseless* part.

"I don't have to answer that," Ilsa replied.

"Maybe you'd like to answer to Detective Locke instead?" I said.

"Fine." Ilsa Skoglund's fingernails tapped out a message. "I knew what JJ was up to."

"What *was* he up to?" I wanted to know.

"He was going to announce his big discovery."

"The whatchamacallit woodpecker." Those were Esther's words.

"That's right," Ilsa said through a heartfelt sigh. "He was going to announce that he had proof of the elusive bird's existence during his keynote address at the American Birding Expo. It was going to be a feather in his cap, so to speak."

"So you knew about the discovery before his intended announcement."

"And then you announced the discovery of this bird yourself, thereby making yourself eligible for a fifty-thousand-dollar reward," put in Esther. "Sounds like a motive for murder to me."

It sounded like a pretty good motive to me too.

Ilsa Skoglund's announcement that she had rediscovered the ivory-billed woodpecker had been a very big feather in her own cap. No doubt securing her lucrative speaking engagements and sponsorships for years to come.

"He sent me a text gloating about it. JJ was a loathsome man."

"So you killed him," Esther insisted yet again.

"No, I did not. In fact, I didn't really believe JJ had any photographs. Certainly none worth murdering him over."

"You thought he was lying?"

"I thought he was faking. It wouldn't be the first time."

"You mean you thought Fuller doctored up some pictures to look like this woodpecker everybody is so worked up about?" Esther asked.

"It wouldn't be the first time he's tried a stunt like that," Ilsa claimed. "JJ was almost as much a whiz on the computer as he was with a camera."

Esther rubbed her nose and started fiddling with my coat on the back of her chair. "You got any tissues?"

"No. Use a napkin." Why was she interrupting our conversation over tissues at a time like this?

Esther plucked a napkin from the tabletop dispenser and blew hard. "Okay," she said, rubbing her nose once more. "Sorry to interrupt. You were telling us how you murdered JJ Fuller and then Peter Porter. JJ to get your hands on the photographs of this special bird and Porter to shut him up.

"What was he doing? Blackmailing you after you had already paid him off?"

I leaned back and looked at Esther in awe and maybe just a little newfound respect—not that I'd ever admit that to her. Despite our differences, she had a way of getting to the point and no fear in speaking her mind.

I, for one, was happy to not be on the receiving end of her verbal attack for a change.

Ilsa Skoglund was looking miserable. I offered her a sip of my drink or any other drink from the bar but she refused. "I don't believe in alcohol."

What was that supposed to mean? We were in a bar with an entire wall lined with the stuff. Believe in it or not, it existed. To prove my point, I sucked the remainder of my drink up my straw and looked around for our waitress. I saw her standing on one foot on this side of the bar talking to Ben Franklin.

Was it my imagination or did she look like Betsy Ross?

I waved my glass for a refill.

"I did not pay anybody off and nobody was blackmailing me." Ilsa Skoglund's jaw barely moved as she talked. "And I have never heard of anyone by the name of Peter Porter."

"That can't be quite true, can it?" I said. "You must have heard about his murder." The entire Expo Center had been abuzz with murmurs, not to mention police and blue lights that had nothing to do with Kmart specials. "Besides, I saw you speaking with Porter in the woods down below the Audubon Center. Remember?"

Her response was a down-turning of the lips.

"What were you talking about?" I asked.

"Birds."

"Birds? You really expect us to believe that?" Esther scoffed.

"Why not? There are millions of bird lovers. It was early morning and we were on a nature walk."

I couldn't picture Peter Porter as a birding aficionado and said so. Zombie bats, maybe. Birds, no. He had not been carrying a pair of binoculars or a camera either. "If you were talking birds, it was one bird in particular, the ivory-billed woodpecker. I think you were talking blackmail."

"I don't care what you think, Ms. Simms." Ilsa Skoglund drew her fingers through her hair.

"Porter demanded a piece of that reward money," suggested Esther, "in exchange for keeping quiet."

"There was nothing to keep quiet about."

"Your word against Porter's." I drummed the table. "And now Porter is dead and we'll never hear his side of the story."

"Convenient." Esther blasted her eyes at Ilsa.

"Mr. Porter's death is unfortunate." Esther snorted but Ilsa didn't let that deter her from continuing. "I am not a murderer. I would never harm a living thing." She crossed her arms and stared me down. "I have nothing to hide."

I sensed she was bluffing. Was it because she was a killer, that she knew Porter would never admit to blackmail or was it something else altogether?

"No," I ventured because I could suddenly picture a possible alternative scenario, "maybe not a murderer—"

"But, Amy—" complained Esther, who seemed determined to pin JJ Fuller's murder on his biggest rival.

I waved my fingers at Esther to hold her tongue while keeping my eyes on Ilsa Skoglund. "But you wouldn't mind picking the pockets of an already dead man, would you? Or in this case, shall I say picking the camera of a dead man?"

Her hard blue eyes beat against me for several seconds before she blinked. "JJ was already dead. I really had no idea if the photos of the ivory-billed woodpecker would be on his camera. I figured there was no harm in looking."

"Weren't you worried about getting caught?" I asked. I couldn't believe the nerve of the woman. The first thing I'd have done after finding the body would have been to run right out the way I'd come. And then phoning for help. "Or leaving fingerprints?"

"Of course I was worried. I got in and out of there as fast as I could. And I was careful to wipe off the camera."

"That explains why the police didn't find any fingerprints on it," Esther said. "They'd been hoping to find mine. You probably hoped they would too. I'd go to prison for murder and you'd be fifty thousand dollars richer and even more famous, you little b—"

"Weren't you even a little concerned that what you were doing was unethical?" I interjected. Let alone illegal.

"JJ was dead." Ilsa Skoglund felt that absolved her of any misdeeds or untoward behavior. "He wasn't going to miss the photographs."

"And if he couldn't get the credit for the discovery, why shouldn't you? Isn't that what you were thinking?" I asked.

"I intended to give the reward money to a bird and wildlife nonprofit organization."

Esther rolled her eyes. I joined her. Ilsa's deplorable behavior and defense thereof was worth at least two sets of eyes rolling.

"How did you happen to discover JJ's body?"

"My dressing room is next door. I heard a disturbance."

"Did you tell the police?"

"Of course." Skoggie looked genuinely surprised. "I told them that, when I opened my door, I saw her." She was pointing at Esther.

Once again, all roads led to the Pester.

It was Esther's turn under the spotlight as Ilsa Skoglund and I pelted her with most curious eyes.

"Ladies' room."

As Esther scooted away, I asked Ilsa Skoglund my next question. "Did you see anyone else loitering around?"

"No. If I had, I would have informed the police."

"You didn't see Peter Porter?"

"No. Apparently he saw me."

"That's odd." I scratched my shoulder blade. "Was there anything else on the memory card besides the photographs of the ivory-billed woodpecker?"

"Sure, a bunch of stuff. Nothing important."

"Such as?"

"Lots of birds. A few people. Just…stuff."

"Did you recognize any of the people?"

"Actually, a couple. JJ had been at a birding festival in Louisiana. There were some shots from the location and some of the attendees and vendors. I was there myself for a day or two."

That gibed with what Lorna had told me about her husband's recent whereabouts previous to the expo. "Did you save copies of any of those photos?"

"No. Why should I? The only ones that mattered were the shots of the woodpecker. I copied those onto my hard drive and deleted the rest."

"But why plant the blank card in Esther's purse?"

"The police already suspected her. So did I, to tell the truth. So why not? It had JJ's initials on it. I knew it would look suspicious."

I could have answered because it was planting incriminating evidence against an innocent woman but I didn't think she'd find it nearly as immoral as I did.

I wondered what was taking Esther so long. I glanced toward the back of the bar. "Must be a long line at the ladies'."

"I don't think so." Ilsa Skoglund was smirking.

"What?"

"In case you didn't notice, your friend took her purse with her."

"And?" I'd done the same thing on more occasions than I could count. As a matter of fact, I felt just such an occasion coming up in my near future. That pink drink was shooting right through me. The waitress had dropped off my refill and half the glass had already magically disappeared.

"And she might have started in the direction of the restrooms but she detoured around and snuck out the front."

"What?" My hands gripped the table. I twisted my neck and looked at the door.

"Doesn't it strike you odd that your friend left the minute an explanation for her being outside a dead man's door was due?"

That it did.

19

Ilsa left me stewing in my own juices. That and what was left of my pretty pink poison.

I'm not a violent person but I could think of several things I'd like to do to Esther the next time I laid eyes—and my hands—on her.

And the next time she claimed she was going to the bathroom, I was going with her and standing watch outside the stall door.

My phone chimed announcing a text. I lifted it from my purse and read the screen. It was from Derek. I felt a stab of guilt.

He'd written that he was feeling left out and wondering where everybody was.

I called him. "What's wrong, dear? Miss me?" I teased.

"You and everybody else." Derek yawned. I heard the sounds of a television in the background.

"How are you feeling?"

"Decent, considering."

"I'm glad to hear it. Karl and Floyd aren't there?"

"No. Floyd texted me a little while ago. Apparently, they took you up on your harebrained idea."

"What harebrained idea was that?" I was only slightly offended. To be honest, I'd had a harebrained idea or two in my short life.

"The one where you suggested they stake out that apartment. According to his text, they are there now."

It took me a minute to process what Derek was saying. "Oh, you mean Bergdorf."

"Right." The droning of the television suddenly ended as Derek turned off the TV. "Who's Bergdorf?"

"Didn't I tell you?"

"No." Derek sounded a little annoyed. "I texted Floyd about it. I got back a text from Karl saying that seeing as I was a lawyer it was best that I didn't know what he and Floyd were doing. Which I find a little scary."

"What are they doing? I suggested they simply keep an eye on the apartment. You don't suppose they…" No, Floyd would never agree to burgle an apartment.

But Karl would.

"Don't suppose they what?"

"Never mind." One of us needed to stay out of jail, better that someone was Derek. Because we'd all need a good lawyer. And a good lawyer needs to be on the right side of the jail bars and have plausible deniability.

I chewed on a pretzel. "Would you mind driving over to Bergdorf's apartment and checking on them?"

"I'd be happy to, but they've got the van and you've got Karl's rental car."

"Right." I frowned for no one's benefit but my own.

"You want me to call a cab?"

"No. You really should be resting." The last thing we needed was more people showing up outside Laurel Cove Apartments. That neighbor of Bergdorf's would probably call out the SWAT team. "Never mind. I'll swing by on my way back to the inn. Are you sure you don't need a doctor?"

"A psychiatrist maybe." I heard the rustling of bedcovers. "You're heading back?" Derek asked hopefully.

"As soon as I check on Karl and Floyd and see that they get back too."

"Great. Wait, what about Esther?"

I sighed heavily. "I just talked to her. And Ilsa Skoglund."

"Did you learn anything?"

"Lots." I promised to fill him in when I returned to the Eagle Inn. For his part, Derek promised to stay awake until I got there.

I pictured a lovely reunion—the two of us, blissfully alone; no spies, no dead bodies, no coworkers and, more importantly, a warm, sexy body to snuggle with. I paid the bill and headed for the car.

I hadn't had so much to drink that I couldn't still walk a straight line and drive but I was experiencing a fierce headache like some sadist was twisting a glowing hot knife sideways into my left temple and the point was protruding out the right side.

Whether that pain had been induced by the pink poison I'd been introduced to by Esther or her inexplicable behavior, I couldn't be certain.

Probably the combination of the two. It was my own fault. Wasn't there some old saying about not mixing your poisons?

What I was certain of was that I had to take control of the situation and my cohorts if I was going to get any peace and pleasure out of this trip.

I googled the address of the Laurel Cove Apartments and fought my way through the crazy jungle of Philadelphia streets. Give me Ruby Lake any day—one main street and a lake. Even the tourists rarely got lost. When they did, we usually just had to turn them around.

I cursed as the third car in a row coming toward me honked and flashed their lights.

"So rude." My eyes teared up. Then I noticed as I turned down a particularly dark one-way cobblestoned street that my headlights were off.

I fumbled for the switch and decided to be the bigger person and forgive everyone.

Deciding it would be best to operate in stealth mode, lest any curious neighbors wonder why half of North Carolina was gathered outside their building, I parked a block and a half away and walked to Laurel Cove.

My headache had receded but not my annoyance with Esther. I yawned listening to the sound of my own footsteps up the cracked and crooked sidewalk leading me to the apartment complex.

There were few lights on in the building. I could not be certain if any of them belonged to my target in 3C.

There was no sign of my van, Karl or Floyd. Was that a good sign or a bad one? I stepped to the shadows next to the building and dialed Floyd's number. My call went straight to voicemail. Dialing Karl got me the same result.

"Where are you guys?" I whispered.

A couple bundled in heavy coats walked past me and entered the apartment building next door.

Fearing that Karl and Floyd might have tried breaking into 3C, I decided to reconnoiter further. Inside the foyer, I pressed the button for the apartment and received no answer.

Glancing at the mail boxes, I noticed a name that did ring a bell, Stevens, Travis, 1B.

Why did that name seem familiar? I stared at the piece of white tape and black marker scrawl. Then I remembered that a Travis Stevens worked for Irving Shipman. If it was a coincidence, it was an odd one.

Then again, the whole week had been odd.

Had it really only been a couple of days since we had arrived in Philadelphia? And only a couple of days before that that Phoebe had reached out to me to tell me I could get a last-minute booth?

If I had to do it all over again, I'd have stayed home. Home seemed far away and my life before this week seemed like a lifetime ago.

For two people it had been just that.

Did Travis Stevens know Marty or the still unseen Mr. Bergdorf? There was only one way to find out. If this was my Travis Stevens and he knew anything about the occupant or occupants of 3C, I wanted to know what.

Despite the lateness of the hour, I knocked on his door.

A skinny, shirtless man in beltless jeans answered the door. "Amy Simms."

"Hi, Travis." I was surprised to see him there in the flesh, having more expected that I'd find this was a completely other Travis Stevens. Speaking of his flesh, I'd seen tundra swans with more color.

"Who is it?" a woman's voice called from afar.

"Ms. Simms from the Expo!"

"Get rid of her."

It sounded like I had interrupted Saturday night date night. I could hardly blame the mystery woman for being annoyed. I should have been enjoying just such an occasion myself.

Travis blushed and cleared his throat. "I'm kind of busy right now." He thrust his hands in his pockets. "Is there something you wanted?" He poked his head out the door. "How did you find me?"

"I didn't. I was coming to visit a friend, a Mr. Bergdorf." I pointed upward. "He lives upstairs. Maybe you know him?"

Travis chewed his lip. "Sorry. I'm only subletting. It's temporary. With the new job, I expect I'll be on the road a lot."

"Of course."

"Is there anything else?" He reached for the door knob.

"I don't suppose you've seen any of my coworkers?"

Travis pulled his eyelids down. "What? Here?"

"Yes. Esther, Floyd and Karl. They work for me."

"I remember." His fingers tightened on the door knob. His voice was filling with impatience and wariness. "Why would they be here?"

"We, uh, were all going to visit my friend, Mr. Bergdorf. It's a party. His birthday. A birthday party." Sheesh. I sounded like a blithering idiot.

"I see." Though by the tone of his voice it was more than clear that he did not see or care.

"Don't worry," I said. "We'll keep the noise down."

"See that you do." Travis shot a nervous look into his own apartment. "Goodnight, Ms. Simms."

I said goodnight and hurried up to the third floor. I tiptoed to 3C. Women like the one in 3B have the ears of an owl. She could probably hear me coming from two hundred yards away.

I whispered up against the marred wood door of 3C. "Mr. Bergdorf?" I tapped lightly. "Are you in?" I pressed an ear to the door and heard nothing but the blood rushing around in my ear drum, I think. Maybe it was the ocean. Some branches of science are a mystery to me.

I tried the door knob just for the fun of it, knowing it would be locked as would the deadbolt above it.

It wasn't. It turned easily and noisily in my hand. I gave a push. The deadbolt had not been set.

"Mr. Bergdorf? Marty?" I held my breath and stepped inside, shutting the door behind me. "Esther? Are you here?"

The glow from a desk lamp lit a small, cluttered desk. The room was carpeted in a dark shade of green and filled with furniture I hadn't seen since the sixties. Judging by the musty odor, the windows probably hadn't been opened since then either.

The out-of-date desktop computer with a boxy monitor on the desk was shut down. I didn't dare touch it. There were a couple of envelopes under a raptor-shaped bronze statuette being used as a paperweight: electric bill and phone bill. The bills were addressed to K. Bergdorf.

A black plastic rotary phone sat within a hand's reach of the computer. I hadn't seen one of those since I was a kid.

If it hadn't been for a fear of leaving fingerprints, I'd have been tempted to make a call just for the fun of it.

A door led to a small bedroom that barely managed to hold a double bed and a tall dresser. The window over the sink of a compact galley kitchen looked out over the street.

There wasn't much about the space to indicate the character of its occupant or occupants. The sole thing of interest in the small apartment were the plethora of stamp collecting books filled with stamps of the world and books on the history of stamps.

Somebody was either an avid stamp collector or a professional philatelist. I flipped through a stamp book on the coffee table wherein stamps mounted on thick black paper were carefully protected by heavy plastic sheets. The stamps were organized by date and country of origin.

Some of those stamps could have been worth good money. Funny that the occupant had left their apartment door unlocked. A thief could easily make off with an armful of stamp albums.

Then it struck me or, rather, my nostrils. A whiff of lime, an undertone of tobacco. The all too familiar scent of two grumpy old men.

"Floyd and Karl." I closed the stamp album and nudged it back into the position I wanted to leave no trace of my presence behind. Unlike Floyd and Karl whom I now had no doubt had been in 3C before me.

Had they broken in or had they been invited?

I shuddered. Had they been bound and gagged and shoved in the closet?

I checked the small bedroom closet plus the one near the entry door anyway. The closets were far from empty, containing the usual clothes and household items, but they were devoid of hostages or even zombies.

I turned slowly around the room one more time, taking inventory both mentally and physically.

The bad news was that I had no idea where everybody was. The good news was that there were no new dead bodies.

A real glass is half full moment in the life of Amy Simms.

As I stood in the kitchen wondering what my next move would be, my cellphone went off. I yelped and clawed for it in my purse. I stabbed repeatedly at the screen until it stopped.

"Karl." I pressed my mouth to the phone. "Where are you?"

"Hey, Chief. This is Karl."

I narrowed my eyes for no good reason. "I know that, Karl. Where are you? Where's Floyd?"

"He's right here with me."

"Where's here?"

"We're at the pen."

"Excuse me?" I glanced at the entry door, praying that no one came home and found me chatting on my cell phone in the middle of their apartment.

"The pen."

I heard Floyd's voice in the background. "Tell Amy she should come."

"I'm trying to do that, Floyd," Karl growled. "That's why we called."

Floyd said something back. I'm not going to repeat it here. Suffice it to say, my ears turned red. I didn't know Floyd had it in him. "Why is Floyd so ruffled?"

"I don't know. He probably needs a cookie."

That sounded like Kim. She gets cranky when her blood sugar sinks.

"So are you coming or what? If so, you'd better hurry."

I pressed my ear harder against the phone. Floyd was whispering at high speed but I couldn't make out the words. "Where is here exactly?"

"I told you, Chief. The pen. We tailed this guy Marty and caught up with him at the pen."

"Hey, look." That was Floyd practically yelling.

"Ouch!" Karl hollered. "What did you punch me for? Hey, is that Esther?"

"Esther's there?" I screeched. "Why didn't you say so?"

"She just hopped out of a cab. If you ask me, Chief, she's come to meet Marty."

"Marty's there, too?" My ears rang in pain. I had no idea my vocal range extended so high. Whatever this pen was, it seemed to be a popular Philly hot spot.

"Yeah. Didn't I tell you? Me and Floyd followed him from the apartment on Laurel Cove."

"Karl, tell me the two of you did not break into the apartment."

"Of course, not," Karl said in full-blown indignation. "That is very much against the law. I am a retired chief of police. Besides," he made the mistake of continuing, "why would I want to look at a bunch of dumb stamp albums."

"If you didn't go inside the apartment, how did you know about the—"

"Esther's going inside, Amy!" Floyd yelled.

"We'd better follow them," Karl replied. "It's dark as coffee beans in there. All we've got are our cellphone flashlight apps and they might spot us if we turn them on, anyway."

"Wait! Karl!" I strained my ear and heard the sound of a van door opening and closing quietly. "Karl? Floyd?"

For a moment, I heard nothing but grunts, wheezes, then a clatter followed quickly by a curse.

"Yeah, Chief." Karl was barely audible. "Our targets have moved inside. Floyd, grab the gear from the back."

"Will do, Karl."

"Quietly," Karl urged.

"What gear?" My brain was bouncing off the walls of my cranium. "What pen, Karl?"

"Eastern State Pen, like I told you, Chief. You gotta listen better. We've got to run before we lose them or they maybe lock the gates on us."

"What gates?" My blood pressure had to be pushing two hundred—and that was the diastolic reading. "Listen to me, Karl. There will be no more breaking and entering."

"No problem. I believe Esther's pal, Marty, has taken care of that himself. Besides, nobody uses this place anymore. Except tourists."

"Tourists?"

"And I've got my thirty-eight," Karl continued, saying things that in his mind were meant to reassure but in my mind only frightened me all the more.

"You brought a gun, Karl? I told you no guns!"

"Don't worry, we'll keep an eye out for you. Over and out, Chief."

"No, wait," I pleaded. "No over and out. This isn't over until I say so and—" *I didn't say so.* Karl had hung up.

A seventy-something, half-blind coot with a loaded gun running around a penitentiary after dark. And there were tourists.

What could go wrong?

I sank to my knees.

Plenty.

I gnashed my teeth and squeezed my phone between my fingers. I heard a crack. A jagged line appeared on the screen, running vertically from the upper right to the bottom left corner of the screen.

It was a symbol.

My entire life seemed to be developing cracks. Great big, gaping cracks.

The phone had been almost new, too. I was still making payments on it. And would be for another year.

The good news was that the phone was still working. I googled the Eastern State Penitentiary. It wasn't far from the Laurel Cove Apartments. I could be there in a matter of minutes.

The penitentiary had ceased its official operations as a prison in 1970, having first opened for business in 1829. It was now operated as a historical site. It was after hours. What on earth had brought them all there in the middle of the night?

I'd find out soon enough.

At least I wouldn't have to worry about prison riots and armed guards clashing with Floyd, Karl, Esther and Marty.

And me.

I punched the prison's address into my phone's GPS and studied the map. There was a fault line running through Philadelphia blocking my route to the prison. After a moment, I realized that the fault line only existed on my screen so I anticipated no problem reaching Karl and Floyd quickly.

Whether I'd be on time to prevent them from doing something dangerous or stupid or a combination of both was another matter entirely.

Taking one last look to be sure I hadn't left a trace of my presence in the apartment, I clutched my cracked phone in one hand and grabbed the door knob with the other.

Bad news was back with a vengeance.

The woman in 3B stood blocking the doorway with an old-fashioned broom. She was clutching the broom by the end of its handle—and I didn't think she had come to tidy up.

20

I was going to have to think fast before she clobbered me like a cockroach that had made the fatal mistake of crossing the threshold into her pristine world.

"Goodnight, Mr. Bergdorf." I tossed my hand in a carefree, over the shoulder wave. "Don't you worry, I'll show myself out. No need to interrupt your phone call for me. By-eee!"

"Hello again." I pretended to see my potential attacker for the first time. Big smile, I told myself.

"I don't believe I formally introduced myself. I'm Amy Simms," I said, sticking out a friendly hand but receiving no skin in reply.

The woman in 3B narrowed her eyes suspiciously. She was holding that thick wood-handled broom like a brawling hockey player getting ready to hit somebody rather than something. "Hello." She peeked in the door.

I gently pulled it shut. "Mr. Bergdorf is on the telephone. Such a lovely man, don't you think?"

"Sorry." She lowered the broom from above her shoulder to the floor. "I thought you was those perverts."

"No." I shook my head to conceal the fact that my entire body was shaking. "No perverts here." Her eyes were fixed on my ZombieFest shirt. Just freaks. I quickly zipped my jacket to my chin. What must she think? "Nice seeing you again. Gotta run."

And I did. I ran all the way down three flights of stairs and didn't stop running until I'd reached the car. I'd half-expected to hear her pounding footsteps chasing or the whoosh of her flying by me on her broom as she strafed me, but I made it to the car unscathed.

I jammed the key in the ignition. Nothing happened. I tried again. Still nothing. Not a hint of life.

I had left the headlights on.

More cracks in my existence.

I waved at passing cars until my hand felt heavy and numb. How some birds, like an Alpine swift or an Arctic tern, could flap for thousands of miles at a time nonstop, I couldn't imagine. I'd poop out going around the block.

Finally, a truck stopped and the driver offered to help.

"Thank you," I said to the Good Samaritan who conveniently carried a set of jumper cables in the back of his truck.

He slammed down the hood of my car and shot off.

A car roared past as I reached for the door handle. I felt a sharp pain on the tip of my nose followed by the sound of glass breaking.

The driver's side window was smashed to bits. The tip of my nose was bleeding profusely. I grabbed some tissues from my purse to stanch the blood and climbed in the car. My eyes fell on a grimy brown brick lying on the passenger seat.

"What the hell?" I looked around nervously. "Somebody could have killed me." I clenched the steering wheel. That was the point wasn't it?

I wasted no time maneuvering into traffic. Whoever had thrown the brick could be coming back for another try. Cold wind blasted me through the broken window as I sped up the street.

My mind was reeling, dabbing my nose with one hand, steering with the other. Floyd, Esther and Karl were prowling around inside an abandoned penitentiary. Who knew what trouble they could get in?

The Eastern State Penitentiary cut an imposing and spine-chilling presence. Massive stone walls rose thirty feet high. I hadn't expected the prison to be situated so close to the city street.

A neighborhood tightly surrounded the eery old prison, which had been built in the neo-Gothic design. No doubt meant to frighten the citizenry of Philadelphia into remaining pious and to steer clear of criminal activities. The penitentiary loomed over them like a dark, foreboding beast ready to swallow them whole should they dare transgress.

I'd have never wanted to be a prisoner in this place. The prison looked like something out of a horror movie, complete with crumbling walls and looming stone towers. It was hard to imagine that this land used to be a pleasant country cherry orchard.

I spotted my van and pulled to a stop behind it. No one was inside the vehicle. As much as I wished I'd find Floyd and Karl there, I had known I wouldn't.

I looked up and down the deserted sidewalk then made my way to the entrance. There might have been more than one entrance to the penitentiary but I was here now and so was the Kia. Hopefully, that meant the guys weren't too far off.

All I had to do was find them.

And drag them all back to the inn. Dead or alive.

The blood coming from my nose had reduced to a trickle. I stuffed my bloody tissue in my pocket and kept moving until I found myself facing a heavy iron gate and a couple of sturdy doors. I tugged upward on the gate and the only thing that budged was my right shoulder, which I was pretty sure I had dislocated.

I cursed and pushed my face into the gate. "Psst. Floyd? Karl? Are you there?" I kept my voice low. Who knew who or what was lurking out there in the inky darkness?

Ghosts of prisoners past?

Karl with a loaded gun?

I received no reply.

Knowing I should just turn around, go back to the inn, get some sleep and focus on making the most of the Expo, I did the next worst thing: I tried the solid wooden door to the right.

Sadly, it creaked open.

I was destined to enter.

Me, Amy Simms, entering an abandoned prison in the middle of the night. "Talk about birdbrains." My whispered words bounced off the damp stone walls.

I meandered down a long, low-ceilinged walkway following the muted light coming from a few fixtures scattered overhead. I passed a long sales counter behind which another door stood ajar.

I pushed through and found myself outside.

Outside being a relative term. I was under the stars. But I was also in the middle of a penitentiary with hewn and squared twelve-foot thick and thirty-foot tall granite walls.

Perhaps a prisoner or two had escaped over the length of its existence, but if I were locked in, I'd have a hard time getting out on my own with anything shy of a helicopter and an ace pilot.

Lesson learned, at least for the near-term, I reached into my pocket and set my phone on vibrate. I had plenty of signal and was ready to use it. At the first sign of trouble, or zombies, I was dialing 911.

And maybe a good zombie exterminator.

I started down the path to the left for no particular reason other than I'd seen a couple of bats whizzing through the night sky to the right.

Bats on the right, go to the left. Always a good rule of thumb.

I hadn't taken a dozen wary steps when a black arm reached out of the shadows and a hand clamped down on my sore shoulder. "Oww!"

"Quiet, Chief!" I felt Karl's cigar breath on my ear as he dragged me kicking and screaming against the façade.

I stopped kicking and screaming once my brain actually realized that it really, truly was Karl I was seeing by the light of the crescent moon above and not some undead version of the ex-cop.

That was Floyd bundled up beside him. With their coats buttoned to their chins and a couple of dark ski caps atop their heads they did, indeed, look like a couple of aging cat burglars.

Or soon to be escaping convicts.

Karl looked the part, complete with a nasty looking gun in his hand. "Put that thing away," I snapped. "Before you hurt somebody."

"Aw, Chief, it's not like it's loaded."

"What do you mean not loaded? I saw you stick a handful of bullets in myself." Floyd pulled at the collar of his jacket. He was weighted down with gear. "What if there's trouble?"

Karl shot Floyd the dirtiest of looks, visible even in the low light, and shoved the weapon in his coat pocket. "Like they say, guns don't kill people."

"No, bullets kill people," I replied. "Why are you standing around inside an abandoned penitentiary with a loaded weapon, anyway?"

"You never know." He patted the pocket with the gun. "Like Floyd says, there could be trouble."

"From who?"

Floyd jostled the camera, scope, tripod and binoculars he was lugging around like a two-legged pack mule. He held a bulging tote bag in his left hand. "That Marty guy. I don't trust him, Amy."

"Neither do I, Floyd. Neither do I." I peered around the corner of the wing. Originally, there had been seven single-story cellblocks arranged in wagon wheel fashion. The thinking at the time was that it allowed a guard in the center of the wheel to keep an eye on all the wings with a simple turn of the head.

More cell blocks, and a second floor, had been added soon after as the penitentiary, like so many others, quickly became overcrowded. Why did it seem sometimes that the world was chockful of people eager to commit some crime? "Where is he? Is Esther with him?"

"Yes," Floyd said.

Karl lit a fresh cigar and inhaled the smoke like it had been sent fresh from heaven as a gift for his lungs. "We followed them to a courtyard around the other side."

I backed up a step and waved my hand frantically in front of my nose.

"They must still be there because they haven't returned this way," explained Floyd. "We came back to wait for you."

"Good. That's good." At least Floyd and Karl had had the sense to wait for me rather than do anything stupid. "Who meets at a creepy old penitentiary after midnight?"

"Esther, that's who." Karl chuckled while puffing on his cigar.

It stank to high heaven but I knew he was nervous—we all were—so I let him smoke.

"Show me," I commanded.

We slowly worked our way across the crumbling prison grounds. It was the absolute spookiest place I had ever been in my entire life. Karl led the way. I was in the middle and Floyd, struggling with the gear, brought up the rear.

"Quiet now." Karl halted, put up his hand and gestured. He slowly stuck his head around the corner of the building we were flanking. "I think I see them." He gave me a nudge. "Take a look, Chief."

Gripping the cold rough stone, I inched my face around. A larger than expected courtyard was framed by the massive wall behind. I could just make out several human-sized black blobs in the distance. "Are you sure that's Marty and Esther?"

"Who else could it be?" said Floyd.

My imagination went wild: ghosts of dead prisoners, specters, werewolves, zombies, the troubled spirits of JJ Fuller and Peter Porter meeting under cover of darkness to plot their revenge on their killer?

I kept such thoughts to myself. Sharing them with Floyd and Karl wouldn't gain me their confidence or respect. "Is that a third person with them?"

Floyd peeked from under my shoulder. "I don't know. I can't be sure. There might be a third person with them." He turned to his partner in crime-solving. "Take a look, Karl."

Karl pulled the cigar from his mouth. He crushed its glowing orange tip against the cell block wall. He stuck his head out, too long for my comfort, before saying, "Hard to tell."

"Have you got some sort of fancy listening device amongst all that gear?" I asked.

"No, but I bet I can get a shot of him." Karl pulled a fancy camera from the American Birding Expo tote Floyd had also been carrying around. "It's got a doohickey for night photography."

"Where did you get that camera? And all this other stuff?" It all looked reasonably new. And expensive.

"We liberated it along with the binoculars." Karl pressed his right eye up to the viewfinder. His hand swiveled the lens.

"Commandeered," Floyd corrected.

I looked in horror at the sleek, long black lens bearing the Ornitho Optics logo. Poor Irving Shipman. Hadn't he noticed how much of the merchandise from his booth had now gone missing?

I promised myself that everything would be returned to him—and in perfect, like new condition.

"Fine." Okay, so I gave in. Just because it was wrong to have it, didn't mean we couldn't take advantage of the fact that we did. "Can you make out faces?"

Karl trained the long-lensed camera on our fuzzy dark subjects. His arm started wobbling. Floyd gripped Karl's elbow to brace it.

I closed my eyes and pictured being with Derek back at the hotel. My attempt at teleportation failed. I returned my attention to the matter at hand. "See anything?"

"It's them all right." Karl's voice was a mere whisper on the light cool breeze tickling my face. "And I believe Floyd is right. I think there's some third guy."

"Who is it?" I asked.

"I can't say. He's blocked by Marty."

"But that is Esther with them?" Floyd wanted to know.

"Yep."

"I've seen enough." I took a step around the side of the cellblock.

Karl blocked me and Floyd clamped his hands around my waist.

"Are you crazy, Amy?" Floyd pleaded.

"Yes, crazy to be standing in an abandoned prison in the middle of the night when I, both of you, and Esther, should be back at the inn, tucked safely in our beds."

I shook myself free of Floyd and Karl. "I'm surprised at you, Floyd," I said, careful to keep my voice low. "That's Esther out there. Don't you want to know what's going on? Don't you want to help her?"

Floyd was fighting with his emotions.

"Maybe we should go say hi," Karl decided.

I nodded my approval. "We'll round up Esther and Marty and whoever else we can lay hands on. We'll find an all-night diner, have some hot coffee, and get to the bottom of this like rational people."

"Yeah." Floyd rubbed his salt and pepper stubbled chin. "Yeah. Rational people. That's a good idea."

I started to move again.

"No," Floyd said, thrusting his arm out in front of me. "Let me go alone. We don't want to spook them."

"Okay." If they saw three obscure individuals coming at them in the dark, who knew what might happen? "Be careful. What if Marty is our murderer? He might be carrying a weapon."

I swung my accusatory eyes at Karl. "Like some people we know." I clutched Floyd's wrist. "I don't want you getting hurt."

"Don't worry about me." Floyd set the rest of the *commandeered* gear on the ground and adjusted the sleeves of his coat. "I'll be fine. Besides, even if that bum is packing heat, an old guy like that probably has poor eyesight. I'll bet he couldn't hit the side of a barn."

Floyd turned to Karl. "I've seen you out at the shooting range. No offense, Karl, but you could use a new pair of glasses. And a bigger target."

"I'm a little rusty is all," sniffed Karl defensively.

Somehow Floyd's words didn't make me feel any easier about the fact that Karl was carrying a loaded handgun in his coat.

"I'll be right back." Floyd rounded the corner and disappeared.

That was when all hell broke loose.

21

The dull thud of madly whirling rotors filled the air and shook the ground beneath our feet.

A black helicopter rose over the prison wall like an invading roc of mythical proportions. A brilliant white spotlight blinked on, illuminating a patch of earth at the far edge of the prison courtyard.

I stretched out my arms and grabbed Floyd. "Come on!"

Karl scrambled for the gear at our feet. "Wait for me!"

"What about Esther?" Floyd fought with me.

"I saw her running toward that building on the left." I bit my lip. Floyd looked miserable. And scared.

I was scared too.

"Let's circle around and see if we can find her. Okay?"

Floyd bobbed his head vigorously.

Spreading the gear between us, we worked our way around the prison grounds, stumbling over broken bits of wall and pushing through the tall weeds.

We stuck to the shadows.

After a couple of minutes, the three of us were out of breath and wheezing. We paused under the light of the dim stars and looked up. The helicopter was veering off. It lifted straight up then angled to the right, hopping over the wall as if it didn't exist.

The sudden silence was deafening.

"Come on," I urged. "I think it's this way."

I tried the door handle outside a building along the edge of the courtyard. "Locked tight." I studied the silent grounds. Not even the crickets had resumed their night song, probably still spooked by the appearance of that great metal insect in the sky.

I cupped my hands around my mouth. "Esther?"

"Yoo-hoo, Esther!" Floyd chimed in. "It's me, Floyd. And Amy and Karl."

"Uh, Chief?" Karl thumped me on the shoulder.

"What is it, Karl?"

"Is that a police siren I hear?"

Bird poop.

"Run!" barked Karl. He scrabbled at the ground, picking up the expensive gear they had borrowed from Ornitho Optics. Floyd and I helped him.

We took off at a trot, leaving one or two items behind, as the sirens grew louder. Just my luck, I'd get arrested. I could just about see the headline now: "Bird Store Owner Becomes Jailbird." Amy Simms and company nabbed by police after breaking *into* a penitentiary.

I'd be the laughingstock of Ruby Lake.

With all the murders that had taken place in and around town since I'd returned, some folks were already calling me the Grim Reaper behind my back. I couldn't afford yet another slanderous moniker.

We hurried back the way we had come. Karl was in the lead. Suddenly he stopped and flapped his arms. "Turn around," he whispered harshly. "Go back. Somebody's coming."

"Where?" I struggled to keep my voice in check. Powerful flashlight beams emanated from the door we'd been planning on escaping through.

Floyd pointed to an inky black opening in the wall. "In there."

We tiptoed inside and held our collective breaths. The metallic scratch of radio communications mixed with the banging of my heart and the call of a faraway train.

Karl took a peek. "There's two of them. In uniform. They are heading up the right side, following the wall. Let's give it a minute."

I waited for what seemed like the longest minute of my life, too afraid to even blink.

"Okay. Let's go," Karl said.

"Wait," I insisted. "What if there are more of them?"

Karl shrugged. "You'd rather they catch us here?"

My mugshot smeared across the front of the newspaper, in a ZombieFest shirt, scraggly hair and the remnants of undead makeup flashed before me. I gave Karl a push. "I'm right behind you."

"Me, too." Floyd gulped in a mouthful of air and followed.

We made it through the inner corridor without incident. A police car sat silently at the entrance, lights flashing. By the reflection on a storefront up the street, I knew another squad car was around the corner. By the sounds echoing all around us, there were more police on the way.

"Somebody must have called the cops." Karl looked up and down the street then stomped toward the rental car and minivan. Fortunately, there were a lot of other vehicles spread up and down the street so ours would not have stuck out in the eyes of the police.

"No kidding." Floyd huffed along behind me.

"A neighbor probably called the police after seeing the helicopter."

"Unless that was the police," I countered.

"What do you think, Karl?" Floyd wheezed.

"I think you two should shut your yaps. You'll move faster."

Floyd and I shut our yaps and doubled our speed. Okay, maybe not doubled but we definitely were moving faster than we had been before being admonished by Karl.

I threw open the rear doors of the van and hurled the equipment I had been hugging to my chest inside.

"Hey, watch it!"

Out of the corner of my eye, I watched in horrified slow motion as Karl yanked his handgun from his pocket and took aim at the person coming out of my van. "Freeze, mother—"

22

I screamed and fell backwards. "Esther? What the—"

Esther loomed out of the door, stooped over inside the van, looking at me like I was the one doing something stupid. "Of course, it's me. You expecting somebody else?"

"Esther!" Floyd helped me to my feet and then rushed to Esther's side. Or rather to the rear bumper, which was blocking his access to her. "Are you okay?"

I pulled Karl's arm down. He was frozen like a statue. "Put that thing away before you hurt somebody."

"Huh?" Karl blinked. "Esther." He chuckled to cover his embarrassment. "Gee. That could have been awkward."

I gaped at him but didn't have time to respond. The shrill sound of at least one more police siren was getting nearer. The pen was becoming a hornet's nest of activity. "We've got to go."

Floyd climbed in the rear of the van with Esther. I slammed the door shut behind them. "I'll take the Kia." I threw Karl his keys. "Meet you back at the inn."

I called Derek from the van and gave him the short version of what had happened.

His reply was a long whistle.

"Can you meet us out front?"

Derek promised to meet the van outside the inn and was waiting at the curb when I pulled up. We dropped Karl's rental off in the parking garage and drove as a group to the first all-night diner we could find.

Karl wasn't happy about his car's busted window and fumed all the way to the diner.

"What happened to your nose?" Derek asked.

"Yeah, I was wondering about that, Chief," said Karl. "You run into a brick wall or something?"

"No, just a brick."

"That explains it," Karl muttered, having noted the brick inside his car.

"What?" Derek gingerly touched my nostril.

I explained what had happened.

"Do you think it was the same person that had been driving that dark sedan?"

"It seems likely but I didn't get a good look at the driver."

Derek told the others what had occurred when we tried to turn the tables on the person following us by following them.

"Did you get conked with a brick too?" asked Floyd.

"I might have been," allowed Derek.

"Weird." Floyd asked for hot cocoa.

I ordered coffee, though the last thing in the world I needed at the moment was a jolt of caffeine. I had more adrenaline going through me than I knew what to do with. I would have ordered a horse tranquilizer but I hadn't seen them listed on the menu.

Esther drank her tea and nibbled at a slice of sourdough toast. She looked worried.

Floyd and Karl flanked her. That was my idea. I did not want her disappearing again.

I sat opposite, next to Derek. The diner was crowded. We occupied a booth nearest the cash register and counter where three members of an emo-thrash metal band were dissecting their night's performance.

A twenty-four-hour news station was playing on the TV over the register. Why anybody would want to have a pleasant meal spoiled by watching what always seemed to be bad news, was beyond my comprehension. I purposefully selected a seat with my back to the noise.

I recounted the remaining events of my night, after leaving Derek at the inn, while demolishing a family-sized serving of cookie dough-filled French toast made with challah bread.

"That's quite a tale." Derek jiggled his glass, listening to the sounds of ice cubes banging around in his cola.

"Do you two have anything to add?" I directed the tines of my fork at Floyd and Karl who were both suddenly looking frail and tired. I kind of felt sorry for them. Especially Floyd. This trip to Philly sure wasn't turning out the way he'd imagined it would.

But then, who among us could have guessed we'd be mixed up in murder?

A thought hit me: Esther. That's who.

"No." Karl had wolfed down a bagel and cream cheese, as evidenced by the traces on his face and shirt. "That pretty much sums it up."

"Right." I eyed him steadily. "Did you discover anything in Bergdorf's apartment?"

"Not a thing," Floyd let slip.

"Floyd." Karl glared at his friend.

"You two bozos were in Marty's apartment?" Esther asked.

"So that *is* Marty's apartment?" I pressed my elbows into the table.

"Of course. Whose else would it be?" Esther rolled her eyes. "I can't believe you two old coots broke into Marty's apartment. You've got no right to do that. I ought to call the police. That's what I ought to do."

"Who are you calling old?" Karl demanded. "And go ahead and call the police. I have a feeling they'd be happy to hear from you." Karl snatched a packet of sugar and ripped it open with his teeth. He dumped the contents in his coffee.

"Don't talk to Esther like that." Floyd draped a protective arm over Esther's shoulders.

"Okay, okay," Karl said gruffly. "Sorry, Esther."

"You should be sorry. You almost shot me, you blithering old fool."

"We were keeping an eye on the apartment building from the van. Marty came out and walked to the market down the block," explained Floyd.

"Yeah, that was our chance," said Karl.

"We only popped into the apartment for a quick look. We were in and out in less than five minutes, Esther," Floyd swore. "We didn't touch anything. I promise."

"Then when Marty came downstairs and hopped into a cab," Karl said, "we followed him. The cab dropped him off at the corner near the pen. You know the rest." He cleared his throat.

Derek rubbed his hands into his face. "Okay," he said wearily. "Now that we are done apologizing and Amy," he said, turning to me, "you can explain to me later how Karl came to almost shoot Esther—"

"Oh?" I batted my eyes in mock innocence. "Did I leave that part out?"

"Yes. Yes, you did." Derek stabbed a plum tomato from the remnants of his tofu scramble and popped it in his mouth. The man ate too healthy for his own good. "For now, let's talk about the murders of JJ Fuller and Peter Porter."

He sounded just like a lawyer, albeit a very tired one. "Esther, how about if you start?"

Esther expressed surprise. "Me? What do you want me to say?"

"What do we want you to say?" My voice rose above the din of the restaurant crowd. The three black-garbed boys seated at the counter even tuned in.

"How about telling us what you were doing meeting Marty in the middle of an abandoned penitentiary in the middle of the night?" I demanded. "How about explaining who Bergdorf is and how he fits into all this? How about explaining—"

"Okay, Amy." Derek patted my knee. "Let's give Esther a chance to talk now."

I caught my breath and pouted. "Fine." I picked up the dessert menu and perused the selections while Derek continued interviewing what I considered to be a hostile witness. The pecan pie sounded good and it came with real vanilla ice cream.

"Esther?" Derek said calmly. "How about starting at the beginning. Tell us about Marty."

Floyd fixed his eyes on Esther while stirring his cocoa.

"In the first place," Esther folded her hands on the table, "I want to go on the record as saying that I never wanted to come to Philadelphia." She aimed her words at me like an accusation.

I dragged my finger through a puddle of real maple syrup as the waitress was about to haul it away. I licked my fingertip. "Probably because you knew there was a warrant out for your arrest." I couldn't help sniping.

"Marty?" Derek nudged Esther along. Me he shot a look of warning.

"Martin Ritter and Klaus Bergdorf are one and the same. Marty is an old friend."

That was one mystery cleared up, albeit a small one.

"Is he really a spy?" Floyd wanted to know.

"What was he, one of those corporate spies?" Karl was quick to add.

"Guys, let Esther tell us." Derek waved his hand. "Go ahead, Esther. I'm sure everyone will hold their questions and comments to the end."

"I wish they would." Esther took a sip from her cup then continued. "Like I said, Marty and I are old friends. I suppose you could say he was a spy."

"You *did* say he was a spy!" I blurted.

"Amy," Derek drew out my name.

"Sorry." I waved to the waitress. I ordered the pecan pie and a double scoop of vanilla ice cream. With whipping cream on top. And two cherries.

"Marty is retired or, rather I should say, Klaus Bergdorf is retired. Marty is supposed to be dead. At least, that's what he wanted his employer and the world to think. You saw his grave at the cemetery, Amy."

I nodded and dug into my pie. At least Esther was making sense for a change.

"Who was his employer?" Karl wanted to know.

"The government," was Esther's reply.

"Which one?" Karl persisted.

"That's not important. Marty gave up the spy business decades ago. He moved to the States. Started a new life."

Esther smiled as her mind conjured up old memories. "He changed his name to Klaus Bergdorf and settled here in Philadelphia. Marty always liked it here. It's where we first met."

I could see Floyd was itching to ask deeper questions about Esther and Marty's relationship. Instead he twisted his napkin into a knot.

I wished my butter knife was a sword and that I, Amy the Great, like Alexander the Great before me, could cut the metaphoric Gordian knot that was Esther.

"Marty, or Klaus, opened a small shop for stamp collectors. About seven years ago, he decided to retire completely."

Derek held Esther's gaze. "Did Marty murder JJ Fuller, Esther?"

Esther's face darkened. "No. And he didn't kill that zombie character either."

"You're certain?"

"Certain as I am that I'm sitting here with you all when I should be out helping Marty."

"I'm sure Marty can take care of himself," Derek replied. "Why were you two meeting tonight at the penitentiary?"

It took a moment for Esther to answer. "Because we were scared. Somebody is trying to set Marty up for murder, bring him out in the open." She tugged at her lower lip. "Maybe try to kill him."

"Who?" I couldn't help asking. "Who would want to kill Marty? You said he retired from the spy game ages ago? Besides, everybody thinks he is dead, right?"

Esther shrugged. "Somebody knows he's alive. Somebody besides me. I think that's why they tried to set me up and why they planted that osprey feather."

"Marty's code name." I nodded. "You know," I shoved aside, the bit of crust remaining of my pie, "in a crazy way, that sort of makes sense."

"It does?" Derek wasn't following.

"Sure. And you," I said, meaning Esther, "took the feather from the crime scene because you knew it was going to implicate Klaus, er, Marty." She nodded and I continued. "Then you placed it on his grave at Laurel Hill—"

"And Marty got in touch with me. It was a signal. We haven't spoken much over the years, but we knew how to find each other if we needed to."

Esther smeared grape jelly over a second slice of toast. "We've been trying to figure out what's going on and who is behind it ever since the first murder. Then when Peter Porter got killed, we really got scared."

"Somebody sure means business," Karl said. "Two dead bodies ain't no joke."

No, it sure wasn't.

I helped myself to Derek's cola. "You still haven't fully explained yourself, Esther. Was Fuller a spy, too?"

"According to Marty, Fuller had gotten mixed up with some people who were willing to pay him big bucks for his photography," Esther said. "And it wasn't birds they were interested in."

I drained the glass and handed it back to Derek. "Lorna, JJ's wife, told me he got angry with her recently when she went into his office and saw him looking at photos on his computer. She said it didn't make any sense because there was nothing special about the photos."

"What were they? Did she say?" asked Derek.

"Just people. Here and there. Funny," I said, "but Ilsa told me the same thing. She found a lot of shots of people on the SD card that she removed from JJ's camera after his murder."

"And now those pictures are gone for good because Ilsa erased them," said Esther.

"Do you think she realized their significance?" Derek said.

"She said not."

"Maybe she was involved in all this espionage too," suggested Karl.

"You might be right." I sighed. It was all too complicated and instead of getting clearer, the situation seemed to be getting cloudier by the minute.

I grabbed Esther's hand and pinned it gently to the table top. "I still don't understand, Esther. Why? Why were *you* looking into JJ Fuller's activities? What does any of this," I said, waving my free hand in the air in complete and utter frustration, "have to do with you?"

"Good question, Chief." Karl nudged her with his elbow. "Tell us, Esther."

Esther plucked my fingers one by one from her hand. "Didn't it strike you odd that we're here?"

"Huh? Are you talking about here at the diner?"

"Here. In Philly."

"Because Phoebe Gates invited us to the American Birding Expo."

I looked at Derek. He was as confused as I was. "Because there was a cancellation and an extra booth," I said.

"Yeah, yeah." Esther waved my words away like they were nothing more than a pesky fly at a picnic. "But why us? Why Birds and Bees?"

I chewed on my lip while my brain got to work on the question. "Because Phoebe had met us last year at the Wings Over Carolina thing. Phoebe remembered us and liked us and when the booth became available, she gave me a call."

"Do you remember what Barbara said when she told you about the phone call she'd had with Phoebe?"

"Mom?" I shook my head. "No. Something about the booth and we could have it if we wanted it. Why?"

"Barbara specifically mentioned that Phoebe had mentioned my name."

My jaw practically hit the table.

"I'll be damned," Karl whispered.

"She did." Floyd bobbed his head. "I remember. Barbara did say that."

"Doesn't that strike you as odd?" Esther pointed her question at me.

"At the time, I admit, it did seem a little strange."

"Why would Phoebe want Esther here?" Floyd asked.

"Something to do with her connection to Marty Ritter?" offered Derek.

"And, thus, to JJ Fuller?" I added. "Tomorrow, I think I'll track her down and ask her."

"If Marty didn't kill JJ Fuller and Peter Porter," I asked Esther, "who do you think did?" With this new bombshell, I realized that I may have dismissed Phoebe and Lorna as suspects too soon.

"Marty and I thought it was Ilsa Skoglund. We'd seen her meeting with Peter Porter on a couple of occasions clandestinely."

"Like at the Audubon Center," Derek commented.

"That's right." Esther bit the end off her triangle of toast. "They met at her hotel once, too. Plus, a fast food joint near the Expo Center. We were pretty sure she was behind the murder after that. Well, Ilsa Skoglund and Peter Porter."

"You believed she had murdered Fuller for the photos of the woodpecker?"

"It seems a likely bet."

"When we met her at the bar earlier, she denied it."

"She didn't deny stealing the SD card or wrongfully claiming the discovery of that woodpecker for herself though," replied Esther. "If she's guilty of those things, she might be guilty of murder, too."

"I agree with Esther." Karl rubbed the tip of his chin. "Once a person crosses the line into illegal activities, it's been my experience that such a person won't feel disinclined to engage in wider and, maybe bigger, crimes."

"You could be right, Karl." That from the lawyer among us.

"It fit with Porter squealing to the police that he'd seen me in the vicinity at the time of the murder." Esther paused and adjusted the navy ribbon at the back of her head.

"And her planting the SD card in your purse," I added.

"It was the osprey feather in the room though. That made no sense. No sense at all."

"How so?" Floyd wanted to know.

"Somebody, Fuller's true murderer, wanted to suggest that the Osprey was behind the killing."

"That's what you said before," I replied. "So?"

"So who besides me knew that the Osprey was still alive? How did they know that leaving that feather would draw him out?" Esther raised her brow in my direction.

But I had no answer.

23

"What if you hadn't found the feather and the police had instead?" asked Derek.

"Then they probably wouldn't have made sense of it at all," Esther answered.

"And Marty or Klaus or whoever he really is, would never have become a suspect and would be sitting in his apartment staring at his stamp collection right now."

"But the police didn't find it," Derek persisted. "You did."

"I received a text telling me that I should go to that room," Esther explained. "JJ Fuller's dressing room."

"Who was the message from?"

Esther shook her head side to side. "We don't know. It came from one of those online services you can anonymously send messages through. Marty dug around on the internet and made some inquiries. He came up emptyhanded."

"Did you show it to the police?" asked Floyd.

"Detective Locke didn't take it seriously. He said I could have sent it myself."

"I don't think I like him." Floyd's countenance darkened.

Esther managed a small smile. "The message told me that I should go to that room and told me explicitly what time to be there."

"And you went." Karl reached across the table and helped himself to one of Floyd's biscuits.

"I went."

Floyd patted her hand tentatively. "I wish you'd told me. I could have helped. I could have gone with you."

"I had to go alone," Esther said. "I didn't want to get anyone else involved."

And now we were all involved.

"That feather was the Osprey's calling card. Marty, for all his flaws, has a sense of humor," Esther went on. "Once he'd gotten the codename the Osprey, he took to leaving a feather at the scene of his various…escapades. He thought it was intriguing."

Escapades? Murder and spying were hardly what I would have called escapades but I kept my mouth shut. We had bigger problems than semantics to deal with now.

"Sounds like more of a taunt to me." Derek rubbed his hands.

He might have been dreaming of gripping his driver. I'd seen that look when he was on his way to the country club. He probably wished he hadn't volunteered to come and had stayed home where he could have played a round of golf every day.

"Who would want Marty dead after all this time?" I asked.

"Marty doesn't know. Neither do I," replied Esther. "Most of the people he dealt with are dead or retired. Like him."

"What about this Porter character?" Derek held up his glass for a refill. "How deeply was he mixed up in all this?"

"Marty and I think he was just a small-time blackmailer. There's nothing suspicious in his background, at least that Marty's been able to uncover."

"Your pal still connected?" Karl asked.

"He has his sources," Esther said rather coyly.

"Right." Karl ran an imaginary zipper across his lips. "So what kind of spy were you, Esther? Do any field operations? Sit behind a desk cracking codes? Ever have to…" Still in imaginary mode, Karl slowly traced his finger across his neck, "eliminate one of the bad guys?"

"Karl!" I yelped.

Esther, for her part, looked like she was about to eliminate a former chief of police. Her white-knuckled fingers were wrapped around a fork. Her mouth opened and closed but no words came out.

"What?" complained Karl. "I'm only curious, is all."

Floyd was looking sadder and sadder. Like me, he was getting to know an Esther that was not what she had appeared to be. "I think I'll get some air." Floyd climbed slowly to his feet.

"Want some company?" asked Karl.

"No, thanks." Floyd grabbed his jacket from the coat tree beside the register. "Hey, look."

Marty's face was on TV.

And he didn't look happy.

24

I spent a fitful, sleepless night, tossing and turning and kicking. The sheets seemed to tighten around my ankles like boa constrictors no matter how hard I fought against them.

Esther had refused to say another word about what was happening, which was infuriating. She had clammed up on seeing Marty's face on the TV screen. The caption stated that he had been taken into custody near the Eastern State Penitentiary. He was being held in the county lockup on suspicion of two murders.

Even more infuriating was Esther's ability to quickly fall asleep once her head had hit the pillow. How could she sleep with her friend in jail?

Wasn't she concerned? Wasn't she worried?

I had asked her both questions, and she had stuck with the clam routine. Although I pried and pried, she refused to release a single pearl—of wisdom or otherwise.

It was the final day of the American Birding Expo. We had driven over in both vehicles, intending to drop the damaged rental car off at a local branch of the rental car agency at the end of the day. In the meantime, the guys had duct-taped cardboard in the hole where the window used to be.

According to the instructions handed out by expo officials on Thursday, we had to be packed and out of the building by 7 p.m.

Had it really only been a matter of a few days since we had arrived all bleary-eyed, bushy-tailed and innocent?

It seemed a lifetime away. There had been two killings, the announcement of the sighting of a bird once thought to be extinct and, oh yeah, Esther was a spy.

Okay, a retired spy. Purportedly. I still couldn't get my mind wrapped around that bit of news.

Truth be told, I wasn't sure I believed it. Esther had always been known to stretch the truth a bit, like the way a candy maker stretches taffy to the near breaking point.

While it seemed quite likely that Marty had a sketchy past that might have involved some sort of cloak-and-dagger activity, I'd need a letter signed by the head of the CIA verifying Esther's vague espionage past before I'd believe it.

The Expo Center was open and doing a brisk business. The parking lot was packed to capacity. A couple of murders hadn't stopped the festivities, dimmed them maybe, but not extinguished them.

That included me. I'd come a long way and paid a reduced yet still hefty sum for me to be in Philly. I was determined to make the best of things—murder or no murder.

We had dropped Esther off at the police station in town. She wanted to check on Marty and would join us later by cab.

Floyd had offered to accompany her but she had insisted he come with us. Karl was doing his best to keep his friend's spirits up. I'd seen puddles of water that looked happier.

The crowd milling listlessly outside the entrance to the Expo Center was a surreal mix of zombies (think weeping wounds, bandages and gore) and birders (think khaki, bird guides and sturdy hiking boots).

I had a hunch both ZombieFest and the American Birding Expo had attracted more visitors than might have otherwise have been the case if there had been no murders.

There were also a handful of uniformed police officers in addition to the regular Expo security team.

Personally, I was hoping our killer was long gone or in jail. If Marty had committed the murders, that was where he deserved to be, ex-lover of Esther's or not.

And if Esther was planning to bust him out of jail and take it on the lam with him, Floyd would be devastated. I, on the other hand, could begin to contemplate more seriously renovating my apartment and expanding into the soon to be vacant apartment below me.

I had a long to-do list for the Expo. You would think that list had something to do with birds. It didn't. It was all about murder. I wanted to speak with Phoebe Gates again, Lorna, too. Then I wanted to look for Peter Porter's friend, Suze, assuming she was at ZombieFest. I had no other way of finding her.

With the Expo ending, I wanted some answers, some closure to what had happened. While I actually would feel bad for Esther if Marty ended up proving to be guilty in the eyes of the law for the two killings, it would mark a nice neat ending to everything. Including the continued cloud that was hanging over Esther. I knew she'd never truly be an accomplice to murder. She might have made the mistake of associating with someone who was a killer but, at heart, the Pester is a softy.

My first goal, however, was to return all of the optical gear that Karl and Floyd had helped themselves to from the Ornitho Optics booth.

To their credit, both Floyd and Karl had offered to accompany me and admit to their transgression, but I was afraid that Irv Shipman might prefer to press charges rather than laugh off their borrowing his expensive equipment. After all, I barely knew the man.

"Hi, Travis." I smiled and showed lots of pretty white teeth. This was definitely showtime. I wished I'd taken my short stint at the community theater more seriously.

I gently laid two totes full of cameras, lenses, binoculars and a spotting scope on the front table of the Ornitho Optics booth.

"Hello, Amy." In a long-sleeved black Ornitho Optics polo and khakis, Travis was the picture of a birder, or at least the picture of a purveyor of birding equipment. I, for one, was just happy to see him with a shirt on.

"Is Irv here?" He wasn't manning the booth but that didn't mean he wasn't close at hand.

"No, sorry. An old buddy of his stopped by. I think they said they were heading down to the food court." Travis relieved me of the gear and set it beneath the front table. "What happened to your nose?"

I'd placed a bandage over my nostrils. "Osprey bite." I didn't know why I'd said that. It was the first thing to pop out of my mouth.

Travis jerked his head back. "Did you say osprey?"

"Just kidding. I wanted to return this gear."

Travis poked his nose in the nearest tote. He smelled of lavender. "What is it?"

"A couple of over-zealous employees of mine borrowed some of your display equipment." That was an understatement. "I wanted to make sure you got it all back."

He stuck his hands in the second tote and handled the various pieces of gear.

"It was all a big misunderstanding." I watched nervously. "I'm sure everything is in like-new condition."

Travis pulled out a long lens and squinted as he held it up to one eye.

"If it's not, let me know and I'll reimburse you."

Travis laid the lens carefully on the table. "No worries," he said with a smile. "I'm sure everything is good."

"You didn't notice this stuff was missing?" I observed several holes on the drapery-covered tables where equipment had probably been lying. A couple of tripods were minus their cameras and scopes, too.

"Irv noticed. I had not."

"I hope we didn't cause him any distress. I was afraid he would report a possible theft to the Expo Center authorities." Or worse, the police.

"Irv said not to sweat it. So I didn't." Travis moved the totes to the floor. "Thanks for bringing them back. I'll tell Irv. Of course, now it's more to pack."

"Thank you. Speaking of packing, where are you off to next?"

"I've got a show up in Boston."

"That doesn't sound so bad. You won't have far to travel."

"No." He looked a bit overwhelmed. "It will be my first solo show though."

"That's right, Irv is retiring."

"Yep." He dug his hands into his pant pockets. "Speaking of retiring, I heard the police arrested that stamp collector guy for killing JJ Fuller and the zombie."

I wasn't sure how Peter Porter's family, assuming he had one, would feel about him being memorialized as a zombie rather than a human being but there was no point giving Travis a hard time about it. He seemed like a nice enough young man.

"So you heard."

"Everybody's heard. It was on the news. Everyone is talking about it." Travis shrugged. "That and Ilsa Skoglund backpedaling."

"Backpedaling?"

Travis grinned. "Yeah. Apparently, she's now saying that it might not have been that ivory-footed—"

"Ivory-billed," I corrected.

"Right. Ivory-billed woodpecker that she'd seen at all."

"Wow. That I had not heard."

"Well, then you heard it here first."

"Heard what?" a woman inquired.

I turned around as Nikki Nilsson passed me and planted a kiss on Travis's cheek.

"Hey, Nikki, babe. Check it out. Amy gotten bitten on the nose by an osprey."

Nikki's face went blank.

"It's a joke." I covered my nose with my hand.

"Heard what?" Nikki asked again, her hand rubbing Travis's neck as if to coax out the answer.

Travis grabbed her hand. "About that guy getting arrested for killing your boss."

Nikki settled her purse on her shoulder. It was a nice brown leather bag that went well with her cashmere sweater and jeans. She'd added a black streak to her blond tresses. A nod to the death of her former boss, JJ Fuller? "Yes, thank goodness," she exclaimed.

"You must be relieved, Nikki."

"Relieved? Relieved doesn't begin to describe it," the young woman said. "I'll bet he's some crazy bird fanatic who tried to rob JJ and ended up murdering him instead. Say," Nikki said out of the blue, "where's Esther? Don't tell me the police are still holding her?"

"No. She's in the clear. What do you think Marty Ritter tried to rob JJ of?"

"The pictures on his camera, of course. What else could it be?"

I didn't have a clue and said so.

"It had to be the pictures."

"The ones of the ivory-billed woodpecker?"

"Yep."

"You saw the bird too? It really was the ivory-billed woodpecker? Because it seems Ilsa's now suggesting it may not have been."

"Beats me." Nikki shrugged.

"Were you with JJ when he took the photos?"

"No. He liked to go birding alone."

"But you saw the pictures before the Expo? You knew that your boss had found the woodpecker, not Ilsa Skoglund?"

"Of course." Nikki frowned. "That woman has a nasty habit of interfering where she ought not. When I confronted her, she said she'd erased everything on JJ's SD card except for the shots of that bird." Her hands curled into fists.

"At least the truth will come out now," I offered.

"Yeah, there is that."

"And the man who has admitted to killing JJ is safely behind bars."

"I only hope he stays behind bars," Travis said. "That guy gives me the creeps."

"You never even met the man, dear," Nikki said.

"Huh? Right, but I saw his face. Definitely the killer type." Travis drank from an open can of cola. "I bet he gets life."

Travis busily dug under his fingernails with a bent paperclip. "It's kinda funny when you think about it. The police nab him outside a penitentiary and now the old bird will probably spend the rest of his life in one. Like a bird in a cage," he added with a big grin.

"I hope he burns in hell." Nikki slapped Travis's hands and he stopped picking under his nails. "Where's Irv?"

"Hanging out with one of his buddies," explained Travis.

Nikki frowned and looked at the slender platinum watch on her wrist. "Tell him I need to see him."

"Sure, babe." The two locked lips. I now recognized her voice as belonging to the woman Travis had been entertaining in his apartment.

Travis moved away and mingled with the browsers wandering the Ornitho Optics booth.

"Are you buying some equipment from Travis?" Nikki asked.

"Actually, Amy is returning some gear she borrowed."

"Borrowed?" Nikki didn't look pleased.

"She borrowed some stuff from Irv." Travis moved back in, apparently unable to long resist the pull of the beautiful young woman.

Nikki rolled her eyes. "There's no money in loans." Suddenly she grinned. "Unless you charge interest."

Embarrassed, I pulled out my wallet. "I could pay you something—"

Travis held up his hand. "Nah. Forget about it. Demoing the products is why we're here." He turned to Nikki. "Right, babe?"

"Nice seeing you again, Ms. Simms." Nikki's lips were swollen and tinged with a violet lip gloss. "Will you and your employees be leaving for home today? Where was that exactly? North Carolina?"

"That's right, Ruby Lake, to be precise. Yes, we'll be up and out. I'm looking forward to being home."

"I'm sure you are." Nikki batted her eyes at me. "Maybe I'll see you at another event?"

"Possibly. After I've recovered from this one."

"Don't let the mayhem get to you," Nikki said. "Usually these things are nothing but fun."

"What about you?" I asked. "Now that JJ is gone, what will you do?"

Nikki shrugged as if she didn't have a care in the world. "I'm not sure."

"No doubt something will turn up," I said by way of encouragement. Maybe Skoggie was looking for a new assistant. Or a publicist to repair her tarnished image.

"It might be time for a career change. Maybe I'll try something different." Nikki appeared to give this some thought. "Don't worry about me."

Nikki helped herself to a handful of butterscotch candies in a small glass dish that she deposited in her purse, saving up for a rainy or sugarless day, sort of like a poor imitation of a western scrub jay, a bird known to cache several thousands of pine seeds and acorns in a single season and then retrieve them during the bleak winter months. "I'm happy as a lark and free as a bird. Speaking of birds, there is a raptor show today. You might want to be careful you do not get bitten again."

"Huh?"

"Your nose?" She put a finger to her own nose.

"Oh, right." I grinned.

Nikki went one way and I went the other.

Free of guilt now that I had returned Ornitho Optics birding equipment to them, I had every intention of operating the Birds & Bees booth for the remainder of the Expo. Maybe I could even find a nearby driving range where Derek could go whack a bucket of balls for an hour or two that afternoon. Although why anybody would want to do that for fun was beyond me.

My intentions, good as they were, would have to wait until I had checked off the rest of the items on my laundry list though.

I found Phoebe Gates hovering over the shoulder of a weary young lady at the registration table near the entrance. I waved to get her attention. "Have a minute, Phoebe?"

Phoebe said something I couldn't catch to the young woman. The woman nodded briskly as she clutched a sheaf of registration papers in one hand and fiddled with the keyboard of a small tablet with the other.

"Hi, Amy. What's up?"

"You seem quite chipper this morning, Phoebe."

"I am. It's the last day of the Expo. And with JJ's killer behind bars, I expect nothing but a family-friendly grand finale with the birds of prey show and some laughs from Donnie Warbler."

Donnie Warbler was really Donnie Weaver. He was known on the birding circuit for his comical imitations of our feathered friends.

Phoebe sipped from a plastic water bottle. "And no dead bodies."

"I'll drink to that."

"Here you go." She thrust the bottle at me. It might have looked like water but it smelled of vodka.

"I was speaking metaphorically."

Phoebe dabbed at the corner of her mouth with her thumb. "Was there something special you need?" Before I could answer, she continued. "I hope you won't let our little distractions deter you from returning next year."

Is that what Phoebe considered two murders? Little distractions?

Phoebe was still talking. "The American Birding Expo gets bigger each year. I've already got a flock of exhibitors signing up to come back." She latched her fingers around my wrist. "You might want to think about reserving a booth early."

"Well…"

"I'll give you a good rate. See me before you leave. We'll see if we can't work something out."

"Sure. I'll do that. On the subject of the Expo—" Out of the corner of my eye, I spotted a vaguely familiar looking, white-haired older man with a ponytail and beard. He was walking with Irv Shipman.

"Yes?"

"I wanted to thank you again for inviting Birds and Bees to fill the empty booth. You must have had dozens of others who would have jumped at the opportunity."

Phoebe lifted the American Birding Expo ball cap from her head. She pushed a hand through her hair before replacing it. "You're welcome. I'm glad you came."

I wasn't sure if I was so glad but it would have been rude to say so. "I still can't imagine why JJ suggested Birds and Bees for the Expo."

"I guess that's one more secret JJ has taken to his grave."

"What do you mean?"

"Oh, nothing." Phoebe shook her head. "It's not polite to speak ill of the dead and rumors are just that." She looked over her shoulder. "Gotta go. If you really want to know why JJ suggested inviting you, ask his assistant, Nikki. She may know something."

"Thanks. I might do that." I had a feeling Nikki was useless. Lorna might know why JJ had recommended me to Phoebe.

"Right." Phoebe took two steps then turned back. "Don't forget. Come find me before you leave and we'll see if we can't get you signed up for a booth for next year."

I nodded in a vague and noncontractual manner. I intended to see that I and my crew got out of this Expo alive and back home safely before scheduling a return engagement.

Worry about Esther crept up in my thoughts. How was she taking Marty's arrest and incarceration?

Behind the cranky, stoic exterior lurked a woman of depth and mystery. And dare I say it?

Heart.

I still couldn't be sure that Marty was not guilty of murdering JJ Fuller and Peter Porter. If he killed JJ, why? Porter's death seemed more clear. He had likely been murdered because he knew too much, probably something about the first murder. So the killer decided he had to go too.

Unless JJ and Peter were involved in something nefarious together. But that seemed improbable.

What had JJ Fuller known or done that had led someone, possibly Marty, to put him permanently out of commission?

That question led me in a circle back to Phoebe Gates. She was more relaxed, carefree today. Was that because Marty was the real killer and he was in custody?

Or, was it because the police had the wrong suspect and the real culprit was looking like they might go free, leaving Marty Ritter aka Klaus Bergdorf—aka whoever—to take the blame? And was that culprit Phoebe and/or her new gal pal, Lorna?

What secrets, if any, had Phoebe been alluding to that JJ Fuller had taken to his early grave?

Which brought me back to why murder JJ?

If Ilsa was not lying about what she'd seen, heard and done, and the others were not lying, then why was JJ killed?

I remembered something Derek had told me once: Find the why and find the who.

I wanted another word with Skoggie.

Unfortunately, Detective Locke wanted another word with me first.

25

Detective Locke saw me at the same time I saw him. He stood a couple of booths down from the Birds & Bees booth feigning interest in a Costa Rican birding expedition.

The detective dropped the brochure he was holding. He nodded to the two men at the booth then began moving in my direction.

I sidled over to the Audubon Center booth and started riffling through the sale items. I wanted the detective as far away as possible from our booth in case Esther showed up. Plus, I thought I might pick up a couple of souvenir sweatshirts for Mom and Kim to thank them for managing Birds & Bees while we were gone.

Detective Locke planted himself in front of me. He wore rumpled blue trousers, a white shirt with narrow blue stripes and a blue sport coat. He didn't look happy. His puffy eyes complemented his sagging jowls.

"A word, Ms. Simms." The detective thrust his hands in the pockets of his sport coat, stretching the material to its breaking point.

"Of course. Good morning, detective, or, should I say, afternoon. You look like you've had a long night." The sweatshirts were nice. But it was the cabana shirts that caught my eye. I held up a blue top for a closer look.

"You might say that."

I almost quipped that I just had but he seemed too tired to be receptive to jokes. "I'm surprised to see you here at the Expo. Tying up some loose ends?" I set it aside. There was a pretty yellow one in Kim's size but I thought she might prefer the sage.

"Where's Ms. Pilaster?" Detective Locke cast his eyes on every passing person as if he knew they were each guilty of something and all he had to do was figure out what. Then he would slap the cuffs on them with the alacrity of a sparrow hawk or, dare I say, osprey, seizing its prey.

"Esther?" I looked around as if she might be in the expo hall, which I knew she was not. "She's down at the police station visiting Marty."

"Are you sure?"

"Why, detective? Don't tell me you have more questions for her." I held the yellow and sage cabana shirts one by one against my chest. "Esther is a dear, sweet woman," I heard myself saying, "I can tell you that she would never be a party to a crime."

Nor would she rat out her old friend, of that I was certain.

"The Expo ends today. And we are all going home." I started to move past him. "I'm sure any questions you have for Esther, she will be happy to answer by telephone long distance. What do you think? Yellow or sage?" I stuck the shirts under his nose.

"Green."

"Thanks." I handed my credit card over to the clerk and she bagged the gifts for me. I thanked her and started to go.

Detective Locke pressed his palm against my shoulder blade. "Not so fast."

I glared at his hand, saying nothing.

The detective removed his hand. "Marty Ritter is missing," he finally said and I had a feeling the words had not come easy.

"You mean escaped?" My mouth went dry.

"Yes. Let's keep that between us, shall we?"

"Don't tell me Esther—"

I clamped my lips together.

"Don't tell me Esther what?" The detective tilted his head at me in question.

I was going to say something stupid, like did she break him out but had caught myself in time. The absurd image of Esther baking a cake with a file in it and delivering it to little old Marty in jail so he could saw his way free sprang into my brain.

Absurd because I didn't know if Esther could bake.

"Don't tell me Esther went down to the station for nothing?" I swallowed. Hard. And hoped he bought it.

"Where is she, Ms. Simms?" He turned a yawn into a frown. "I went by your booth. Mr. Harlan tells me she hasn't been in."

"Where did I put that receipt?" I dug around in the bag holding my new shirts, buying time.

"It's in your other hand."

"Oh, right." I tossed the balled-up receipt in the plastic bag. "I haven't seen Esther since we left the inn. If she's not here and she's not at the station, then I honestly don't know where she might be. She said she was going to the police station."

The bandage on my nose was slipping. I shoved it back in place. Who knew noses could sweat so much?

"Come to think of it, she must have meant the police station in Philadelphia." It was the Philadelphia police who had made the arrest. "Maybe you should check with them there."

"Maybe." Though he said it, he clearly didn't believe it. "What happened to your nose?"

"Some jerk tossed a brick out of their car and it nicked me." I pinched my nose just enough to see that it still hurt. A lot. "That's all."

"Are you sure that's all it was?" The detective seemed almost happy with the news. "Maybe it's someone's way of telling you that they don't like you sticking your nose into something that does not concern you."

He had a point. A scary one. Another six inches and I might be dead.

My brain was working furiously. Where, oh where, was Esther? What trouble had she gotten herself into now? Was she harboring a fugitive? Was she a fugitive herself?

"Something about those two doesn't add up."

"You mean Esther and Marty?"

"You know two other senior citizens up to their eyeballs in a double homicide?"

I wasn't sure that two killings on separate days qualified as a double homicide but, again, I thought better of pointing this out to the harried detective.

"What was Marty Ritter doing in the middle of a deserted penitentiary in the middle of the night?" Detective Locke wanted to know.

Too bad I had no answer. Esther merely spun a tale of meeting some third party who shall remain nameless. He was a contact of Marty's who was helping them piece together whatever was going on. He had gotten away.

"How should I know? What did Mr. Ritter tell you?" Floyd, Karl, Esther and I could thank our lucky stars that we hadn't been rounded up along with Marty.

"I never got the chance to ask him the question."

"How is it that the police happened to go to Eastern State Penitentiary last night in the first place?" I asked. "Did you receive a tip?"

"Not us. The police in Philly got a call from a resident who happened to see some odd goings on, as they put it. The police responded. Ritter was caught just outside the prison and taken into custody. Lucky for the police, he snagged his coat on a chain-link fence and couldn't wrestle out of it in time to disappear into the night."

"So what happened? I mean, how did you lose him?"

Locke glared at me. "I did not lose him. The police transport lost him." He rubbed his palms against his cheeks as if hoping to erase all traces of himself. "It seems there was an incident on the road."

"What kind of incident?"

"Two banged up cars on a remote intersection. A bloody accident victim lying on the pavement. The driver got out to assist. When he got back…" A long sigh filled what would have been an otherwise awkward silence. "Ritter was gone."

"I hadn't heard."

"Like I said, we're trying to keep it under wraps for now. We haven't released news of the escape."

"Why not?"

Detective Locke shifted his feet. "We are working some angles," he said rather unconvincingly.

Working some angles or trying to avoid being embarrassed by recapturing Marty before the public caught wind of his escape?

Or was there something going on that Detective Locke was not being made privy to? That would hurt him right where it counted. In the ego.

So Marty had vanished. Where was he now? Back at the apartment? With luck, I'd find Marty and Esther at Laurel Cove. I knew better than to mention that to the detective. I needed to find Esther first and see what was going on before putting the police on her trail.

"I did some checking up on their backgrounds," continued Detective Locke. "Did you know there are serious holes in their pasts and in their stories?"

"No, I can't say I did." Why had I never thought of that? At least, when it came to Esther. Maybe I had never been curious enough or didn't think it had mattered. Pasts were just that, the past. Except in this case, the past might have something to do with what was going on now. "What sort of holes?"

His lips twisted like a worm on a hot sidewalk. "Holes. If I knew, they wouldn't be holes now, would they?"

The detective was losing his cool.

"One thing I am not clear about," I said. "According to the news reports, Marty Ritter is believed responsible for the deaths of JJ Fuller and Peter Porter. What makes the police so sure?"

For the first time since I'd laid eyes on him that day, the detective smiled. "I guess you didn't hear everything."

"I guess not."

"He confessed."

I sucked in a breath. "Does Esther know?" She must be devastated.

"You tell me."

"Did Ritter say why he committed the murders?"

"Ms. Simms, he didn't even give us a hint." Locke's hands went back into his pockets as if seeking refuge. "And now he's gone. His ID listed an apartment in West Philly. We interviewed his neighbors."

That didn't match with the apartment I knew him to be living in as Klaus Bergdorf, which meant that the police were probably unaware of it. "And?"

"And the few people we talked to claim never to have seen him. Even the manager of the place only saw him the day he moved a few sticks of furniture in."

"How does he pay his rent?"

"The guy in the apartment next door claims Martin Ritter is some kind of trained assassin." Locke chuckled. "Ritter told him himself one night when they were knocking back a bottle of Bacardi and the guy believed it." He shook his head. "Some people sure are gullible."

"I'll say."

"Fill me in, Ms. Simms." Locke pulled his right hand from his coat pocket and wiggled his fingers.

"What do you mean?"

"Tell me about Ms. Pilaster's past. Where is she from? Who are her friends? Does she have family? Specifically, does she have any family or friends in the greater Philadelphia area?"

"I know very little about her, detective."

"I'll take anything you've got."

"Like I said, I don't know much." That was suddenly a scary thought. Who was the crotchety old woman I shared a house and business with? Was she a trained assassin who could sneak up on me while I slept and slit my throat?

"Come on, Ms. Simms. The woman works for you. You share a house with her and you don't know anything about her? Where is she from? Where did she go to school? Does she have any family? Hell," he tossed his arm, striking a passing man, "does she have a dog?"

"I know she has a sister."

"A sister, good. That's good." He massaged the back of his neck. "Tell me about her."

"Her name is Gertie. Gertrude Hammer. I bought my house from her. She lives in Ruby Lake." I could have added that she was a curmudgeon but that probably was not pertinent.

"What did Esther do before she came to work for you?"

"I honestly don't know." Esther had said she'd been some sort of agent once. I still didn't quite believe her. Was there a tombstone at Laurel Hill with her name or some alias of hers on it too?

I did not want to know. That would be creepy. What did I know about Esther besides the fact that she doted on a real or perhaps imaginary cat?

A uniformed officer stepped between us. "The captain wants you at the station, sir. The guys from Philly are here."

"Oh, joy. Has there been any word on Ritter?"

"Not that I've heard," related the officer.

"The DA is busting our butts on this," Detective Locke addressed me. "We need to solve this case before the Expo ends and everybody spreads to the four corners of the world. We can't expect people to stay in town once everybody packs up," he complained. "There's too many of them. Bad for tourism, too, according to the DA and the mayor."

"I understand your concern but I don't know what I can do, detective."

"What you can do, if you see Ms. Pilaster," Detective Locke said, sounding beaten down yet unrelenting, "is let me know. Better yet, hold her until I get there. Promise?"

"I'll do my best." Equivocation is one of my best qualities. Just ask my mom.

26

With the detective out of my hair, I was free to ruffle Ilsa Skoglund's feathers. "You never did give me a good explanation for why you were meeting with Peter Porter, Ms. Skoglund."

"You again?" Ilsa looked up. "We were just talking. It was nothing." She signed her name to the title page of her latest book, a memoir of her year-long Central American birding adventure.

"Thanks." I stuck the book in my purse. "Then why all the skullduggery?" I had ambushed her at the signing table near the hall entrance.

Lucky for me, she didn't seem too popular at the moment. Her fans might have already come and gone but I had a feeling there would be fewer adoring fans flocking around her since her so-called discovery of the ivory-billed woodpecker blew up in her face. "Why meet in the middle of the woods?"

When she made no reply, I continued. "Before he was murdered, Peter Porter told me that someone had paid him to point the finger at Esther. That was you, wasn't it?"

She clicked the cap of her signing pen furiously, sounding like an angry blue jay. "Don't be ridiculous, Simms. I told you already, I wouldn't harm anyone, let alone kill them. Leave, please, I have books to sign."

I took a quick look behind me then back. "Sorry, I appear to be the end of the line. Tell me why you were meeting with Peter Porter and I'll get out of your hair."

Ilsa scanned the area to be sure she wasn't being overheard. "If you must know—and I'll deny this if you so much as tell a single soul," she warned aiming the pen at me. "Porter heard about the announcement of my discovery and the reward. He said he felt he deserved a share."

"Oh?"

"It seems he had figured out or at least suspected that I may have been involved in some chicanery."

"I'd call theft and murder more than chicanery."

"I told you," Ilsa Skoglund hissed at me. "I did not kill anyone. JJ was already dead when I found him. Besides, I wasn't the only woman Peter Porter was trying to squeeze money out of."

"There were others?"

"Try Lorna." Ilsa's face, normally so pretty, was dark and full of anger.

"JJ's wife?"

"Wealthy widow, you mean." Skoggie shoved me aside and shot past me. I let her go.

Watching her go, I couldn't help thinking that hearing the truth out of anyone lately was about as likely as seeing a long-tailed São Paulo marsh antwren on the streets of downtown Philly.

Not very.

Skoggie had pointed me in the direction of Lorna Fuller but I didn't have to look for her. She was looking for me.

She grabbed my arm and yanked me towards the ladies' room. "What did you say to Phoebe?"

"Uh..." I struggled to remember. "Nothing special." I glanced at my reflection in the ladies' room mirror. Hideous. What was it about mirrors in bathrooms that always made my face look pasty and my shape look so flabby? Were all mirrors designed and manufactured by men?

I turned toward the stalls. Anything was better than looking in the mirror. Lorna seemed to have no trouble facing herself. She had dressed for the last day of the American Birding Expo in a black silk pantsuit and pearls.

"She said you upset her, practically accused her of having had something to do with JJ's death. And the death of that other silly man."

"Silly man? You mean Peter Porter?"

"Imagine, a grown man getting dressed up like a zombie. It's preposterous."

"In case you hadn't noticed, the convention hall next door is crawling with them."

Her face displayed utter distaste. "I wish you would leave poor Phoebe alone. She's going through a difficult time."

"Believe me," I said, not understanding where all the anger was coming from, "it was never my intention to upset her. We were only talking."

"About murder you were talking. This is a birding convention. Why don't you talk about birds for crying out loud? I'm surprised. You are a birder. Why can't you be more like JJ?"

"You mean dead?"

"No, Ms. Simms. Birds. Birds are practically all JJ ever wanted to talk about. Try it. There are thousands of people here dying to talk to one another about birds."

"Murder trumps birds, Lorna," I replied. "I think even JJ would have agreed."

"My husband's death has nothing to do with Phoebe or me or anyone else around here. The police have their killer in custody." She pulled open her purse and extracted a cigarette.

A passerby snapped at her. "This is a no smoking facility."

She cursed him out and tossed the cigarette back in her purse.

"Is that a gun?" I had noticed what appeared to be a black pistol grip wedged down inside the purse.

"My husband was murdered. I intend to protect myself." Lorna snapped her purse shut.

"You said yourself that JJ's killer is in jail." I didn't bother to update her on Marty's escape.

"Really, Ms. Simms, you can be quite tiresome."

I ignored the dig. "Did your husband know Martin Ritter? Can you think of any reason he would have wanted to murder your husband?"

"I was not privy to all of JJ's friends and acquaintances. Thank goodness. Whether he knew the person who killed him or not, I could not answer. I'm sure the police will get to the bottom of the matter. And you should leave it to them, Ms. Simms."

"Your husband had expensive habits and a lavish lifestyle." There was no sense rubbing salt in the wound and pointing out that he shared that extravagant lifestyle with multiple playmates—mostly on her dime. Even the most successful birder is still that, a birder. They couldn't possibly command movie star or NBA money.

Lorna's eyes darkened. "If you are trying to imply something—"

I cut her off. "I'm not trying to imply anything. I'm only saying that it's good that you won't have to worry financially."

"My finances are none of your business."

"I'll bet you didn't think they were any of Peter Porter's business either, did you?" I noticed a flash of anger and continued. "I'll bet it made you angry when he asked you for hush money."

Lorna bit down on her lip. "Who told you that?"

"Ilsa."

"That b—" Lorna caught herself. "He tried to." Lorna appeared amused. "Porter told me he had seen me coming out of JJ's dressing room around the time of the murder."

"So you did meet with Porter. How did you react to his accusation?"

"I laughed in his face," she said with a smile. "In the first place, JJ was my husband, so I had every right to be there. Nothing suspicious about it at all."

"And in the second place?"

She thought about my question a moment. "In the second place, I've explained everything to the police. To their satisfaction, I might add. Now, I really must go."

And go she did. But after a hip-swaying three steps, she twirled and faced me. "If you ask me, Porter was nothing more than a cheap hustler. I believe he tried that same *I know what you did* line on a lot of people after the murder.

"Surely in an attempt to blackmail them to one degree or another. Unfortunately for Mr. Porter, one of them took him seriously and decided to put an end to his ambitions. Maybe your Esther."

"What about Phoebe?"

"What do you mean?"

"Did Porter try his line on her?"

Lorna's eyes turned to nasty slits. "Don't be ridiculous. Phoebe is completely innocent. You think she murdered JJ? Why?" Lorna demanded. "Why would Phoebe kill him?"

Lorna didn't give me time to answer. "Leave Phoebe out of this, Ms. Simms. Better yet," she said pointing a red-nailed finger at me, "keep your nose out of it. Two murders are enough, don't you think?" she added with an evil grin.

That was a good question—not about whether two murders were enough. Two murders were more than enough. No, the question was why would Phoebe want JJ dead? I had thought it might be because she was furious with him because she had left her husband to be with him.

But if Phoebe was actually involved with Lorna, what if Phoebe then murdered JJ because she wanted him out of the way?

Permanently.

That way she could have Lorna to herself. And the Fuller estate. The two women would be free to share everything.

Could Phoebe have been part of all this? She was at the Expo Center all day, every day. She would have known where JJ's dressing room was. She had probably assigned it to him herself.

Maybe Porter had tried to shake Phoebe down. And maybe, instead of succumbing to blackmail, Phoebe's answer to him had been a knife.

And maybe, just maybe, Lorna had an inkling of the truth and was worried that I was getting too close to the truth about Phoebe. Maybe Lorna was afraid that Phoebe would crack.

The problem was that life was filled with too many maybes. I needed some answers but the farther in I waded into the waters of the truth, the more tangled everything was becoming.

And what was that crack of Lorna's about keeping my nose out of it? Was she trying to tell me something? Had she sent me that brick?

Parting the dense sea of last day visitors, I headed for the Birds & Bees booth. I was happy to see a flock of customers in attendance. Derek and Karl were handing out flyers with our store's website and info about our town location along with the remaining samples of my mom's bird bars.

The folks next door at Back to Nature Tours were slammed with customers eager to sign up for their tours. I'd been reading through some of their brochures in my spare time. I had seen one to Belize that I was hoping maybe Mom and I, and Derek and his dad, could take in the spring.

Fingers crossed.

I hadn't broached the subject with any of them yet, but intended to the minute we got settled back home. Once they'd forgotten all about spies and murder and mayhem and zombies—which could take a while.

"Derek, have you seen Esther?"

He excused himself from a customer at the table. He planted a kiss on my lips. I returned the favor. "Nope. Detective Locke was by earlier and I told him the same thing. What's up?"

The dear man looked harried. I appreciated that he kept his complaints, and he must have had a dozen, to himself. I owed him big time. Maybe a new set of golf clubs. "I don't know." I pulled him aside and whispered in his ear. "I saw Detective Locke myself. He's looking for Esther."

"Whatever for?"

"Marty's escaped."

Derek whistled. "Wow."

"Wow is right."

Derek nodded somberly. "It doesn't sound good."

"It isn't good. You haven't seen her at all?"

Derek shook his head. "Sorry."

"What about you, Karl?" I called out.

Karl dropped a couple of bird bars in the ABE-logoed tote of a woman about his age. "Trick or treat," he said as the bars hit the bottom of the bag.

She laughed and thanked him.

"I haven't seen her since breakfast. Shouldn't she be here helping us out? Esther's an actual employee. She's getting paid to do this, not me."

"I'm sorry, Karl. I shouldn't be asking you to do all this work. And for nothing." Especially if it was true that he had dropped a bundle of cash in the casino. "I'll pay you for your time. I promise."

Karl blushed. "I was only joking, Chief. I don't need no money." He grabbed his leather belt and hitched up his trousers. "I've got me a nice pension. Enough for two." He winked at Robin who stood on the other side of the divider.

"You are incorrigible," Robin said with a grin. "I hope you plan on behaving yourself in Costa Rica."

"Costa Rica?" I asked.

"Robin talked me into taking one of their nature tours," Karl explained. "I always wanted to see the jungle."

"Sounds like fun," I replied. I'd have to warn her about making him keep his gun at home. "Speaking of seeing things, where's Floyd?"

Karl answered. "He read the note that fella left you and high-tailed it out of here. He said he was going to look for you."

"That's odd." I scanned the crowded aisle. There was no sign of Floyd. Or Esther for that matter. "What fellow and note are we talking about?"

"Some bozo in a costume came by looking for you, Chief."

"For me?"

"Who?"

"I don't rightly know," Karl answered.

Derek laid a hand on Karl's shoulder. "By bozo, Karl means zombie."

"A zombie came by looking for me?" Peter Porter was dead. Who could it have been? "Was it a woman by any chance? Was it his girlfriend, Suze?"

"Nope. It was definitely a guy." Karl outlined a straight shape with his hands. "The man needed a shave. And a shower. You get a better look at him, Derek?"

"I don't know about the shower but it was definitely a man," was Derek's answer.

"That lets Suze out then. I wonder who it could have been. I don't know any other zombies personally. Except for Stalker."

"Who?" asked Derek.

"Never mind," I said. "It's a long story."

"Well, this zombie had a note for you, Chief. He didn't act like he knew you personally. It was in an envelope with your name on it."

"How long ago was this?"

"Maybe ten or fifteen minutes," Derek answered after a look at his wristwatch.

"I hope whoever it was comes back. What did the note say?"

Karl shrugged. "Like I said, he handed the envelope to Floyd when he saw you weren't here. He said somebody paid him to deliver it. I asked him who but he said he'd never seen her before."

"Her?" My head was throbbing.

"That's what he said," answered Karl. "After the zombie lurched off to wherever it is zombies go during the daytime, Floyd read the note. He said he was going looking for you."

"You think it's important?" asked Derek.

I chewed my lip. "It could be. Floyd opened the envelope and read the note. Now he's disappeared. I wish I knew what was in that message. It wasn't attached to a brick, was it?"

The guys looked at me blankly.

"Never mind. What did this zombie look like? Maybe I can find him at ZombieFest. At the very least, he might be able to identify the woman who'd given him the message to deliver."

"Like he should have been buried six feet under," answered Karl. "One zombie looks pretty much like another."

"Derek?" Maybe he could give me a more helpful description.

"Like Karl says. Just your average run-of-the-mill zombie."

That wasn't helpful at all.

"And neither of you two read the note?"

Both shook their heads in the negative.

"Floyd tossed it in the trash can on his way out," Karl said.

"He did?" I grabbed our plastic trash can from under the table and started sifting through the garbage.

"Not that one," Karl explained. "That big one over there by the exit." He pointed. "You want me to fetch it?"

"Thanks, but I'll do it myself." The note was intended for me, after all. Maybe it was a note from Stalker wanting to hook up with me. In which case, the trash was the best place for it. I pecked Karl on the cheek and Derek on the lips. "Hold the fort, would you?"

Derek chuckled. "Do we have a choice?"

"You could tell me no."

"What, and break a perfect string of yeses?"

"Ha-ha." I hurried to the trash barrel only to discover a clean black plastic bag lining the inside. I cursed and scanned the hall. A man in gray overalls was deliberately pushing a maintenance cart through the crowd.

I stopped him as he was about to make his exit. The cart held a mound of bags and a pair of brooms. After a little haggling and the promise that I would haul the bag to the dumpster, the worker allowed me to take the top bag. He stated with certainty the bulging bag contained the trash from the bin Karl had indicated.

I dragged the bag to the ladies' room. Ignoring the occasionally amused and often disgusted glares of the women moving in and out, I spread the trash out on the floor.

"Lose something?" asked a stout woman washing her hands in the basin next to me.

"I lost an earring," I said, sifting through the soggy debris.

"Good luck," she quipped, drying her hands on a paper napkin she'd plucked from a basket between the sinks. "All I see is trash."

Icky trash was all I saw too. Frustrated, I dumped the second half of the trash on the tile floor. Pushing scraps of paper, plastic bottles and crumpled brochures around with the toe of my shoe, I spotted a coffee-stained white envelope. I fell to the ground and snatched it up. *Amy* was written in scroll near the center of the envelope. A little more digging and I found the typed note: *If you want to see Esther, bring Marty to the Bowlarama. You have until 3 p.m.. Come alone or the old lady dies.*

Gripping the counter, I hauled myself off the floor and yanked open the bathroom door.

"Hey! What about all this rubbish?" a woman with a British accent remonstrated.

"I'll be back!" I promised.

I shoved my way outside and climbed in the minivan. I read the crumpled note again. Derek had said the message had been delivered ten or fifteen minutes before I had arrived at the booth. I had lost time with the maintenance worker and then more time sifting through the trash in the ladies' room.

It was quarter to three now.

What was I going to do? I had no Marty and very little time left. Even if Marty was at Laurel Cove, which I doubted, there wasn't time to drive into Philadelphia, explain the situation to him and drive all the way back.

I had no choice but to go and hope that I could convince whoever had sent me the note to let Esther go. Besides, whoever was behind the sinister message couldn't possibly harm us in the middle of a bowling alley. I pictured bowling shirts, beer and quirky shoes. What harm could come to anyone in a place like that?

The worse thing that happens at bowling alleys is a 7-10 split or the occasional gutter ball—except in my case, in which they occurred all too commonly.

We'd be safe. And I'd talk our way out of it. Whatever *it* was.

Pulling out of the Expo Center parking lot, I realized I had no idea where this Bowlarama was.

I slammed on the brakes, rolled down my window and waved at the first oncoming car. "Can you tell me where the Bowlarama is?"

"Bowlarama?" The leonine-faced driver furrowed his brow a moment and rapped the steering wheel with his knuckles. "Two blocks down on your left."

"Thanks." I lifted my foot from the brake.

"But I wouldn't bother, if I was you, lady. The joint closed down two years ago."

His parting words echoed in my brain as I rolled up the window and sped off. An abandoned bowling alley sounded like just the place to find a killer.

There was no time to spare.

The Bowlarama, with its busted signage, stood at the corner of a long-neglected shopping center. The asphalt parking lot was buckled and sagging and filled with potholes and litter. Many of the storefronts had cracked and broken windows. There was something spooky about the crumbling shopping center.

A weathered sign had been thrust into the asphalt up near the street: *This Site Available.*

For what, I couldn't imagine. Somebody would have to tear all these crumbling buildings down and start from scratch.

I parked near the street and cut the engine. Fishing my binoculars from the back of the van, I studied the bowling alley. It appeared deserted.

All hopes of being able to count on being surrounded by the public had vanished. If I went in, I'd be on my own.

And without the one thing I was supposed to bring to the party: Marty.

What had made Esther's kidnapper think that I would have him? Let alone that I might have convinced him to turn himself over to this kidnapper in exchange for her safe return?

As these thoughts rolled round and round in my much-bruised brain, my binoculars fell on something that made my stomach turn queasy and my blood turn cold.

Karl's rental car.

It was tucked away behind the corner of the shopping center to my left, sticking nose out. It might have been another car but what were the odds?

I lowered my binoculars and drove over for a closer look. I came to a halt beside the vehicle. There was no sign of the driver.

I left the van and peered in the dirty windows of the car—what was left of them. Cardboard took the place of glass on the driver's side. An American Birding Expo tote drooped over the back seat. Several empty coffee cups were strewn about, including one holding the remains of a cigar—somebody was going to be in trouble with the rental agency for that—yesterday's newspaper and a multitude of fast-food wrappers.

And there was my brick, on the floor of the passenger side. I picked it up and turned it over in my fingers. *Back off* had been scratched into the short end on one side. I hadn't noticed that before.

Definitely Karl's rental.

Floyd was somewhere nearby.

I did a slow turn of the narrow strip of broken glass and rock-strewn pavement. I was out of sight of the bowling alley.

"Floyd?" I said softly. "Are you here?"

A cold wind whistled past. Two liter-sized plastic soda bottles rattled past my feet and bounced off the drab concrete block wall.

I hoped Floyd had not done something stupid.

But in my heart I knew that he had.

27

I moved slowly to the van, grabbed my purse from the passenger seat and pulled out my cellphone. I massaged the dark screen to life. My finger hovered over the number pad. I should call the police. I should call Derek.

I should run for my life.

But I couldn't. Not with Esther being held by someone who had killed twice before. If whoever Esther's kidnapper was so much as caught a whiff of police, Esther and Floyd could both end up dead.

Floyd was probably up to his farsighted eyeballs in trouble.

Realizing that there was no good answer to my current dilemma, I slid my phone down my sock between my boot and my ankle. I wanted it with me but not someplace obvious that a kidnapper-slash-murderer might find it.

Returning to the rental car, I retrieved the brick that had almost been the end of me. I slid it inside my coat pocket and zipped up.

I started walking, keeping to the edges. If I drove the van up to the bowling alley, there was every chance of being seen—if I hadn't been spotted already. I had the uneasy sensation of being watched.

I was also worried that anyone passing by car might get suspicious of me wandering around an abandoned shopping center and stop to see what mischief I was up to. Worse yet, report me to the police.

Skirting the empty storefronts, I angled across the parking lot to the rear of the bowling alley. There was no sign of movement and no other vehicles were in sight. The clouds had rolled in with the promise of rain and the sky had grown visibly darker since my arrival.

Trash was heaped up outside the back wall of the bowling center. Someone had once been sleeping there too. A rusting shopping cart and a battered cardboard box large enough to hold a refrigerator lying lopsided against an eggplant-colored velvet sofa that itself looked like it had been gnawed on by hundreds of sharp little teeth.

I didn't want to know what those sharp little teeth had been attached to. I prayed the beasties were nocturnal.

I tiptoed up to the windowless back door and pulled on the rusty handle. As decrepit as everything appeared, the door was solid and held. I wasn't getting inside that way.

I rounded the building, coming at last to the main entrance. It had been boarded over but several pieces of lumber had fallen or been pulled off by looters, squatters or the weather—probably a combination of all three.

The building had an airlock entry to protect the main facility from the elements. Being careful of the broken glass, I squeezed myself through the hole created by a pair of crossed two-by-six boards. That left me facing what was left of an inner set of doors. The steel security curtain was hanging askew. Someone had managed to pry open the metal bars designed to keep out intruders, a long time ago by the looks of it.

A single scuffed bowling pin was wedged between the two main doors, propping them apart. I pulled open the door on my right.

Inside, all was silent and dark. I bent quietly and picked up the bowling pin. It wasn't much, but like the brick, in a pinch it would do as a weapon.

Testing the weight of the pin in my hand, I was surprised. It was heavier than I had imagined it would be, several pounds at least.

I waited as my eyes slowly adjusted to the darkness. I'd read somewhere that it can take upward of thirty minutes for a person's eyes to adjust to the dark. I did not have that kind of time to spare.

I moved forward tentatively, with shuffling steps. The low ceiling hung like a dark cloud over my head. I decided that the chest-high, blurred shape to my right was the main counter. To the left, I could make out the outline of what had once been a dining area.

"Hello?" I said softly. "Esther?"

Hearing no reply, I moved to my right. A ragged hole in the ceiling let in a cold light rain that hit me in the face. I grunted in surprise. A blur of rustling feathers shot out from the edges of the hole.

I recognized the distinctive high-pitched twittering of chimney swifts.

The bowling pin in my hand was growing heavier by the second.

"I ought to shoot you right now."

The words had come out cold and venomous somewhere ahead of me. I froze.

"Where the hell is he?"

It was a woman's voice. There was a familiarity to it but I couldn't quite put a face to it. Whoever she was, she wasn't happy. I sensed she was a good fifty feet away.

"Do you mean Marty?" I asked.

"Marty, Klaus. Call him whatever you want. He is *supposed* to be here. You were *supposed* to bring him."

There was a sudden flash of fire with an accompanying bang. I jerked, fearing that she was shooting at me. But I was unscathed and all I heard was the sound of falling debris in the distance. "The next bullet is for you, Amy. Where's Ritter?"

"He—he's been arrested. The police have him." I squinted into the darkness. My vision was getting a little better. "Nikki? Is that you?"

"Don't play games with me. I know he never made it to jail. The man's a snake. But one way or another I'll see him dead."

"Why?" My brain was struggling for answers. "Because he murdered JJ, your boss?"

Nikki's laughter echoed throughout the bowling alley. "You're not so smart after all, are you? I murdered JJ," she gloated.

Which meant she had probably murdered Peter Porter too. "Why? Why would you murder JJ?"

"Let's call him a sacrificial lamb."

"I don't understand." I bent down and slipped my cell phone from its hiding place. There was no way I could handle Nikki alone.

She was armed, dangerous and crazy.

"I knew that if I killed JJ and made it look like the Osprey had been involved that it would flush him out. Why do you think I sent an email from JJ's computer suggesting I invite this old coot?"

I suddenly understood. "That's why Birds and Bees was invited to the Expo. That's why Esther was specifically asked. You were using her to get to Marty."

"And it worked."

"How did you know that Marty knew Esther?"

"Let's just say our families go way back. Marty and my dad had some run-ins."

"Run-ins?"

"Marty ruined my dad's reputation. He was branded a double agent. It was a lie," she hissed. "It was all Marty's fault. He set Dad up."

"Where is Esther? Let me talk to her."

The bright light of a cell phone flashlight app suddenly lit up a face in the distance. It was Esther. Black duct tape covered her mouth.

"Esther, are you all right?"

She nodded once and the light went off.

"Let her go, Nikki. Please."

"Gee, I'd like to do that, Amy, but we had a deal. Marty for Esther." I finally understood that Nikki and Esther were standing at the far end of one of the old lanes.

"So you can kill him?"

"That's the idea. He's lived too long, too well. While my dad's been stuck living the lousy life of a traveling salesman," she said. "He's lived. Why didn't you bring him? Your friend told me I could count on you."

"Marty has disappeared." I heard a slight movement and scanned the shadows. Was it chimney swifts or rats? Or was there somebody else here with us?

"No. I am over here." Marty's voice called firmly from my far left.

A gunshot rang out, followed by the sound of running feet.

"Esther!" I shouted. "Are you all right?" Nothing. "Marty?"

Nikki cursed. "Give yourself up, Marty. I'm counting to five and then Esther takes a bullet."

"Marty!" I hollered. My fingers danced over my phone, punching in 9-1-1. "Please, do as she says." I didn't want to see him hurt any more than I wanted to see Esther hurt. I hoped his acquiescence would buy us some time.

"You win, Nikki," Marty said calmly. "I'm old and I'm tired. You win."

A flashlight popped on coming from the direction of Nikki's voice. "Come closer where I can see you." The beam of light danced along the walls, finally alighting on the former spy as he moved sideways across the bowling lanes. But it wasn't the Marty I was expecting to see. This Marty had long gray hair tied in a ponytail.

This was the man I had seen in the company of Irv Shipman. Marty in disguise.

"Marty?" I whispered. Bits of sunlight fell through the holes in the ceiling and squeezed through the smudged windows, like pieces of a shattered sun. The sky was clearing outside. Shapes were taking on definition and color.

The voice on the other end of the phone kept repeating, "Hello? Hello? What is the nature of your emergency? Hello?"

A shot rang out and Marty fell to the ground.

"No!" another man's voice rang out. "I insist you stop this now, Nikki!" the voice commanded.

"Irv?" I said. "Irv Shipman, is that you?"

"Daddy?" Nikki sobbed.

Had Nikki just called Irv Shipman 'Daddy'?

"Put down the gun, Nikki." Nikki aimed the beam of light at Irv Shipman and held it there. "Give the gun to me," he urged softly.

"No, Daddy. Don't you see? We can end it all here."

"Give me the gun." He was moving towards her slowly.

A hunched-over shape lunged at Nikki, hitting her low.

I didn't have time to wonder who the new player might be.

Nikki fired wildly a couple of times and ran, dragging Esther with her. I hurled the bowling pin I'd been strangling. It clunked against the side of the gutter and bounced harmlessly off the maple flooring.

Shipman was shouting and giving chase.

The bowling alley had become a carnival madhouse.

"Esther!" I decided to give chase too.

"Back off or she gets it!" snarled Nikki.

"No you don't!" A blurry figure slammed into Nikki from behind. She lost her grip on Esther's arm and went down hands first.

Esther dodged to the right and fell into Marty's arms.

Nikki scrambled to her feet and fired off another round.

Her assailant opened fire. I heard five shots before he fell to the ground.

Shipman threw himself on top of Nikki. "Stop this at once!" He lifted her up like a ragdoll and shook her.

The gun in her hand bounced loose. I kicked it down the lane. It landed in the gutter and skidded to a stop.

She screamed and fought against Irv Shipman to no avail. Marty and Esther scrambled to us. Marty yanked the tape from Esther's mouth, leaving a deep red welt.

I ran to the fallen man and gaped. "Floyd?"

"Hi, Amy." Floyd grimaced, clutching his right leg. "You won't tell Karl I borrowed his gun, will you?"

Somehow I thought that cat was already out of the bag.

28

"Are you crazy, Floyd?" Esther loomed over the fallen man.

Marty held back.

Irv Shipman had Nikki's arms pinned behind her. She was steaming. It didn't look like she'd be calming down anytime soon.

I realized Esther was still yelling at Floyd. "You could have gotten hurt, you crazy old fool!"

"Uh, Esther." I tapped her on the shoulder and pointed. A line of blood showed along Floyd's trouser leg.

"Oh, Floyd!" Esther fell to her knees and began ministering to the wound.

Marty and Irv conferred in hushed tones.

I heard sirens and they were coming closer.

"Thank goodness," I said. "Marty, I think—"

But there was no sign of him. Marty was gone.

"What the devil…" I spun in a circle. "What happened to Marty?"

"Let it go, Ms. Simms. Please."

"But Daddy!" shrieked Nikki.

"Not another word from you, young lady." Shipman released his grip on Nikki with some reluctance. "And you will say nothing about any of this." He straightened his coat and adjusted his sleeves. "It is time I lived up to my past."

The police came in all armed and dangerous and not just a little wary and confused. They did their police thing, followed by the EMTs who did their emergency services thing. Most of which involved carting Floyd off to the hospital. Despite their protestations, Esther clung to him like a crusty old barnacle.

* * * *

Floyd was carried off with the keys to the rental car still in his trousers. I telephoned Derek to break the news and give him and Karl a lift to the hospital. The staff of Back To Nature Tours promised to keep an eye on our booth. Not that it mattered much, the Expo was all but over.

"Is he going to be okay?" Karl kept repeating as we exited the minivan and hurried through the entrance doors of the hospital.

I kept repeating that Floyd's wound had appeared serious but not at all life-threatening.

We were told at the desk that Floyd had been seen, treated and sent to a recovery room. Following the blue line on the floor, we found Floyd sitting up in bed. Esther sat in a chair at the bedside. She and Floyd were holding hands.

"Floyd," I cried. "Are you all right?"

"You moron!" barked Karl, folding his hands under his armpits and blocking the doorway. "You might have gotten yourself killed." His head shook violently side to side. "This is why civilians should never get involved in police investigations."

Floyd looked at him sheepishly. Esther looked like she was about to strangle the ex-chief of police. Floyd was restraining her.

"Next time you decide to try to get yourself killed," Karl said as he stomped to the foot of the bed, "call me. Maybe that will save your dumb ass from getting shot by a crazy woman."

"Karl," said Derek. "Don't you think you're being a little rough on Floyd?"

"Huh?" Karl looked abashed. "Oh, yeah." He patted Floyd's toes beneath the sheet. "Glad you're okay, buddy."

"How are you feeling, Floyd?" I inquired.

"Not so bad."

I grabbed the pitcher of water from the tableside and poured a glassful. It was a habit I'd picked up from my mother. A nice cool glass of water from the hand of a loved one is sometimes as good as any medicine.

Floyd took the glass and drank then handed the glass to Esther who said, "Do you all mind taking your act someplace else? Floyd needs his rest." She squeezed his hand. "Don't you, dear?"

Dear? I shot Derek a look and he smiled at me.

"At least the police got the crazy woman that shot you." Karl downed the remains of Floyd's drink and wiped his mouth with the back of his hand. "Women. They're all crazy."

Esther snarled. She looked like she was about to bite Karl's head off.

"Actually," Floyd said rather tentatively, "you might as well know…It's going to come out sooner or later."

"Know what?" I asked.

"It wasn't Nikki Nilsson who shot me," Floyd answered.

"It wasn't?" I replied. "Who then? Who shot you?" Had it been Irv Shipman? Marty? One of the chimney swifts?

"You see, actually I sort of…well, I, that is—"

"Tell us who shot you already, you old buzzard, before I shoot you myself," threatened Karl.

"Karl!" I said.

"That's okay, Amy. The truth is I sort of wounded myself." He tucked his chin against his chest.

Karl hooted. I sent him a dirty look special delivery. That didn't stop him from speaking. "Wait. You shot your own self? With my gun?" He pressed his hand to his temple. "Oh, Lordy. There's gonna be paperwork. Tons of paperwork."

Karl slumped into a chair near the window.

Floyd looked humiliated. I planted a kiss on his forehead. "Come on," I said to everyone. "Let's let Floyd get some rest." Before coming inside, the doctor treating him had said he could be released in the morning.

"I'll be back in a minute," Esther said to Floyd as she fluffed the pillow behind his shoulders. "Press that buzzer if you need anything."

Esther followed us out.

We reconvened in the waiting room.

"That Detective Locke came and went." Esther took a seat in the chair beside me. "He said he'll be back later today with more questions."

I lifted my legs and twisted sideways in my seat so I could rest my feet on Derek's knees. "I have a question or two myself."

"Me, too," Karl said. A passing nurse shook her finger at him as he stuck a damp cigar in his mouth. He cussed and dropped it into an empty paper coffee cup. Karl liked his cigars almost as much as he liked air. "Like how did that bullet hole get in your jacket, Chief?"

"What?" I jumped up and examined my coat. "What the—" Brown brick showed through the hole. Only now there was a quarter-size chink in it.

"My god, Amy. You've been shot." Derek looked horror-stricken.

I pulled the brick from my pocket. "If it hadn't been for this…" I couldn't bring myself to finish my sentence. That brick was going in a special place of honor in my apartment.

"Didn't you notice?" asked Karl.

"Let's change the subject," I said quickly. I was never going to hear the end of this from Derek. "Tell us what happened, Esther."

"If you must know—"

Derek raised his hand to cut her off. "Wait. As a lawyer, and possibly the attorney who is going to be forced to represent the lot of you—"

"*Pro bono?*" I interrupted.

"*Pro bono,*" Derek agreed with a small frown. "Then I should wait for you all outside. I'm not sure I want to be privy to anything that you have to say, Esther."

"That might not be a bad idea," I said.

"Suit yourself." Esther shrugged. "I've got nothing to hide."

"Nothing to hide?" My feet hit the floor as Derek stood. "All you've been doing is hiding things."

"Go easy on Esther, Chief," Karl interjected. "She almost got killed herself."

"I suppose," I huffed and crossed my arms over my chest after waving goodbye to Derek. "I'll fill you in later," I mouthed.

I turned my gaze on Esther. "You were saying?"

Esther pressed the creases out of her slacks with the palms of her hands.

"When the SD card went missing, Nikki went into panic mode—"

"Because Ilsa Skoglund stole it," I interrupted.

"Yes." Esther gave me a dirty look of warning and I knew better than to interrupt again. "Nikki was certain that Ilsa Skoglund was somehow involved. Once Ilsa made her quote-unquote discovery, Nikki figured out that Ilsa had stolen the ivory-billed woodpecker photographs with the intent of claiming the discovery for herself.

"She followed Skoglund and saw her take the disk from my purse. Nikki was furious that I had been released, frustrating her plans to expose the Osprey."

"Marty Ritter aka Klaus Bergdorf." Karl plucked his soggy cigar from the coffee cup and stared at it unhappily.

"Nikki was desperate to draw the Osprey out of hiding. She hated Marty and wanted him exposed or, better yet, dead in retaliation for what she felt he had done to her father."

"Irving Shipman," I couldn't help saying.

"And her entire family. Her mother had committed suicide and she blamed her death on Marty, too."

Nikki Nilsson was devious and deadly. She had taken the name Nilsson and wormed her way into JJ Fuller's life. Probably seduced him. As it turned out, she had also phoned the Hikers and Bikers Tours and, pretending to be Phoebe, cancelled their booth.

According to Esther, she'd also enlisted him to work as a part-time freelance operative, taking photographs of people, places and things for murky customers whom Nikki had links to.

Nikki had also wormed her way into Travis Stevens's life. She had duped him into helping her. Esther had already explained how Nikki and Travis had gotten the drop on her and taken her away from the convention center at gunpoint.

He was now being held in jail as Nikki's accomplice.

Her father, Irving Shipman, had hired her the best lawyers he could afford. I didn't think that was going to be enough to save her. She had murdered two men in cold-blood. Even discounting the fact that one of those was already undead, didn't make the deed any the less heinous.

Irving Shipman, not his real name, had once been in the spy game, too. Irv and Marty had been nemeses. As Esther talked, I realized what a perfect cover being a birder or a birding optics salesperson was for a spy. Shipman circled the globe, moving from town to town, country to country, all under the guise of being nothing but an innocent bird lover.

Esther had no answer to the question of what fate and the feds had in store for Irv. I couldn't help wishing him well.

Esther stood finally. "I'd better be getting back to Floyd."

"Wait." I reached for her arm.

"What now?"

"What about Marty?"

"Marty is gone. Forget about Marty."

"I'd be glad to but the police are looking for him."

She managed a smile. "They can look all they want. They aren't going to find him."

"Is he up to more spy stuff?" Karl asked with a glimmer of jealousy.

Esther rolled her eyes. "Marty is retired. All he wants to do is sit and watch the birds and flip through his stamp collection."

"Speaking of which, the police are bound to go to his apartment or, should I say, apartments?"

"They already have. Both are about as empty as the space between your ears." Esther pointed a finger at Karl.

"Hey." Karl straightened. "There's no call for abuse."

"No?" Esther loomed over him. "It was your gun that Floyd shot himself with."

"I didn't give it to him." Karl cowered.

"If we're done here, Floyd needs me."

"Of course, there's just one more thing," I raised a single finger.

"Yeah?" sighed Esther.

"Are you, you know, I mean," I twisted in my seat, "were you a spy? I asked through narrowed eyes.

Esther stared at me for a moment that seemed to last an eternity. "Like they say, if I told you, I'd have to kill you."

Esther winked archly and turned on her orthopedic heels.

I stared at the Pester's retreating backside and kept my big mouth shut. Some things were better off left unknown.

About the Author

In addition to writing the Bird Lover's mystery series, **J.R. Ripley** is the critically acclaimed author of the Maggie Miller mysteries and the Kitty Karlyle mysteries (written as Marie Celine) among other works. J.R. is a member of the American Birding Association, the American Bird Conservancy, and is an Audubon Ambassador with the National Audubon Society. Before becoming a full-time author, J.R. worked at a multitude of jobs including: archaeologist, cook, factory worker, copywriter, technical writer, editor, musician, entrepreneur and window washer. You may visit jrripley.net. for more information or visit J.R. on Facebook at facebook. com/jrripley.

Made in United States
Orlando, FL
10 April 2023

31945403R00125